nevermore

To Dawn —
We hope you
enjoy!
Best wishes,
Marilyn Zacu
Jill Steel

Praise for *everafter*

ForeWord Reviews 2009 Book of the Year Awards Finalist for Horror

"Stark and Tam have managed to scare the bejesus out of me in their highly skilled effort to introduce Valentine and Alexa, two professional students, who are thrust into the forbidden realm of Vampires and Weres...the writing is superb, the characters believable, the plot strong...I have to give these authors kudos."—*Kissed By Venus*

What Reviewers Say About Nell Stark's fiction:

"In this character driven story, the author gives us two very likeable and idealistic women that are without pretense. The growth these two experience from their involvement in an important cause, as well as the friendships that they make throughout the year, is moving and refreshing. Kudos to the author on a very fine book."—*Curve* magazine

"*Running with the Wind* is a fast-paced read. Stark's characters are richly drawn and interesting. The dialog can be lively and wry and elicited several laughs from this reader…the discussions of the nature of sex, love, power, and sexuality are insightful and represent a welcome voice from the view of late-20-something characters today. The love scenes between Corrie and Quinn are erotically charged and sweet."—*Midwest Book Review*

By Nell Stark and Trinity Tam

everafter

nevermore

By Nell Stark

Running With the Wind

Homecoming

nevermore

by

Nell Stark and Trinity Tam

2010

NEVERMORE

ISBN 10: 1-60282-184-4
ISBN 13: 978-1-60282-184-2

THIS TRADE PAPERBACK ORIGINAL IS PUBLISHED BY
BOLD STROKES BOOKS, INC.
P.O. BOX 249
VALLEY FALLS, NY 12185

FIRST EDITION: OCTOBER 2010

CREDITS
EDITORS: CINDY CRESAP AND STACIA SEAMAN
PRODUCTION DESIGN: STACIA SEAMAN
COVER DESIGN BY SHERI (GRAPHICARTIST2020@HOTMAIL.COM)

Acknowledgments

nevermore is our first foray into series writing, and we are particularly indebted to our editor, Cindy Cresap, who helped us weave together the many threads of this narrative. Stacia Seaman's careful fine-tuning of the manuscript is also very much appreciated.

We are likewise indebted to Radclyffe for sowing the seed of this idea years ago and for the opportunity to publish with Bold Strokes Books. We'd like to thank all of the wonderful, hardworking, and selfless people at BSB—Connie, Lori, Lee, Jennifer, Paula, Sheri, and others—for helping to put out and market quality product year after year. The members of Team BSB, including our many fellow authors, continue to inspire us!

Finally, our thanks goes out to each reader who picks up one of our books. This series is, above all, for you, and we hope you recognize yourself in it.

Dedication

To love, ever after.

valentine

CHAPTER ONE

The deep rumble of the Jeep's engine throbbed in my ears, its rhythm increasing as we accelerated. I looked out my window over the fraction of Serengeti plain we had just crossed, appreciating the aesthetics of deep blue sky converging with tawny earth at the horizon. Alexa's fingers, entwined with mine, tightened. When I turned to glance at her, I was held captive by the elegant lines of her profile: the dark hair cascading in subtle layers along her jawline, the thick eyelashes that curled up ever so slightly at their tips, the delicate curve of her mouth. Her beauty pierced me.

Thirst flared, a link of fire arcing down my throat, and I swallowed hard against the sudden urge to lean over and sink my teeth into the pulse that beat steadily beneath her neck. I had been sated that morning, but already, my need had returned. This wasn't surprising, given the fact that for the past two months, I'd only been able to see Alexa for a few days at a time—too-short bursts of togetherness between endless weeks of separation.

Originally, we had planned to spend the summer together in New York—she interning at a corporate law firm, and I interning at a microbiology lab. But at the last minute, she had received an offer from her sire, Constantine Bellande, the man who had sent his blood across the Atlantic more than six months ago to help her become a Were so she could feed me indefinitely, saving my soul and assuaging my thirst. I owed her. And in a way, I owed him. So despite the screaming demands of the vampire parasite that ruled my bloodstream, I hadn't objected when she had wanted to spend the summer in Telassar with Bellande in order to learn more about her inner panther. Because Alexa was special. Already, she had more control over her beast than did many older shifters. Spending time in Telassar was a way for her to enhance her relationship with the panther that emerged every full moon, and I was glad that she had decided to go. But being apart from her had been even harder than I'd anticipated. My thirst, always a compulsion, was now laced with desperation.

I breathed in deeply, struggling to regain some equanimity. The tension manifested in a sharp ache in my jaw and a hard knot between my shoulder blades—a stress reaction that was automatic now after months of fighting against my own need. But at that moment, I didn't have to fight. I could relax. Alexa wasn't an ocean away—she was sitting right next to me, and she would gladly let me take her blood and her body as soon as we returned to the lodge. Anxiety had no place here. I focused on the sensation of our palms pressed together, and my heartbeat began to slow.

Our hands were a study in chiaroscuro, my pale skin contrasting with the deep tan she had developed during her time in Africa. And she was leaner than she had been—even in relaxation, the muscles in her upper arms rippled. Life in Telassar was hard work. The city was essentially medieval, unencumbered by modern conveniences like electricity. Alexa had described it as "camping in a castle." Not for the first time, I wished that I could have a glimpse of its walls—just enough to feel connected to Alexa when we were apart. But vampires were not invited, and its location in Africa was a jealously kept secret. Rumor had it that no one without four legs could even so much as approach the city.

This was my third and final visit to her. Each time, we'd met somewhere different: once in South Africa, where we'd learned to surf; once in Casablanca, where I had dipped into one of my "emergency" bank accounts and splurged on a fancy hotel; and now here, on safari in the Serengeti. I had no idea which of the locations was closest to Telassar. Alexa had made her travel arrangements privately. I didn't like having secrets between us, but I could understand the shifters' paranoia about maintaining the secrecy of their most treasured city. From the little I'd heard of it, Telassar sounded like a welcome haven for those who wanted or needed distance from the human world. I hoped Alexa was happy there. Sometimes it was difficult to tell, since she could say so little.

I was surprised that she hadn't yet noticed my scrutiny, but she seemed entranced by the view out her own window. I didn't see the allure—her line of sight was almost completely blocked by a large outcropping of granite that our driver, Amiri, had referred to as a koppe. At that moment, she leaned over so her mouth was next to my ear.

"On the other side of that rock," she said, her warm breath cascading over my sensitive earlobe, "are two giraffes, four elephants, a herd of gazelle, and five…hmm, no, six wildebeest."

I laughed and rested my hand on her knee, feeling the last of my anxiety melt away. "Compared to you, our guide is useless." I nodded toward Amiri, who had bragged about his ability to seek out exotic animals.

Alexa smiled. "It's comforting to know that this could be my backup career if the law doesn't work out."

"Bite your tongue. You're going to be an amazing lawyer."

"Mmm. How about *you* bite my tongue, when we get ba—"

The car lurched to a halt; we had rounded the leading edge of the koppe. "Just as I promised," Amiri declared smugly as he pointed toward a small watering hole that had attracted a wide variety of herbivores. "Look at all of those animals!"

I snickered quietly as he began rattling off the different species that we were seeing—which, of course, corresponded precisely with Alexa's list. We lingered for a while as late afternoon gave way to dusk. I found myself captivated by the improbable grace of the giraffes and the playful antics of a young elephant. Alexa, on the other hand, looked bored after about ten minutes. Given the fact that she'd been spending most of the summer in panther form, it made sense that the wildlife here no longer held her interest the way it once would have. I wondered just how many gazelle she had consumed over the past few months and barely managed to suppress a shudder. The irrational, human part of me didn't want to think about her sharp teeth tearing at the flanks of such a beautiful creature. But the predator that lurked in my bloodstream understood that kind of hunger all too well.

Amiri started up the Jeep again, taking us back not the way we'd come, over the plain, but around the watering hole and into a forest of acacia trees. I closed my eyes, letting the rich smell of growing things wash over me, and trailed my fingers up and down Alexa's thigh.

The muscles beneath my hand tensed. I opened my eyes to see

Alexa staring into the forest's canopy, surprise and apprehension warring on her face. Before I could open my mouth to ask the question, a massive cat, its tawny fur mottled with dark spots, dropped from the thick tree branch above us and onto Amiri. He screamed in pain and fear, and the sharp tang of blood sliced through the air, parching my mouth. The car lurched—listing first to the right before sharply curving left toward one of the larger trees. I curled one arm around Alexa's waist and used the other hand to brace myself against the seat in front of me. The impact reverberated up my arms, and I set my teeth against the cry that wanted to escape from my chest.

I raised my head to the sight of Amiri draped over the steering wheel, blood streaming from a furrow across the width of his shoulders. "Alexa." I forced myself to wrench my attention away from the tantalizing red ribbons that were pooling on the vinyl seat below Amiri. "Are you—"

"Just bruises." Her voice was terse and low, her gaze focused on a point outside the Jeep. The collision had thrown the leopard at least fifteen feet, but even as I watched, it rolled over fluidly onto its huge paws. "The gun, Val. Quick."

I reached for the long box beneath my seat. Before we had set out from the lodge, Amiri had stowed a rifle inside. But he had locked it, and my strength, though superior to a human's, was not sufficient to free the bolt. I dropped the box back to the floor and returned my focus to Amiri. "The key. It's in his—"

Alexa's touch on my arm was fleeting. "No time." I followed her line of sight and tensed as I saw the feline, crouched menacingly, its tail lashing. It was going to spring.

"Take care of him." Alexa vaulted out of the Jeep before I could protest, and as her feet touched the ground, she called out a word I'd never heard before. "Uje!"

Her body collapsed in on itself. There were no seizures, no bitten-off cries of agony as the transformation took her. She flowed effortlessly into her panther self, leaping forward to intercept the pounce of the leopard. Snarling and spitting, they rolled along the forest floor, claws sparkling in the dying light that filtered through the trees.

I forced myself to look away from the battle, knowing Alexa could handle herself. I gripped Amiri beneath his arms and dragged him into the backseat. When I felt for his pulse—thready, but present—my fingers came away bloody. The thirst broadsided me, and I clenched a trembling fist. No. I would not tear into him, finishing the work that another predator had started. I would not. I would resist, and honor the Hippocratic Oath I had yet to officially swear. *Do no harm.*

Breathing through my mouth helped a little, and I managed to blink the haze from my eyes. Carefully, I rolled Amiri over enough so that I could inspect his chest. When I raised his shirt, I was unsurprised at the mass of bruises, a perfect circle matching the circumference of the steering wheel. That complicated things. He probably had severe internal bleeding. There was nothing I could do about that out here.

I pressed him against the seat, hoping the pressure would curb the flow of blood from his shoulders. I rummaged first through one pocket and then the other, until I found the keys to the box. It contained some first-aid supplies, too, but the rifle was my priority.

It fit snugly into the curve of my arm and shoulder, and I raised it with confidence. Index finger on the trigger, I sighted down the long barrel, waiting for the perfect moment. Alexa's black fur mingled with the leopard's dappled coat as they writhed, snapping at each other's necks with their curved, deadly teeth…but in the next instant, Alexa had managed to put a few inches of space between them with one powerful shove of her hind legs.

I pulled the trigger and fired into the leopard's shoulder. It grunted, staggering at the impact, and Alexa seized the opportunity I'd given her. She sank her powerful jaws into the leopard's neck and shook her sleek head once, twice, three times. The leopard's spinal cord snapped with an audible pop. Immediately, she tore into the meat of its flank, driven by the desperate hunger that always accompanied the change.

I turned back toward Amiri, tossed the gun onto the floor of the Jeep, and rummaged through the other contents of the box. The only useful supply was a handful of gauze pads, which I unwrapped and applied to his back. As his blood soaked through them, my brain raced, suggesting and discarding possibilities. He needed medical attention, posthaste. Driving back now would mean leaving Alexa behind. But I'd have to do that anyway—her clothes had been ruined during her transformation.

Decided, I vaulted into the driver's seat. The call of Amiri's freshly shed blood was even stronger here, and I gripped the steering wheel hard. *Alexa.* I had to focus on her. To tell her what I was going to do.

"Alexa," I called softly, not wanting to startle the panther into an instinctive reaction. She raised her head from her feast, and I couldn't suppress a shiver at the sight of her gore-stained muzzle. Her ears were flat against her head, and her breaths came out in low, snarling rasps. For the first time, I noticed that she was favoring her left hind leg, and my heart clenched at her obvious pain. Thankfully, the injury would heal when she changed back.

"Amiri is in bad shape," I said. "I'm going to drive him back to the lodge. Meet me after dark, near the pool."

She stared at me for a long moment, and I wondered what she was feeling behind those beautiful, alien eyes. Did the panther experience Alexa's mental presence as an interloper? Or had the past few months of study in Telassar enabled them to build on the tenuous common ground they'd discovered during our pursuit of the rogue vampire?

But now was not the time for speculation. Silently praying to whatever deity ruled the Serengeti, I twisted the key in the ignition. The engine coughed a few times in protest before catching, but when I shifted into reverse, the Jeep cooperated, and I swung back onto the road.

The movement blasted me with the alluring scent of Amiri's blood, a delicious wave that momentarily swamped my best intentions and left me wanting to take his life instead of save it. I clenched my teeth against the persistent burn in my throat, letting the ache in my jaw ground me against temptation. And then I pressed the gas pedal to the floor and left the forest behind.

The panther prowled out of the darkness, a living shadow, green eyes reflecting the light of unfamiliar constellations. I held out the robe in my hand as an offering. Her stretch was a sinuous motion that only continued, elongating and blurring until she stood before me in her human form. Naked.

I held open the robe and wrapped both it and my arms around her when she walked forward. She leaned against me and I breathed in, filling my lungs with her distinctive fragrance, at once comforting and exciting.

"How is Amiri?" she said.

"The staff took him to the nearest hospital right away. I don't think we'll know anything until tomorrow." I spun her to face me, then bent to brush a kiss across her lips. I meant for the gesture to be loving and reassuring. Tender. But she must have sensed the sharp need at the very core of me. She leaned in before I could pull away and slid her tongue deep into my mouth. Instantly the fire leapt up, crackling between us.

"Inside," I gasped when I felt her fingertips dip beneath the waist of my cargo shorts. When she responded by flattening her palm against my skin, I laughed breathlessly and somehow managed to pull back. "Not like that. Not just yet. Room. Now."

As we stumbled through the nearest door and down a dimly lit hallway, I tried not to think about the fact that after tonight, we had only one more full day together before I returned to New York. I didn't want our union to be marked by that kind of desperate urgency. I wanted to take her body because it was the best way to communicate my emotion—not because I was in a race against time to fill myself up with her before the distance could once again intervene. Sliding one arm around her waist, I put everything else out of my mind but the heat of her flushed skin against mine.

When we were finally behind the closed door, she pushed me up against it. One hand tangled in my hair, forcing my head back while her teeth and lips grazed my neck. The other divested me of my shorts, then cupped between my thighs.

"I love you, Valentine," she whispered against my skin in response to my wordless groan. "I love you. I love you."

She released her grip on my hair to cup first one breast, then the other, even as she began to stroke me languidly. My hips thrust into her touch, needing more. She laughed softly, teasing me, reminding me who was in charge.

"I'm going to taste you, Val. I'm going to drink you in, make you come in my mouth…and then?" She paused to mark the skin of my neck with a long, pulling kiss. "I want to come with your teeth in me."

I breathed a plea without conscious thought. Her hand never left my breasts as she sank gracefully to her knees, as she twisted two fingers deep inside me, as the heat of her mouth enveloped me and every nerve became a storm of sensation. The room cartwheeled across my field of vision. Alexa's name burst from my throat.

Over the pounding of my heart, I heard my own harsh gasps and the soft sounds of her lips kissing my thighs. For a moment, I felt deliciously emptied by the passion that had wrung me out so thoroughly, but then thirst rushed in to fill the vacuum, tinting the world red.

Alexa rose to her feet. My tongue curled around one of my sharp canines—an involuntary response. Her glistening lips curved seductively in a slow smile that bespoke her desire. But her eyes—those beautiful emerald eyes that she shared with her panther—were soft and loving. In one smooth motion, she undid the knot of her robe and let it fall to the floor. I reached out one finger, tracing it along her jaw and down, down over the ridge of her collarbone.

"Yours," Alexa said, her voice trembling on the simple syllable.

"Mine." I closed the gap between us and kissed her hungrily, urging her toward the bed. When she stretched out on it, I followed her down, entranced by the way her tan skin stood out against the white coverlet. I ended up with my lips pressed to her neck and one hand curled around her breast. The urge to sink my teeth was overwhelming, but I fought it, gentling my lips against her skin and rubbing her nipple between two fingers. My jaw ached with the effort of holding back.

"Val," she whispered, hips undulating against mine. "Oh, God."

I shifted my hand to her waist and pressed down, holding her in place. "No," I said, rising to meet her gaze. She looked as hungry as I felt. "Slowly. Be patient."

Her answer was inarticulate, half frustration and half anticipation. I took my time, caressing the taut muscles of her stomach before stroking along her thighs, forcing us both to wait. When I finally touched her, I felt every muscle tense.

"Please—"

The entreaty inflamed me. I dipped my head and took her into my mouth, thrilling to her low cry. It was all I could do to keep from pressing my fingers all the way inside and claiming her. Instead, I went as slowly as I could, fluttering my tongue against her as I slid deeper, one fraction of an inch at a time.

She was incoherent below me, above me, and when her body clutched at me, she cried out. I yielded then, shifting my mouth to her thigh and sinking my teeth, prolonging her climax and assuaging my thirst. Her blood was richer than the finest brandy—bold yet gentle, subtly complex. The essence of Alexa. My love.

I felt her fingers in my hair, pulling me up. But when I obliged, she guided me not to her mouth, but to her neck. "More," she said, fitting one muscular leg between mine. "Take more."

My own cry was muffled against her skin as I obeyed. Her intoxicating flavor burst again under my tongue, and she arched beneath me, shivering in pleasure. We slid down the wave of passion together, moving in tandem, urging one another up the other side until we found the glorious crest together.

For a long time afterward, I held Alexa as she dozed, savoring the sensation of her heart beating under my palm and the sound of her deep, even breaths. Fatigue tugged at me, but I didn't want to lose awareness. Our time was running short.

After a while, her eyes opened. She leaned in to kiss me before pulling back, blinking sleepily. "Mmm. How long was I out?"

"About an hour." I rolled onto my back, carrying her with me. She smiled at the change of position, settling the slight curve of her belly into the dip of my rib cage and kissing my chin.

"That was incredible," she sighed. "We are so good together."

"And a formidable team," I said, thinking back to our encounter with the leopard.

She raised one eyebrow. "We do seem to have a routine, don't we? I do the wrestling, you do the shooting."

"It works." I trailed my hands down the back of her neck to massage her shoulders. "What was that all about, anyway? The leopard, attacking Amiri out of the blue."

"I don't think it was after Amiri. I think it was after me."

I stilled my hands. "You?"

"It probably perceived me as a threat to his territory."

"Even though you weren't in panther form?"

Alexa kissed my chin again, trying to soothe me. "I'll ask Constantine about it," she said, wriggling against me—a cue that I should continue my massage.

"What was that word that you said?" I asked after a few minutes. "Just before you changed." I tried to remember what the two syllables had sounded like. "Oo-dyay."

A deep shudder racked Alexa's frame and she rolled away, turning her back to me. Her body trembled violently, as though she'd just been outside in the bitter cold. Startled, I touched the shoulder I'd just been rubbing. "Baby?"

"Just...a minute," she said, her voice strained. "I'm sorry— just..."

I lay as still as I could, trying to stave off my own apprehension. For a second there, she had sounded as I remembered from the early days of her infection with the Were virus—tense, distracted, and struggling to maintain control.

Finally, she turned back to me and buried her face in my neck. When she spoke, her voice was thick with regret. "I'm sorry, love. Clearly, I still have lots of work ahead of me."

"What happened?" I asked, running my hand down along her side and back again in what I hoped was a soothing motion.

She took a long breath. "That word is a...a trigger. It's an imperative, in Swahili. My way of calling the panther."

I thought about that for a minute. "Well, it seems very effective. I've never seen you transform that quickly and with no struggle."

Alexa's laugh was shaky. "That's the goal, certainly—it's a significant step on the road to fully integrating my two halves. According to Constantine, anyway. But I think..." She pulled back to look at me, and her eyes were troubled. "Apparently I'm a little too trigger-happy. When you said it, just then, the panther almost got away from me. I am so sorry."

"Baby." I kissed her once, then again, then a third time. "Alexa. This is a *process* for you. A long process. Remember telling me all about it, back at the beginning of the summer?" When she nodded, I smiled to reassure her. "It's so clear to me that this time you've spent in Telassar has been very good for you. And for the panther. You're remarkable. You have nothing to apologize for."

She didn't answer right away—just kept looking into my eyes, as though searching for something. I wasn't sure what, but I stared back, trying to convey every ounce of love and pride and affection that I felt for her. Trying to shield her from the raw need that, even now, still tore at the depths of me.

Because that was my battle. And she had her own to fight.

CHAPTER TWO

I landed in New York early in the morning and had a cab take me directly to Tisch Hospital, where I was interning. There was no sense in going home to lie around the apartment missing Alexa—better for me to do something productive and exhaust myself in the process. I never slept well without her.

Besides, my supervisor, who was a stickler for proper protocol, would be out on vacation this week. In her absence, Sean, my best friend at the lab, had promised to show me how to operate the scanning electron microscope. I'd never had the opportunity to work with technology that sophisticated and was eager to learn, especially since it was an integral piece of equipment to a microbiologist's research. Maybe, if I felt competent enough after a little while under Sean's tutelage, I could sneak in some samples of vampire and Were blood to examine.

Not for the first time, I wished that Harold Clavier, the Consortium's chief physician, would be more forthcoming in granting me access to the Consortium's research facilities. I had practically begged him to allow me a place as an intern on one of the teams currently conducting medical research, but he had argued I didn't have enough experience to be useful. He had a point, but I got the sense he was using my inexperience as an excuse to stonewall me. The only real question in my mind was whether he had a personal bias against me, or whether his orders were coming from Helen. Either way, my lack of access was symptomatic of their distrust. Not that I could blame them; I'd already demonstrated that I wasn't very good at following orders when they didn't suit my purposes.

As I was paying the taxi driver, my cell phone rang. The number was blocked. When I answered, I was greeted by the voice of Helen's secretary.

"Valentine. Ms. Lambros requests your presence at ten o'clock this evening."

I bit back a laugh at her choice of verb. Helen didn't request things; she demanded them. "My schedule's clear," I said breezily. "May I ask why she wants to see me?"

"She will inform you upon your arrival. Ciao."

The connection clicked off before I could open my mouth again. "What on earth," I said under my breath, staring at my phone as though it could offer me some answers. I hadn't so much as seen Helen since she'd shown up in our apartment the day after Alexa and I had tracked down and killed the rogue vampire known as the Missionary—though not before he murdered Detective Devon Foster and her partner.

I pushed aside the familiar twinge of guilt and walked toward the entrance to the hospital. What Helen wanted with me, I couldn't guess. She had been kind and attentive while I adjusted to my new circumstances, but by now, I was just another vampire, doing the best I could to make a place for myself. Alexa was the special one.

As I drew close to the front doors, I fumbled in my bag for my ID badge. There was no sense in getting anxious. It was time to focus. My questions would be answered soon enough.

❖

When I stepped into the antechamber to Helen's office at a few minutes before ten o'clock, her secretary waved me through right away. Helen's floor-to-ceiling windows, specially tempered to allow her to work there during the day, looked out over the dark swath of the East River and the sparkling lights of Long Island City. For a moment, I stood captivated by the view before I realized that Helen and I were not alone. A man leaned against one corner of her desk; tall and thin, with his hair drawn back from his face in a long ponytail that fell well past his shoulders. The off-white shade of his linen shirt and slacks matched the color of his sandals perfectly.

"Valentine." Helen walked around the desk and beckoned me

closer, then grasped my shoulders and kissed both cheeks. "It has been too long. Please, allow me to introduce Henri Alençon."

When Henri pressed his cool cheek to mine, my suspicions were confirmed that his olive skin was the product of genetics and not time spent in the sun. Like us, he was a vampire.

"A pleasure," I said. He simply inclined his head. Having been born into a family of what amounted to American royalty, I recognized snobbery when I saw it.

"Monsieur Alençon has sought you out from across the Atlantic." Helen's intent gaze reminded me of my mother's scrutiny during the important social events I'd attended as a child. Helen looked as though she were silently compelling me not to misstep, but in this case, I had no idea what constituted a faux pas.

"Oh?" I asked, completely in the dark as to why a vampire from overseas—French, by the sound of his accent—should wish to seek me out.

Henri clasped his hands behind his back. "René Valois, Blood Prime of the Clan of the Missionary, has summoned you to Sybaris."

I blinked, having no idea what three-quarters of that sentence meant. "Excuse me?"

When Helen's eyes narrowed, I knew that I was not performing to her expectations. Henri wore a puzzled frown. In that fraught moment of silence, I decided on honesty. "I apologize for my ignorance. What is a blood prime, and where is Sybaris? And why should I be summoned there?"

Henri seemed taken aback. "You are…unaware…of your clan affiliation?"

The Clan of the Missionary, he had said. Why would I want to be affiliated with the vampire who had turned me and almost killed Alexa? The memory of rage welled up hot under my skin, pushing politeness aside.

"I killed the Missionary several months ago," I said harshly.

"We are, of course, aware of this." Henri spoke as though we were conversing in a foreign language in which he was fluent and I a neophyte. Maybe the metaphor was apt. "The clan will convene to elect another Missionary in a week's time. All members must be present."

Now I was the one lost for words. Henri already knew that I was the one responsible for the death of the Missionary, but despite being a part of his so-called clan, he didn't care? Was he particularly callous, or did the entire organization embrace the same Darwinian "live and let die" imperative?

"That bastard made me a vampire!" I was unable and unwilling to keep my vehemence in check. "I have no desire to elect his 'successor.' Why the hell would you want to turn what he did into some kind of... office?"

Henri's mouth clicked shut and he crossed his arms over his chest. I'd affronted him, but frankly, I didn't care. His mission was anathema to me; I wanted nothing more to do with the Missionary, and I certainly didn't want anyone else to suffer as I had.

"Please forgive Valentine, Monsieur Alençon," Helen said. She angled her body away from me to give him her full attention. The message was clear; I was in the doghouse. "She is new to our community and our ways. She does not understand her place."

But Henri would not be appeased. "I am afraid that my visit was in vain," he said stiffly. He crossed the room and opened the door, then looked over his shoulder at me. "Your willful ignorance is foolish, Valentine. As are your scruples."

The silence in his wake was deafening. I turned back to Helen, feeling as though I were facing my executioner. Her face was stony.

"He is right." From a snifter on her desk, she poured a finger of amber liquid into a glass, and the aroma of fine scotch filled the room. "You are a fool not to have paid any mind to your heritage, your history."

It was true that my knowledge of vampire and Were history and politics was woefully thin—the price I paid for splitting my attention between two realities. But I had good reason to do so. "I've been a little preoccupied," I said hotly, unappreciative of having been put in my place like some kind of delinquent schoolgirl. "I'm doing everything I can to prepare myself to research the parasite full-time. I know we can find a cure."

For a moment, Helen looked murderous. But in the next instant, she was offering me the glass and smiling. I shifted on my feet, feeling as though I were trapped in the eye of an unpredictable storm.

"The parasite is, of course, important. And I understand your obsession with it." She ran one deep red fingernail along my jaw, and I struggled not to flinch. "But stop and consider for a moment, Valentine. Are you really so poorly off?" She moved away from me toward the windows, and I couldn't help but admire her silhouette against the skyline. "You will always be young, always be strong. Your lover has made it possible for the two of you to be together for eternity. Why not embrace your new life?"

The problem with Helen's rhetoric was that some of it was always right. Unlike any human couple, Alexa and I could truly have a happily ever after, and I was thankful. The sticking point was that I hadn't chosen this existence, the way she had chosen to become a Were in order to sustain me. And I didn't like being dependent on her for my sanity and survival. Finding a cure for the parasite would allow those vampires who wished to, to have their humanity back. To have a choice. But I didn't speak my thoughts. Helen would only twist my words.

She turned, and our gazes locked. When I was the first to look away, I caught the ghost of a triumphant smile. Exhaustion washed over me then, compounded by the long plane ride, the full day at work, the fatigue of missing Alexa. I wanted to go home and sleep until she returned—to forget all about political maneuvering and machinations. But Helen had other ideas. She sat at her desk and gestured for me to take one of the chairs.

"All the information you could ever want on the history of the vampire clans is in the library," she said, "and I strongly urge you to take full advantage of those extensive resources. But before my next appointment arrives, I have some time to tell you about your particular clan."

Part of me still wanted to lash out, but I decided that civility was the best option. "Thank you."

"There are seven vampire clans in total. You in particular will be interested to learn that the number is not arbitrary; one exists for each subspecies of the parasite."

No one had ever mentioned that particular detail to me before, and my fatigue retreated to the background. "The vampire parasite has subspecies? Did they evolve alongside each other, or are they derivative from a common source, or—"

Helen held up her hand to forestall my barrage of questions. "As I told you in our first meeting, you were infected by *Plasmodium sitis*. In Latin, *sitis* means 'thirst.' The name is not a coincidence. Your parasite engenders a thirst in its hosts that is significantly stronger than that produced by the other subspecies. When that thirst is assuaged, however, *Plasmodium sitis* also makes its hosts stronger and faster than the vampires of any other clan."

I remembered watching the Missionary nearly drain four people, as well as the unearthly speed with which he'd dodged my bullets and the crazed strength that had allow him to wrestle Alexa nearly into submission. I fought down a shiver.

"It has been theorized—though not yet proven—by a group of our scientists that *Plasmodium sitis* is in fact the original vampire parasite, and that the other strains are derivative. Because it demands such large quantities of blood, it often kills its hosts during the transitional process. As a result, it has been necessary to charge one vampire with the task of perpetuating the existence of your clan. He, or she, is elected to the office of the Missionary."

I bit my lower lip to keep from making an outburst. The knowledge that I had been turned—and many more others killed—in a perverted attempt to thwart the extinction of a vampire clan made me want to leap across the table and throttle Helen where she sat. I'd been angry enough when I thought I'd simply been a victim to the same kind of thirst that tempted me now. To hear instead that I was part of a deliberate project made me want, for one absurd moment, to throw myself in front of a bus just to spite them all. And Helen expected me to be grateful?

"You are upset." When I continued to say nothing, still fighting my desire to lash out, she sat back in her chair and sighed. "Your self-righteousness is vaguely amusing. I felt certain that you, of all people, born and raised in a prominent political family, would understand the principle of expedience. We are far more fragile than the legends make us out to be. Your very existence is a triumph for our species."

"You told me once that no one ever has to die at the hands of a vampire." I gripped the arms of the chair hard and kept my voice low. "Yet the damn Missionary sacrifices lives right and left, just to find the occasional person who survives. How is that just?"

"Just?" Helen laughed. "You know nothing of the operations of justice. Your youth has made you myopic. Millions of people throughout the history of the world have died insignificant, nihilistic deaths by comparison."

I didn't want her to have a valid point. I didn't want some small part of me to feel compelled by her argument. I wanted to stand up and leave the room so I didn't have to hear anymore, but that would be childish. So instead, I gritted my teeth and changed the subject.

"Something else that Henri said confused me. He mentioned the 'blood prime.' What is that?"

"He was referring to his lord and master. The natural, biologically appointed leader of each clan is called the blood prime."

"Biologically appointed?"

"As you and I both know well, vampires cannot be born—they can only be made. A distinct genealogical tree can thus be drawn from one vampire to another, but with a clear and discernable point of origin. That origin, the eldest vampire in a clan, is the blood prime. He or she governs the clan, usually from its capital."

I frowned, trying to remember the place Henri had referred to. "Which, in my case, is called Sib…"

"Sybaris, yes. It is located in western Algeria, and was founded long ago by turned members of the French royal family." At that moment, Helen's phone rang. She murmured an affirmation into the receiver and then hung up. "My next appointment has arrived. I hope that this conversation has been helpful, Valentine. And that you reconsider your refusal to travel to Sybaris for the election. It is both your right and your blood duty to participate in the choosing of a new Missionary."

I rose and threw back the last half-inch of scotch. Helen was either trying to bait me or bully me or both, and I wasn't going to give her the satisfaction of an emotional response. "I appreciate your taking the time to share your knowledge with me," I said. "Good night."

And then I set the glass down on her desk and left without looking back.

CHAPTER THREE

The apartment door closed behind me with a hollow sound, and I stood still for a moment, discomfited by the hush that greeted me even after nearly an entire summer of coming home to empty rooms. I dropped my bag on the scuffed hardwood floor and shucked off the loose polo shirt that concealed the gun tucked into the waistband of my jeans. It went on the nearest shelf, behind the middle row of books. I'd started carrying it regularly a few days after my meeting with Henri and Helen, almost two weeks ago. It had seemed, then, as if someone was following me around. Now I wasn't so sure. The thirst and loneliness and fatigue were probably just making me jumpy.

I sank into the cushions of the couch and flipped on the television to take the edge off the silence. My shoulders ached from too many pull-ups at the gym, followed by an hour of target practice. On the screen, a commercial for antidepressants ran in black and white, and I found myself jealous of its audience. Modern medicine had no way of alleviating my symptoms, no drug to even out the imbalance in my blood. In my soul, if you believed that kind of thing. My jury was still out where the soul was concerned, but it was clear enough that for whatever reason, my condition was declining in Alexa's absence.

My throat burned just thinking about her, and against my will, I went to the refrigerator. In it was a half-empty pizza box, a few bottles of beer, and two bags of her precious blood. I almost mustered a laugh at how quintessentially bachelor the scene was—with a twist. The crimson bags called to me, but I forced myself to grab a beer instead. I still had ten days to wait until her return, and the urge to drink would only grow stronger.

Not that bagged blood had anything more than a placebo effect—the vampire parasite would reject anything that wasn't fresh. In Alexa's absence, it had defaulted back to consuming my own red blood cells. Left unchecked, it would transform my entire circulatory system, eventually rendering me a full vampire. I would be even stronger, even faster, my senses even keener, but as my human failings waned, so too would my human compassion. I would become distant. Cold. Ruthless.

Alexa was the only one who could save me from that fate—hers was the only blood that the parasite would accept as a substitute. I never would have wished on her the burden of sustaining me, but it was comforting to know that she was my soul mate all the way down to the chemical level.

My phone rang, piercing the white mumble of the television. When I fished it out of my pocket, I hesitated. Sebastian Brenner, prominent nightclub owner and one of the celebrities in the up-and-coming generation of werewolves, was calling me at eleven o'clock at night. Either it was some kind of emergency, or he was bored.

I answered the call. "Hey."

"Valentine," he said, drawing out the first syllable.

"You're drunk."

"Am not." The two words would have sounded petulant coming from anyone else. "I'm just glad to hear your dark and broody voice. Come to Luna, and I'll make you feel better."

I had to laugh. For some unfathomable reason, Sebastian persisted in flirting with me. "Who's with you?"

"Karma is right here and promises to protect your virtue. And I think I saw your bloodsack friend Kyle on the dance floor earlier. Now will you come?"

I bit back a suggestive reply. "Maybe."

"Maybe," he said, a note of disbelief coloring his voice.

"Maybe." And I hung up.

❖

Half an hour later, I trudged up the stairs from the subway, hoping that it would be cooler on the streets than underground. But the mid-August night was sweltering, and my gun, tucked into the back of my jeans, shifted uncomfortably against the moist skin of my lower back. Above the skyscrapers, the bulging moon, draped in haze, ruled the sky. It would be full in a week. Three days later, Alexa would finally come home.

The line to get into Luna stretched for half a block, but I didn't so much as slow my pace. The bouncer, Damian, had biceps as thick as my quads and spiked hair that looked bleached but wasn't. I'd seen him shift only once—a few weeks ago, when some Were turf skirmish had spilled over into the club. It wasn't every day that a polar bear materialized on a dance floor. I'd been tempted to snap a picture with my cell phone.

"He's on the roof, Val," was all Damian said as he pulled the rope aside for me.

"Thanks." I threaded through the crowd inside and made my way up to the second floor. As I paused at the bar to order a scotch, I couldn't help but reflect on my relationship with the Weres of New York. Many of them hated me, holding me responsible for Alexa's rebirth, choosing to believe that I'd manipulated her into deliberately infecting herself with the Were virus so that I could be fed for eternity. Others sympathized with us and treated me as one of the family. For whatever reason, Sebastian had gone so far as to include me in his inner circle—which was otherwise populated by shifters. It was curious. It was confusing. But on a night like this one, when the loneliness was riding me just as hard as the thirst, it was a comfort.

The door to the roof was guarded by another bouncer. I'd never seen him before, but when I approached, he moved aside. I stepped out onto grass and paused to admire the view, familiar by now, but still breathtaking. An immaculately groomed lawn—real grass, not turf—covered the expanse of the roof, contrasting sharply with the surrounding cityscape. Ten feet away, several people were lounging on blankets. Karma gave me a small wave as I approached. I smiled back as warmly as I could before turning to the alpha of the group.

"I knew you wouldn't be able to resist." Sebastian was dressed as casually as I'd ever seen him, in slim-fitting khaki shorts and a tight black T-shirt. He was rolling the stem of a half-empty martini glass between his fingers, daring the liquid to spill over. "You look like shit. How long has it been since you've had a decent meal?"

I sat in the space Karma made between them, trying not to betray the thirst his question inspired. "Almost two weeks. And another ten days to go."

Sebastian arched his shaggy eyebrows. "Plenty of snacks downstairs, if you'd quit being so picky."

Karma tsked her disapproval and brushed one palm across my shoulder blades before lightly massaging the back of my neck. "Stop baiting her. What she's doing is admirable."

"Suffering is not admirable." He drained his glass in one long swallow. "Don't fool yourself. Nobility has no place here."

Karma's solicitousness needled me in a way that Sebastian's callousness had not, and I had to struggle not to shrug off her hand. Even that slight, platonic touch made my skin ache, desire and thirst twining together like the strands of a double helix.

"That's a fine thing to say, Prince Sebastian," I said, focusing on the verbal spar that he wanted. As a pureblood, he was effectively Were nobility himself.

His laugh was short and sharp. "Being a Brenner doesn't mean as much as you seem to think. After four hundred years, my father has spawned whelps on every continent. Even if he wanted to care, he'd be hard-pressed to find the time for all of us."

For the first time, I felt empathy for Sebastian. "Our fathers are cut from the same cloth. What does yours…do?"

"My father?" When Sebastian looked surprised at the question, I realized that I was already supposed to know the answer. At least he wasn't haranguing me as Helen had. When I nodded, Sebastian bared his perfect teeth. "Pisses off your kind."

I sipped at my scotch to hide my uncertainty. There had always been tension between vampires and Weres, and in the past, that tension had boiled over into outright hostility. But the Consortium was an alliance of the two species—created and maintained to help them survive and even thrive in secret amongst the humans. Did Sebastian's father distrust the alliance? Or just vampires?

The sounds of reveling from the club below penetrated the hush that had fallen over the group, and I decided to change the subject to something more mundane. "Luna's crowded tonight."

Sebastian drained his glass. "Unsurprising. This is the first night we've been open in almost a week."

I frowned. "Why?"

"You didn't hear? The annoying bloodhounds at the DA's office shut us down."

"They suspended our operations while they questioned the management," Karma added.

"For what reason?" I asked, hearing the outrage in my own voice. Suspicion prickled at the corners of my mind. "Who was in charge?"

"Olivia Wentworth Lloyd." Sebastian spoke the name as though it left a bad taste in his mouth. "And I have no idea what she was looking for. I suspected drug trafficking at first, but her questions made it sound like she was investigating some kind of violent crime."

"Damn it," I said. "She just won't give up, will she?" I knew Olivia well—we had been born into the same social circle. One year older than I, and from just as politically prominent a family, she had often been held up by my parents as a model to which I should aspire. Until she had come out, of course. I admired her, but she and I were too alike for me not to feel competitive. We'd never had to compete over women, but I could tell that she was attracted to Alexa. That hadn't bothered me until I'd been turned into a threat to Alexa's life.

"Val?" Karma asked. "You know what she's looking for?"

"Olivia was attacked by the Missionary, a few weeks after I was turned. He was interrupted before he could do enough damage, and she's fine now. Fully human."

"Fully irritating," Sebastian groused.

I stared at the smoky amber liquid in my glass, trying to make sense of what was happening. "I'm sure she's still trying to find him. The question is, how did the Missionary's trail lead her to Luna? Shifters had nothing to do with her attack."

"Do you think she might be on to us?" Karma's voice was laced with alarm.

"She's clearly on to something," Sebastian said. "I've upped security, and I know our people will be careful, but…"

"But you're worried that someone will make a mistake while she's watching."

He shrugged. "We're volatile. You know that."

I thought back to the early days of Alexa's life as a shifter—back when something as simple as a loud noise had triggered her panther's snarling emergence. The majority of shifters fought hard for every modicum of control over their beasts. Sebastian was right. If Olivia looked hard and long enough in the right places, she would find something.

"Maybe we can throw her off the scent. Or ease her suspicions, somehow."

"Somehow," Sebastian echoed skeptically.

Karma patted his shoulder. "What are you thinking, Val?"

"Well, either we feed her information, or we try to convince her that Sebastian's harmless."

"I'm not harmless." His voice was flat but his eyes glittered, and I knew that his wolf was suddenly close to the surface. Resisting the instinctual urge to move away from him, I took another long drink of scotch.

"Knock it off. I'm trying to help." Feeding Olivia information would be dangerous because she was a good investigator. So how could I convince her that Sebastian wasn't connected to the attacks, while still maintaining the Consortium's secret?

"I've been invited to a fund-raiser on Thursday night for a few of the Democratic candidates for state senate," I said. "I bet Olivia will be there. Maybe I can talk to her then."

Sebastian leaned toward me, abandoning his threatening attitude. "Need a date?"

I felt my eyebrows try to climb into my hairline. "Is *hell no* emphatic enough for you?"

But he persisted. "If I were there too—if Olivia sees me with you, someone she presumably trusts—then she might back off."

My stomach churned as I thought of how little Alexa would like Sebastian accompanying me somewhere. "She'll be more likely to open up if I'm alone." Actually, she would be more likely to open up for Alexa, but I didn't want to think about that, either.

"You owe me a favor." Sebastian's change of tactics was unexpected. "For pointing you in the direction of the Red Circuit, all those months ago."

"You're calling in that favor now? For this?"

When his gaze locked onto mine, I realized that he was serious. "Take me with you."

Much as I didn't want to admit it, I really did owe him. "Fine," I said. "Just as long as we are perfectly clear that this is *not* a real date. You're accompanying me as a friend because Alexa happens to be out of town."

Sebastian inclined his head like a king on his throne. "So…what color is your dress?"

I bared my teeth, ignoring Karma's sudden laughter. "Excuse me?"

"Well, you know," he said, dropping the deadpan for a rakish grin, "I would like my cummerbund to match."

"There will be no *dress*," I hissed. "And if you buy me a corsage, I swear to God I will gouge your eyes out and eat them for breakfast."

Karma's laughter doubled. Sebastian cocked his head, seeming to consider my threat.

"Mr. Brenner!" A shout from the doorway interrupted our banter. The guard was in a flat-out run toward us. Sebastian rose to his feet with preternatural speed, and I was only a second behind him. Most situations that arose in the club were handled discreetly by security and didn't require Sebastian's personal attention.

"What is it?" His voice was quiet but urgent.

"Medical emergency, sir. On the second floor. I've never seen anything like it."

That was all I needed to hear. I took off for the door, Sebastian's footfalls pounding in counterpoint behind me. A few moments later, I burst into the club and shouldered through the crowd that had gathered. When I broke through into the space that had formed around the spectacle, I skidded to a halt, my confidence dissipating.

A pool of vomit at the foot of the bar. A man foaming at the mouth, convulsing, held down by two more of Luna's security staff. His eyes had rolled up in his head. As I watched, his body began to shimmer and blur, its molecules defying the conventional laws of physics and biology. I hung back, knowing what would happen next. He would change into whatever animal lurked beneath his skin and psyche. The guards backed away and raised their guns—loaded not with bullets but with tranquilizer darts, to subdue the beast when it emerged.

We watched. We waited. But there was no transformation. After one particularly wrenching spasm that propelled him into a sitting position, the man vomited before collapsing back onto his elbows. I hurried over then, urging the guards to help me turn him onto his side lest he choke on his own bile. They hesitated.

"Do as she says," Sebastian ordered from behind me. "What the hell is wrong with him?"

"No idea." As I crouched and helped to hold him in position, snarls erupted from his throat, raw and menacing. But he continued to writhe without relief. Fully human. "Why isn't he making the change?"

"I don't know." Sebastian's voice was tight with anxiety.

"We need to get him to the Consortium," I said, keeping one hand pressed to the sick man's back. His face nagged at me. I'd seen him before. Somewhere. I glanced over my shoulder, my eyes meeting Sebastian's as he flipped open his phone. When he nodded once, I turned back to my patient.

Wereshifter physiology was complex, but it was based on one principle that I had thought to be unshakable. Until now. When shifters were threatened, they transformed. Pain was an especially effective trigger, a fact I had witnessed many times. It had taken Alexa months of internal struggle against her panther before she had been able to endure my bite without shifting. The man who quivered and moaned under my gentle grip was clearly in agony. Either he had the most superb self-control I'd ever seen in a Were, or something was preventing him from making the change. I ground my sharp canines against my molars, frustrated by my own ignorance.

"Someone get me some towels," I said as blood began to trickle from his nose. When several dark blue towels were dropped into my outstretched hand, I used one to cover the mess on the floor and the other to wipe the man's face. He was pouring sweat now, even as his teeth chattered. I opened my mouth to reassure him and then shut it again. Any words of comfort that I offered would be hollow.

Under the buzz of the crowd, I picked up on the sound of quick footfalls on the stairs. A moment later, the crowd parted for two men carrying a stretcher. I had expected Harold Clavier, the head Consortium physician, to come himself—or to send his assistants, at the very least. But the two vampires who began strapping the Were man onto the board for transportation were from Helen's security detail.

"Valentine," one of them said. "What did you see?"

I frowned at the question. Why hadn't he asked me what had

happened, or what symptoms I had observed? Suspicion joined my unease.

"He was convulsing. He vomited. And he has a nosebleed." I kept my answer as terse as possible.

"We'll take care of it." The guard turned away, and the vampires bent to the stretcher only to jump back in surprise as the Were bolted upright, snapping through two of the straps that had held him down. He looked right at me, his pupils so wide that his eyes seemed black.

And that's when I recognized him. Vincent. I had only seen him once, in the dogfights at the first Red Circuit party that Alexa and I had attended. He had fought another shifter to the death for money and glory. I had watched him transform into a black wolf that had torn the opposition to shreds and eaten his heart in victory. Now he was helpless.

I watched the consciousness fade from his eyes—watched him slump back bonelessly against the rigid surface of the stretcher. One of the vampires checked his pulse. "Out but stable."

"I'm riding with you," I said. They both looked up sharply, and the one who had spoken to me seemed on the verge of protesting before he finally acquiesced with a nod.

Before I could step forward, Sebastian laid a hand on my shoulder. His palm was warm and heavy, and my needy skin hummed under even his touch. "Let me know, Val."

"I will."

But when the Consortium's black Suburban pulled up to the curb of Headquarters—a tall, concrete building on the East River—the guards ordered me to remain outside. Harold Clavier stepped out from under the awning over the back door as Vincent's body was carried into the facility.

"Hello, Valentine."

"Dr. Clavier." I tried to peer surreptitiously over his shoulder but only caught a glimpse of the doors swinging closed. "Do you know what's wrong with him?"

"I'm sure it's nothing. I'll take it from here."

We were almost the same height, and I stared hard into his deep brown eyes, refusing to back down. His evasiveness wasn't surprising, but I felt disconcerted nonetheless. "It looked like he wanted to change but couldn't. Does that mean anything to you?"

Frown lines developed across the bridge of his nose. "Interesting. I'll be sure to investigate."

"I want to help." It wasn't an idle offer. As a second-year medical student, I was at least somewhat qualified.

But Clavier shook his head. "I have everything under control, Valentine."

I hesitated, wavering on the edge of saying more to argue my case, but the knowledge that my words would be futile killed them before they could leave my burning throat. I nodded once before spinning on my heel. For now, I had to walk away, if only to make my capitulation look convincing.

For now.

CHAPTER FOUR

Sebastian insisted on sending a limousine to collect me. I had the champagne open before the dark car pulled away from the curb, and I perversely hoped that traffic would be heavy enough for me to kill the bottle before the driver could reach Sebastian's Upper West Side apartment. Of course, there were probably several more bottles stashed away somewhere in the vehicle.

It had been a while since I'd ridden in a limo. As I sipped at my Dom Perignon and stretched my legs out in front of me, I felt regret at not ever sending a car for Alexa, especially during our courtship. While I would never inherit the trust fund left to me by my grandfather, with the stipulation that I marry a man, I had several other bank accounts to draw from. I preferred to leave them untouched and simply live on what I earned, but once in a while they came in useful. Alexa's engagement ring was a perfect example—the beautiful Etoile band that had been taken from me by the Missionary and later returned to me by Helen. The ring that was still languishing in my safe deposit box. Someday, at the right moment, I would use it. Perhaps I'd splurge for a limo on that day.

By the time the car pulled into a space between two idling taxis, I had managed to drain the Dom down to half. Resigned, I poured a glass for Sebastian and then peered out the window at his building. Its baroque façade gleamed in the molten light of the sunset, and I found myself speculating on what the inside looked like. Did his décor match the ornate exterior? Or did his tastes run more to the Spartan aesthetic?

He slid into the car and looked me up and down, his expression inscrutable. I wondered if he was disappointed that I hadn't worn a dress. I didn't even own one anymore. My sleek black slacks and matching short-sleeved jacket were far more rakish than feminine, and he was just going to have to deal. Silently, I held out the champagne glass.

"You certainly look happy to be here." His voice was dry with irony.

"You're the one who bullied me into this." I downed the rest of my glass and poured another. "And if *any* of my family members were going to be at this event, no debt in the world could have moved me."

"They want to see you with a man."

My heart constricted in memory of the pain of a hundred heated arguments. "More than you can imagine. And my father in particular takes his anger at my 'choice' out on me in any way that he can." I laughed mirthlessly at the memory of one particularly unpleasant confrontation. "A few years ago, he made a donation to one of those right-wing religious groups in my name. I insisted that he either withdraw the money or change the name associated with it, but he refused until I threatened to expose his campaign finance law infractions." Twirling the champagne flute between my fingers, I watched bubbles rise to the surface. "We're at war."

Sebastian was silent for a moment. "I think you're right," he said, "about our fathers being cut from the same cloth."

"Tell me more about yours." After our enigmatic conversation a few nights ago, I was curious.

Sebastian turned his head to watch the cityscape slide by. "He is old and very cunning. We're estranged—if that's what you call it when he doesn't give a shit about anything except the beast he put under your skin."

"What do you mean?"

He crossed one leg over the other and rested his head against the plush leather to stare out the limo's moonroof. "I began to change when I was fourteen. The month after it first happened, my father showed up on my mother's doorstep: unexpected, unannounced, unwanted. He took me deep into the Adirondacks, then told me that I had to live as a wolf for an entire month—to survive on my own until the next full moon. And that if I turned back before the time was up, he would kill my mother in punishment."

I couldn't help it; I gasped. "That's barbaric!"

Smiling grimly, Sebastian met my gaze. "From what I can gather, he considers that one task to be his sole paternal duty: to force each of his offspring into some kind of harmony with their animal half."

"But why does he care about that so much?" I asked, trying to figure out the logic behind such an extreme stance. While I was happy that Alexa had begun to find common ground with her panther, I had also seen just how difficult any kind of equilibrium had been for her to attain. To force a mere boy to subordinate himself to the will of his beast—to struggle to retain enough of his own essential self so that he could return to human form after an entire month of living as a wild creature—seemed far more cruel than wise.

"There are several schools of thought on what, precisely, a Were is," Sebastian said. "Are we genetically altered humans? Schizophrenic animals? Or are we an entirely different species?"

As I mulled this over, I realized that I was getting a crash course in Were politics. Alexa had decided to infect herself with the virus for me. For us. In so doing, she had joined a community divided on the most fundamental question possible: identity. I wondered how Alexa saw herself, and whether her time in Telassar had changed her perspective.

"My father is a rabid champion, pun intended, of the third position. He believes that Weres represent a step up on the evolutionary chain, and that to subordinate ourselves in any way to 'mere' mortals is to deny our very DNA."

"He can't be happy about the Consortium, then," I said. "Given that the alliance's main purpose is to help our kind live under human radar."

"Oh, he isn't. And while he considers vampires to also be an evolved species, he thinks that they are flawed. Weak. Unfit partners for Weres."

I thought of Alexa—of our best moments together. Waking up entwined to a new morning. Laughing as we walked the city streets, hand in hand under the sunlight. The loving triumph in her eyes as I confessed how much I needed her—blood, body, and soul. The sensation of her naked body rising sensually beneath mine as I slid my teeth into her neck. Unfit partners? We were perfect together.

I held Sebastian's gaze. "What do you think?"

He laughed again. "Like you, I have serious political disagreements with my father. By celebrating my humanity and associating with members of the Consortium, I turn my back on everything that he stands for."

"My family battles seem paltry compared to yours."

Sebastian threw back the rest of his drink and stowed the flute in a side compartment as the car pulled up to the Mandarin Oriental. "Paltry? No. But at least you have bargaining chips to use against your father. I have none."

He offered me a hand as I exited the car, and just this once, I allowed the chivalrous display. His stories had roused my sympathy. But when he would have retained my hand to escort me into the hotel, I pulled away.

"Not a date, remember?"

He rolled his eyes. "How could I forget?"

We were directed to a large room overlooking Central Park South, and I paused to admire the view while Sebastian went to the bar. My gaze followed the march of apartment buildings up along the borders of the trees, their lights twinkling in the summer dusk. Someday, perhaps Alexa and I would splurge on a penthouse apartment with floor-to-ceiling windows and a roof deck. Her panther would love the airy feel of such a place, and I had no reason to fear the sun while she was with me.

The daydream shattered as I was engulfed in a bear hug from behind. Exerting a touch of my vampire strength, I spun in my assailant's arms, only to feel a smile break over my face. Bryce Nealson—Olympic ski champion, gay activist, and the eldest son of my father's chief of staff—grinned back at me.

"Val! It's been for-ev-er!"

My smile widened at Bryce's hyperbole. I didn't use that word casually anymore, and it was somehow refreshing to hear him do so. As children, Bryce and I had naturally gravitated toward each other, perhaps out of some instinctual recognition of shared difference. But we hadn't done a good job of keeping in touch since then, and it was nice to forget Consortium intrigue for a few minutes as I caught up with an old friend.

When Sebastian returned with a pair of neat whiskeys, I introduced him as a friend who had "volunteered to keep me company since Alexa's out of town" and was gratified to see Bryce take me at my word and go into full-on cruise mode. I didn't blame him—Sebastian exuded a raw and powerful sexuality that defied the traditional boundaries.

"Your name sounds familiar," said Bryce as he took a step closer. "Where would I have heard it?"

"Sebastian owns Luna," I said, knowing that Bryce would recognize the name of one of the most exclusive nightclubs in town. Bryce took yet another step, lightly grazing Sebastian's arm as he continued to ask questions.

I had no idea how word spread at these kinds of events, but it always did. Within an hour, we had amassed a small group of inquisitive souls who wanted to learn more about the elusive businessman. Sebastian was enjoying the attention, and as I scanned the crowd outside our knot of admirers, I wondered whether any of these new connections would lead to his opening another exclusive establishment—one geared more toward humans, perhaps.

And then I saw her. Olivia was standing alone, which was uncharacteristic—she was almost always surrounded by a few hangers-on. Maybe Sebastian's presence had enticed them away. Her attention was riveted to him, and when she noticed me looking, she beckoned me over. This was my chance to try to pump her for information, but I would have to be discreet about it.

"Hi, Val." Olivia never fully uncoiled, as far as I could tell, but tonight she seemed particularly tense.

"Good to see you," I said easily, as though I didn't know the cause of her discomfort. "It's been a while. How are things?"

She shrugged. "Fine. The usual. How's Alexa?"

Despite the surge of possessiveness that raced like an electric current beneath my skin, I kept my voice even. Olivia's interest in Alexa never failed to bring out my own inner beast. "Doing well in Africa. I spoke with her a few days ago. She'll be coming home in a week."

"Good, good." Olivia's voice was absent, and she had gone back to looking at Sebastian. "What made you bring Brenner along for the ride?"

"You know Sebastian?" I asked, feigning surprise.

"We've met," she said evasively. "How do *you* know him?"

"Alexa has some contacts in the club scene," I lied, thinking it clever to associate her with Sebastian given Olivia's not-so-secret crush. "We got into Luna one night. I guess we made an impression, because next thing we knew, the man himself was buying us a drink."

Olivia made a noncommittal noise. "I'm not sure he can be trusted."

I paused, pretending to think this over. "Ah. You're investigating him. For what?"

"I can't tell you that." Olivia's response was automatic.

"Sure, okay," I said, wanting to keep her talking, not give her a reason to clam up. "But honestly, Sebastian seems like a great guy, and I've never gotten any kind of sinister vibe from him. You sure your information is accurate?"

Wrinkles appeared in Olivia's brow, and I forced myself to maintain a casual demeanor even as I paid close attention to her body's little tells. "My source is…well, let's just say that his information has proven to be very valuable." She put a hand on my shoulder. "Watch yourself, Val. Please."

In that moment, I became certain that she was still investigating the rash of "muggings" a few months ago that had almost taken her life and my own. I wanted to reassure her that that particular monster was no longer a threat—that I'd taken him off the streets myself. But I couldn't. And someone was feeding her bad information.

I was spared the necessity of coming up with a reply when Sebastian joined us. Olivia stood ramrod straight, but Sebastian gave no sign that he noticed. He extended his hand. "Hello, Olivia."

She took it briefly. "Sebastian."

He turned to me. "I need to get back to work, Val. But I'm happy to leave you the car if you're planning to stay."

Instantly, I was on full alert. He had emphasized "back to work" subtly enough that Olivia wouldn't have noticed. The phrase was meant for me. Had something else happened at the club?

"You know, I think I'll catch a ride with you," I said. "Early morning at the lab tomorrow. Good night, Olivia."

As we left, I made a show of waving to Bryce, who was still schmoozing. "Call me!" he mimed across the room—whether to me or to Sebastian, I didn't know. But my lingering amusement faded when Sebastian picked up his pace as soon as we were in the hallway. Minutes later, I was ducking into the car.

"What's going on?" I asked as soon as he shut the door behind us.

"I just got a call from one of my contacts. He was at a private party when one of the guests went into the same kinds of spasms that we saw at Luna the other night. Except this guest ended up dead."

Anxiety settled in my chest. I hadn't really believed that Vincent's case could be an isolated incident, but hearing positive confirmation was disturbing. Besides, Vincent had been unconscious when last I'd seen him, not dead. What was going on here? Were we witnessing the outbreak of some kind of disease?

"If you're going to check it out, then I'm coming in with you."

"A vampire at a private Were party? I don't think so."

"Are you a doctor?" I shot back. "I don't think so."

"Christ, Val, neither are you." Sebastian actually raised his voice, which was rare. And unsettling. When I continued to look at him expectantly, he sighed and ran one hand through his shaggy hair. "All right. Fine. You can look at the body."

As we drove, I thought back to Vincent's episode, trying to pin down all of his symptoms. Thirst flared deep in my throat as I remembered the blood trickling from his nose, and in that moment, I loathed the parasite that lurked in my veins. What kind of monstrous impulse made me thirsty at the memory of a man's agony? It would be such a relief when Alexa returned—when my thirst would subside to a dull murmur and no longer threaten my self-control.

We stopped in front of an elegant apartment complex in Tribeca, and I exited the car on Sebastian's heels lest he change his mind. He went around the side of the building to a private entrance labeled "Penthouse" and rang the bell. Only a few moments later, a man opened the door. The red of his hair matched the crimson stains on his shirt sleeves.

"What's this?" he exclaimed, staring angrily at me.

"A friend. She's here to help." Sebastian's voice was soothing but also firm. "James, where is—"

"Gone! *Her* kind came to collect, not more than ten minutes ago. And when I protested, I got a call from Blakeslee himself, ordering me to surrender the body."

Sebastian cursed under his breath. James continued to look at me accusingly. "I had nothing to do with the Consortium's involvement," I said, "and I have no idea why they're being so secretive. Will you just tell me exactly what you saw?"

"It was Martine. Her nose began to bleed, out of nowhere. She's young, you know, and when she saw herself like that, her face covered in blood..." He trailed off when his voice choked up.

"She began to change," said Sebastian.

James nodded. "But she couldn't." He swallowed hard. "I've never seen seizures like that before. As though they would tear her apart. When they finally stopped, she wasn't breathing." Anger flared again as he turned to me, displacing his grief. "Happy now?"

"I'm terribly sorry for your loss," I said, refusing to rise to the bait.

Sebastian squeezed his shoulder. "I'm not going to rest until I find out what—or who—is responsible. We'll be in touch."

We walked slowly back to the street, but when we reached the car, Sebastian didn't open the door. "I need to get back to my office." His voice was quiet and restrained, but the tension that rippled beneath his skin was not fully human. I fought off a shiver. "Do you mind making your own way home?"

"No, of course not. You'll let me know how I can help?"

"I will." He leaned forward slightly, as though to touch me, but apparently thought the better of it. "Good night, Val."

I watched as his car pulled away, then I began to walk toward the closest subway stop. Sebastian had looked more upset than I'd ever seen him. But his distress was nothing compared to James's. Clearly, he had cared a great deal for Martine. And now she was dead. How would I have felt, if—

Clenching my teeth, I increased my pace, as though by doing so I could outrun my own fears. I didn't have to imagine how I would feel if Alexa had been the one to die before my eyes. I knew exactly how that felt because once, not so long ago, I had believed that I'd killed her. The worst day of my life.

I fished my phone out of my pocket then, afraid that I'd missed a call from her while at the party. But there were no messages. It had been almost four days now since I'd heard from her—longer than normal.

Tamping down my unease, I descended into the subway. She was fine. She would call tomorrow. And within a week, she would be in my arms.

CHAPTER FIVE

I couldn't sleep. Instinct nagged at me, a dull ache in my head insisting there was something terribly wrong with the world. The afterimage of James's dark, anguished eyes was burned into my memory, but that wasn't all that had been keeping me awake. In the two days that had passed since the fund-raiser, Alexa still hadn't called. Before now, I had heard from her at least twice a week, despite the fact that the nearest telephone was in a village over two hours' run from Telassar. I had no way of contacting her. And despite my rational brain's calm assurances that there was a logical explanation for her silence—the phone had broken, maybe, or she was busy as she prepared to come home—images of her alone in danger, injured or even worse, flooded my imagination. Last night, in a frenzy of need and anxiety, I had downed one of the two remaining bags of her blood. The taste, a fading echo of the glorious ambrosia that ran through her veins, had only sharpened my thirst.

This morning I had caved, calling first Karma and then Sebastian to enlist their help. Karma worked closely with Malcolm Blakeslee, the Weremaster of New York. If something big had happened in Telassar, he would know and she would be able to find out. If I was being honest with myself, though, I was counting more on Sebastian's underground contacts and unofficial channels. It made me crazy to have to count on anyone at all, but without knowing Telassar's location, I had no choice, no power, no control.

I stared at the fine cracks in the ceiling. They seemed to warp and twist in the flickering ambient light from the city that filtered through

NELL STARK AND TRINITY TAM

my window. They reminded me of Vincent's seizing body—how he had writhed in pain, unable to take refuge in his wolf. What force was powerful enough to keep a shifter from changing? Some kind of drug? A pathogen? Were others in danger? Would Alexa be in danger, if…no, no, *when* she returned? Sighing, I checked the clock. After two a.m. Either I could lie there spinning my mental wheels until the sun came up, or I could do something about the other source of my dread. The one on *this* continent.

Half an hour later, I walked into the lobby of the Consortium, heading directly for the bank of elevators. I spared a glance for the receptionist and wished I hadn't. Giselle. She had tried to seduce me once at Helen's behest. It hadn't worked, but the memory of how she had drawn one long fingernail across her own skin, parting it to allow her blood to rise and tempt my thirst, set my throat to throbbing.

"Hello, Valentine," she called, her voice low and teasing.

I ignored her and stepped into the open elevator, then punched the button marked "L." The library was the floor below the penthouse. It boasted all of the standard features, with the added bonus of a librarian who had been born in the nineteenth century. At two thirty on a Friday morning, it was busier than I'd ever seen it during the daylight hours. It was surprising how often I forgot that Alexa's blood was the only reason I could still walk unharmed in the sunlight. And that the majority of my people could not do the same.

I sat at one of the computers, nodding to the vampire who occupied the seat next to mine, and called up the Consortium's database. I squeezed my gritty eyes shut and forced myself to relive the sequence of events at Luna. Then I input every search term I could think of: bloody nose, seizures, vomiting, failure to shift.

Nothing. No hit results at all. So I tried a different tack and entered the broadest search I could think of. "Unable to shift." This time, I got results, but they weren't at all what I was expecting.

Were-women didn't shift when they were pregnant. I sat back in my chair, working through the medical logic. It made sense: the transformation of a pregnant shifter would be catastrophic for her fetus. Suddenly, my senses were assaulted by the mental image of Alexa, her face radiant with joy as I rested one hand on the swell of her belly—as I felt the first kick of our growing child. The vampire parasite had rendered me sterile, but Alexa could bear as many children as she wanted. As we wanted.

I closed my eyes in agony as that unexpected desire clashed with the uncertainty of our reality. Clenching my jaw, I struggled to regain equilibrium. She was fine. She would make it back; I would see her in just three more days. I had to focus—to make sure that New York was a safe place for her to return to.

Link after link took me to more information about shifter pregnancy. Consortium scientists hadn't yet positively identified the mechanism by which the change was suppressed, but they suspected it was hormonal. The science distracted me for a few minutes before I got back on task, skimming through the remaining hits for anything that resembled Vincent's condition at Luna. I found a few interesting entries on the herb wolfsbane, which, when diluted and injected into a shifter, could delay transformation for up to an hour, depending on the size of the dose. But according to the official Consortium records, there was nothing that could prevent a male shifter from making the change.

Whatever had happened to Vincent and Martine was either too new to be in the archives, or too secret. Given the alacrity with which Helen's security guards had responded to both emergencies, combined with Clavier's refusal to share any information, I suspected the latter. Which meant that I couldn't go to either of them for help.

I closed my browser window, stood, and slowly spun in a circle. Rows upon rows of bookshelves. Multiple computer banks—and off to one side, even a card catalogue. But none of these resources were of any use. I looked at my sandals, picturing the medical wing several floors below my feet. I had last visited it months ago, shortly after being turned. My stomach churned at the sudden, visceral echo of remembered fear, and I dispelled the sensation with one swift shake of my head. I wasn't about to let those ghosts deter me.

Within minutes, I was exiting the elevator on the third floor. It was busier than I remembered, perhaps because of the lateness of the hour. As I watched, a man in a white lab coat exited one room and a woman ducked into another. The Consortium version of orderlies. I wondered if they were all vampires, and if so, how they treated their patients without killing them.

I walked down the hall, scanning each room as I passed. I didn't think anyone would question my presence there, but I didn't want to pause too long lest I seem suspicious. Most of the rooms were empty. The few that were occupied held vampires—I could tell from the thick blackout curtains that swathed the windows. Vampires would sever themselves from the natural rhythm of the outside world by banning sunlight from a room.

By the time I reached the end of the corridor, I was confused. Not only was Vincent nowhere to be found, there were no Weres at all on the floor. Shouldn't there have been at least a few—if only the recently infected, who required supervision and confinement while they adjusted to their inner beasts? I turned and walked back the way I'd come, rolling my neck in a futile attempt to loosen the knot that was growing tighter between my shoulders. When a female orderly emerged from a room several doors ahead of me, I made a snap decision and hurried to catch up.

Her heart-shaped face turned toward me when I put a hand on her arm, and I saw her pupils dilate at the same instant that I realized she was human. My gaze was drawn by a days-old bite scar just above her collarbone. Saliva flooded my mouth as the heat ripped through my throat. *No.*

"Can I help you?" she asked coquettishly, oblivious to my struggle.

"I'm looking for Vincent."

The bridge of her nose crinkled. "We don't have any patients by that name." She took a step closer to me. "But what's yours? Mine's Tonya."

I took shallow breaths in an effort to dull the effects of the warm aroma wafting off her smooth skin. It didn't help. "He was brought in just under a week ago."

Some note in my voice must have clued her in to the magnitude of my concern, because she stopped her advance and bent her head to the digital tablet in her hand. After scrolling through it, she shook her head. "I have no record of him. I'm sorry."

"Is there a different facility just for Weres?" I asked, wondering if the shifters had a wing that I wasn't aware of.

"No, this is a mixed-use facility." Tonya frowned again. "But we haven't admitted any Weres in a while."

Aimless dread made my throat constrict. "How long?"

"Maybe two weeks?" In a heartbeat, the flirtatious glint returned to her eyes. "To be honest, I don't pay all that much attention to them. I'm much more interested in your kind."

"So I gathered." I spoke the words more softly than she could hear.

"You look so thirsty. And it's been days since the last time I…" Her eyes glazed at the memory. "Won't you let me? Harold says I taste like rose petals."

I licked my lips. I couldn't help it. But I could help whom I sank my teeth into. "You're very generous. But no. Thank you."

Before she could respond, I was gone.

The trail for information, barely lukewarm to begin with, had gone cold. I could think of only one other tactic, and it was a long shot. I had seen Vincent twice: once in a dogfight on the Red Circuit, and once on the floor of Luna, seizing in agony. If I went back to the Circuit, I could ask some of the regulars about him and maybe learn something that way.

I walked across the width of Manhattan in the pre-dawn, enjoying the stillness of the city at this hour—the hush as it took a deep breath in anticipation of the frenetic day to come. By the time the sun broke free of the horizon, I was in Hell's Kitchen, staring at the marquee of the Vixen Theater. Every week, the marquee announced, in code, the location of the next Red Circuit party. But if this was a code, it wasn't one I was going to be able to decipher. The marquee was blank.

Despair rose in my chest, a black wave of longing and fatigue that set my entire body aching in empathy with my throat. Why was my search being thwarted at every turn? And did whatever was happening here in New York have any connection to why I hadn't heard from Alexa?

I needed to feel her hands on me, to hear her soothing murmurs of love, to taste the bright, hot flavor of her under my tongue. I wanted to go home—to crawl into bed, pull the covers over my head, and escape into oblivion. But I knew I wouldn't sleep. And I couldn't give up. Sebastian would know what was going on with the Circuit. He was the one who had told us about the marquee in the first place.

He picked up on the second ring. "Hello, Val." His voice was deeper than usual and harsh with fatigue. I could only imagine the pressure he felt to get answers about what had happened to both Vincent and Martine, especially in the face of the Consortium's secrecy.

"Breakfast?" I said. "I'm buying."

"Where?"

I rattled off the name of a greasy spoon near Times Square and hung up. He'd probably have his chauffeur drive him, which meant that I had to hustle. I walked uptown briskly, welcoming the warmth of the sun on my arms. Too much direct sunlight without any sunblock would leave me with a mild rash and some nausea, but it was a small price to pay for the ability to move about freely during the daytime. Thanks to Alexa.

When I reached the restaurant, Sebastian had already claimed a booth. He was clean-shaven and dressed in clothes that fit him too well to be store-bought, but his face was drawn and his eyes bloodshot. I slid in across from him and nodded to the waitress when she asked if I wanted coffee.

"Invite me to breakfast but keep me waiting." Sebastian raised his own ceramic mug in a mock salute. "You wouldn't treat me like this if I were a woman."

"You don't fool me," I told him. "What's going on?"

He sat back and spread his arms along the width of the booth. "You first."

"Still no word from Alexa. I presume you haven't heard anything."

"Nothing. But that's not unusual where Telassar is concerned. I don't think you understand just how isolated that place is." He shuddered delicately.

"All right." I battled down the urge to take out my frustration on one of my only allies. "Thanks for looking into it."

The waitress returned at that moment, and I snatched up my coffee gratefully. Once we had ordered, I leaned in over the table. "What's the deal with the Red Circuit?"

His shaggy eyebrows arched. "You're looking to party? I was under the impression that you hated that whole scene and only did it under duress."

"I'm looking for Vincent."

Sebastian's bravado dissipated like mist over the East River. "What have you heard?"

"Heard? Not a damn thing that's useful." I scrubbed one hand through my hair. It was getting long. Alexa liked it when I was a little bit scruffy. I wouldn't cut it yet because she would be home soon. Because the village phone was broken. That was all.

"I called Malcolm's office the morning after Martine's death, asking about Vincent. I was told by some secretary that he had been treated and released." Sebastian's eyes were dark with an emotion I'd never seen him express before. Fear. "She seemed to believe her own story. But no one can reach him."

"I talked to an orderly in the medical wing just hours ago," I said, sitting back as the waitress deposited a stack of pancakes in front of me and an omelet in front of Sebastian. "She said that no one named Vincent had ever been admitted. And that they'd seen no shifters at all in the past two weeks."

Sebastian's eyes narrowed. "That's odd. There's always a Were or two at the Consortium—either a newbie dealing with having been turned, or a drug addict trying to get clean."

"You mentioned drugs before," I said, remembering that he had first assumed Olivia to be investigating trafficking at Luna. "Are drugs a big problem?"

"They're one way to deal with an animal in your head."

"Makes sense." Alexa had been on several prescription medications after being turned—antipsychotics like Klonopin that had muted the will of her panther while she adjusted to the unfamiliar presence in her psyche. I could imagine the ease with which some shifters became addicted to drugs like that.

"Look," I said, trying to get the conversation back on track. "I've only seen Vincent twice in my life: once on the Red Circuit, and once last week. Since the Consortium is putting up information roadblocks, I thought I'd go back to the Circuit. But the marquee is blank."

Sebastian laid down his fork and grimaced. "More of your friend Olivia's work. She's taken her fight up the Consortium food chain, asking questions she shouldn't know how to ask. Malcolm ordered me yesterday to put the Circuit on ice for a while."

"Damn it." I swallowed the coffee dregs and shifted my mug to the end of the table in the hopes that it would be refilled. "Where the hell is she getting her information?"

Sebastian's jaw bunched. "I think we have a leak."

"A traitor? Really?"

"How else do you explain it?"

I shrugged. "You could be right. All I know is that her source is male."

"Well, that narrows it down."

Ignoring the gibe, I glanced around the diner to be certain the waitress wasn't nearby. Maybe I was paranoid, but then again, given the unanswered questions both Sebastian and I were wrestling with, maybe not. He still hadn't told me what I wanted to hear, and I wasn't about to let him off the hook.

"You can't expect me to believe that the Circuit has actually ground to a halt," I said. When Sebastian opened his mouth to protest, I raised one hand and fixed him with what I hoped was my most intimidating stare. "You know as well as I do that our people need that kind of outlet. So tell me where they're getting it now."

He pushed the plate aside and leaned in close enough to kiss me. I didn't move. "The Chinatown tunnels. Tomorrow night." Uncertainty flashed over his face—an unfamiliar expression. "You really think the Circuit has something to do with what's happened to Vincent?"

"It's your baby. You would know better than I." When Sebastian shook his head, I flashed my sharp canines to forestall him. "Don't try denying it. 'I put the Circuit on ice,' you said."

He grimaced. "So I did. Damn it. I can't afford to slip like that right now." He squeezed his eyes shut for a moment. When he opened them, they telegraphed his anger. "I don't like coincidences. The ADA starts snooping around at the same time a sick Were goes missing?"

"And there's been no word from Telassar," I reminded him. It wasn't surprising that urbane Sebastian didn't have a strong connection to the isolationists in Africa, but I knew somehow that Alexa's silence was part of this puzzle.

"Fine, yes, that too."

I looked at my watch. I needed to be at the lab in an hour. "Will you be there tomorrow night?" I asked as I threw a few bills down on the faux granite tabletop. "Come to think of it, I've never *seen* you on the Circuit."

Sebastian's grin was pure wolf. He stood with a subtle grace that was both masculine and animal. "Nonetheless," he said softly, "I'm always there."

CHAPTER SIX

I reached the Bloody Angle just as it began to rain. Earlier in the evening, dark clouds had rolled in from the west, smothering the sunset. But the storm had held off until I'd set foot on Doyers Street. Probably a bad omen.

At the turn of the century, crooked Doyers had been infamous as a good place to get mugged by one of the gangs warring over the turf of Chinatown and Little Italy. Now it was a tourist attraction. As the skies opened, I made a dash for the Wing Fat Arcade, stepping down into the tunnel only seconds before the first crack of thunder rent the night. In the moments it had taken me to get indoors, the rain had plastered my hair to my head and my shirt to my torso. Rivulets of water streamed down my face to drip onto the stone steps leading into the bowels of the city.

Shops, all closed for the day, lined the narrow underground street: acupuncturists, an apothecary, English schools. When I reached the first intersection, I looked right, then left. Both corridors ended in barred doors with signs in English proclaiming "Keep Out!" and signs in Chinese that probably said the same thing. The one on the left also featured a beautiful woman lurking in the shadows. The gatekeeper.

She pressed close as she handed me a raffle ticket. "Haven't seen you in months." When she breathed in deeply, frown lines materialized on her forehead. "Hmm."

"What?"

"The cat. Her scent has faded." Her lips skated lightly across my neck. "She shouldn't be so cavalier about her territory."

I stiffened and stepped away, tamping down a blistering surge of anger that made me want to sink my sharpened teeth into the tattoo just below her collarbone. Instead, I reached for the door handle. It didn't budge. The gatekeeper smiled provocatively as she pulled her cell phone from the front pocket of her skinny jeans. When she punched three numbers into the keypad, I heard a click as the lock released.

"Have fun," she said as I stepped into the gloom beyond. As soon as the door slammed shut, I crumpled up my ticket and tossed it onto the floor. I wanted what it offered too much to trust myself.

The corridor was sinuous, twisting every ten feet so that it was impossible to make out its destination. Naked lightbulbs hung from the ceiling, their harsh light illuminating doors that were set into the uneven stone walls at regular intervals. The fifth door on the right had been propped open with a brick, and I slipped into a large, low-ceilinged room that might once have been a warehouse but now functioned as a club. Several folding tables had been lined up to form a bar along the near wall, and a makeshift plywood dais across the room served as a stage on which a blond woman, wearing nothing but stilettos, danced for the crowd.

In another room nearby, I knew, would be the dogfights. I needed to find them and ask around about Vincent. But first I needed a drink. Being here reminded me of the last time I'd braved the Circuit—the night when the Missionary had made an appearance. The night I'd almost died at his hands a second time. If it hadn't been for Alexa…

Suppressing a shudder, I worked my way to the bar and ordered a double of whiskey, neat. After a long sip, I took a look around, intending to head for the fights, but at that moment, the lights dimmed and a spotlight focused on the stage. When a woman, dressed head to toe in black leather and holding a bullwhip, stepped into the bright circle, I sighed in relief. The Record was much easier for me to handle than the Raffle for some poor homeless soul's lifeblood.

As the dominatrix dramatically cracked her whip, two men, shirtless and barefoot, led a naked woman out onto the stage by a chain clipped to the collar around her neck. I sucked in a surprised breath when I recognized her.

"Gwendolyn was reborn in India one hundred and eighteen years ago." The disembodied voice ricocheted around the room, soft and sibilant. As though it were inside my head. "The last time she stood before us, she nearly broke the Record. Tonight, she wishes to try again. Will you welcome her?"

Applause thundered beneath the low ceiling, and I felt my pulse increase to match the beat of the crowd. Gwendolyn's skin shone under the spotlight, and for a moment, I thought she had used oil, until my keen vision caught a bead of sweat trickling between her breasts. I frowned. These tunnels were cool. If she was nervous enough to be sweating profusely, she wasn't going to last long.

The dominatrix's crimson lips twitched below the cruel beak of her falcon mask, and I wondered what she was feeling. Power? Lust? Perhaps even a little trepidation? The collar around Gwendolyn's neck looked heavy and the chain strong. But only months ago, I had watched her transform into a Bengal tiger and snap those iron links in one powerful lunge. She had been beautiful in her ferocity. And I had no doubt that she would have killed her tormentor if given the chance.

A hush fell over the room as the dominatrix moved into striking distance. In the pause before she raised her arm, I took a deep breath. I didn't want to feel anticipation for the spectacle, but the mood of the crowd had caught me up. I walked the streets above among mortals with the face of a woman and the appetites of a monster. Down here in the belly of the city where the veneer of civility had no place, we were all unmasked. It would have felt like a relief, had I not been so desperately thirsty.

My throat pulsed greedily as a streak of red opened along Gwendolyn's flank. Another followed it below her left shoulder blade. Another, and then another, until her flesh was weeping and it was all I could do not to vault onto the stage and kneel beneath her to catch the red drops as they fell upon unyielding wood.

The crowd counted. Twenty-four. Thirty-seven. Forty-nine. The Record was fifty-seven lashes; I knew that from the last time Gwendolyn had attempted it. Her tiger had leapt free at fifty-one. Now, on the cusp of fifty-five, the energy in the room was nearly unbearable. She was shaking, convulsing against the pillar, held up only by her chained hands as her feet skidded over the rough floor. How was she not shifting?

The room went berserk at the fifty-eighth lash. It felt like Times Square on New Year's Eve, and I clutched at my glass, struggling to keep my feet. Once I'd found my balance, I looked up at Gwendolyn again, wondering how long she would be able to hang on…only to realize that something was terribly wrong. She was jerking in her chains, and her eyes had rolled up in her head. Spittle foamed over red lips drawn back in a rictus of agony. And that's when I knew: it wasn't self-control that had allowed her to break the Record. Like Vincent, like Martine, she couldn't shift.

The dominatrix had lowered the whip. It trembled against the floor, an extension of her shaking hand. The crowd was starting to quiet now, their exultant shouts subsiding into confused murmuring. Cursing, I pushed forward, shouldering through the wall of people. I didn't know what I could do when I reached Gwendolyn, but I had to try something. When her body began to blur, I felt a surge of hope that she might transform after all, but she continued to spasm, human and helpless, the chain clanking hollowly against the pole as the seizures racked her flayed body.

And then, as though a switch had been flicked, the paroxysms stopped. Her chin lolled on her breastbone as she swung slowly from the bonds around her wrists. When blood seeped out of her nose to join the crimson smears at her feet, I knew she was dead.

An uneasy hush fell over the room. Those who came to the Red Circuit came to watch death. But not like this. I kept pushing toward the stage, but I was still twenty feet away when Sebastian's cronies emerged from the shadows. They made quick work of disposing of Gwendolyn's broken body, then disappeared into the mass of black curtains. When I looked around for the dominatrix, she was nowhere to be found.

"Damn it," I breathed. At least Helen's guards hadn't been the ones to collect the corpse. With Sebastian in control, I would have access to Gwendolyn's body.

"Ladies and gentlemen," the sibilant voice announced. "Do not be alarmed, but for security purposes, this room must be vacated. Please make your way to the adjoining chamber, where we will continue with the Raffle." Several more men dressed in black emerged from behind the stage to direct people. The procedure was orderly and efficient, and while many in the throng looked troubled, no one was panicking.

I spun in a slow circle in an effort to locate Sebastian, but all I saw was the seething crowd. Working my way toward the front of the room made me feel like a salmon swimming upstream, but after several minutes, I succeeded in skirting around the stage. I ducked behind the curtains, only to be brought up short by the sight of two guards flanking a door set into the wall.

"I'm a doctor," I fudged. "I need to get back there." The left guard stared at me, expressionless. The right shook his head.

"And a friend of Sebastian's," I said.

"No one passes."

I bit back a frustrated retort. "Call him. My name is Valentine Darrow."

When neither made a move to activate the mics strapped to their wrists, I thought for one insane moment about taking them on. Gwendolyn and Martine had died because they couldn't shift. Vincent had come close, and was perhaps even now lying on his deathbed. The most likely explanation was that they had contracted some kind of pathogen, but it was impossible to tell for sure without more information. And I had to know now, because Alexa might be coming home to an epidemic. But without my gun, I was no match for two shifters.

I was just about to turn and head for the surface, where I'd have cell reception and could leave Sebastian a message, when both guards put their left hands to their ears.

"Yes, sir," the right one said into his wrist as the left one beckoned me closer. He pushed the door inward and as soon as I'd stepped into the shadows, he closed it behind me. Sebastian was there. I could smell his distinctive cologne before I saw him step around a bend in the tunnel ahead. A surgical mask dangled around his neck.

"It's a pathogen?" I asked, fear coiling in my gut.

"I don't know. The mask is a precaution." The muscles along his jawline flexed ominously. "I want the Consortium kept out of this. Do you have a way of testing Gwendolyn's blood?"

"At the lab where I intern, yes."

But instead of showing relief, he rocked back on his heels. "You're sure? You're no medical examiner, Val. And this has to be done right."

My fists clenched and I took a step toward him before I could help myself. "You think I don't know that? Goddamn it, Sebastian, Alexa's supposed to come home in two days! I need to know what the hell she's coming home to. We all need to know. I'll make sure it's done properly."

"Okay. Come with me."

He led me back the way he'd come, around one bend in the tunnel and down a steep slope to a T-intersection. He turned left and froze.

"Fuck!" He took off sprinting down the corridor before I could tell what was wrong. And then I saw it as he skidded to a halt next to a recessed doorway: a crumpled human form lying across the threshold. By the time I reached them, Sebastian was rising from his crouch.

"Is he—?"

"He's alive. Tranked."

I knelt to feel the guard's pulse and was reassured by its steadiness. Sebastian was leaning against the door, his face turned toward the room. When I followed his gaze, all I saw was an empty table.

"Someone took the body."

"Lambros." Sebastian spat the word, and I had to fight not to take a step away from him. He was angry. So angry that he was struggling not to shift.

"Why?" I moved into the room, searching for even the slightest trace of blood that was still salvageable. There was nothing. "How did they clean up so fast?"

"There was nothing to clean. We had her in a bag, in case of infection."

Inspiration struck. "What about the stage? Her blood was all over it."

Our pace was hurried as we walked back the way we had come. A dozen feet from the doorway, however, Sebastian broke into a run.

"What?" I called after him.

"Bleach!"

Puzzled, I followed close behind as he burst through the doors. The guards that had blocked the passage now lay on either side of it. I bent to check their vitals. "Tranked, too."

"Can't you smell it now?" he asked bitterly. "I bet her fucking commandos covered the stage in bleach while we were in the tunnels."

He was right—the acrid smell of bleach pricked my nose when I breathed in. Together, we walked up the crude wooden set of stairs that led to the back of the stage. When we pushed through the thick curtain, my eyes began to water. Sebastian was right—someone had dumped a large quantity of bleach over the pool of blood. The mixture had trickled over the left side of the stage and was pooling onto the floor. Not a drop of it would be viable for testing.

"Damn it!" What was Helen covering up? It had to be big, or she wouldn't have gone to such efforts. I stood still, listening to Sebastian take deep, even breaths in an effort to calm his wolf, and tried to figure out what to do now. I could either stick with my original plan and ask questions about Vincent, or I could follow the body. It had to be at the Consortium somewhere. And this time, I wasn't going to stop looking until I found answers or was forcibly removed.

"I'm going after the body," I said. I expected Sebastian to try to argue or tell me it was hopeless, but he only nodded. This version of him, weary and fighting for control, was unsettling.

"I have to deal with the aftermath here. There are going to be a lot of questions."

"What are you going to say?"

"I don't know." He closed his eyes and slumped against the side wall of the stage like a prizefighter who had taken too many punches. "If I tell the truth—that I have no fucking clue—the uncertainty will cause a panic. If I cover this up, then I'm no better than Lambros."

"What if you tell half the truth?" I flashed back to Gwendolyn's last moments. "You could say that you're not sure what happened tonight, but that it might be drug-related. Given what you've told me about the drug abuse in the shifter community, people might buy it. They'll have something to latch on to, but you won't actually be lying."

Sebastian's taut triceps finally ceased their rapid flickering as he pushed off from the wall. "That could work. You'll call me if you find something."

I knew what he wasn't saying—that even given our friendship it was difficult for him to trust me, a vampire who had a close relationship with Helen. "I will," I said softly. "Nothing's more important to me than Alexa. Nothing."

He nodded once, then gestured for me to follow. As I let him guide me through the warren of tunnels, I wondered where the dominatrix had disappeared to. Had she pulled off her mask and blended into the crowd? Or had she been part of Helen's cover-up attempt? Remembering the agonized curve of her mouth and the anxious trembling of her arm, I rejected that suspicion. She had been as surprised as the rest of us. And the pain in her eyes had been palpable.

"Sebastian," I said as we ascended into an alley just off Mott. The rain had cleared, but puddles filled every divot in the street. "The woman with the whip—do you know her?"

"No." He was already thumbing through his BlackBerry, eyes flickering rapidly as he scanned his messages. "She leaves me a message before every party, but she only uses burn phones."

"If I don't get anywhere at the Consortium, I want to find her."

His head snapped up. "You think she has something to do with this? Why?"

"No," I said. "But I think she might be connected to Gwendolyn somehow."

"I'll look into it." His gaze flickered between my face and the backlit screen in his palm. "Be careful."

Normally, his proprietary concern would have grated on me, but tonight I didn't mind. I even touched him on the shoulder as I turned toward the subway station. If what we both suspected was true, he was the one at risk here—not me.

I avoided the front door. Vincent had been taken into Headquarters via the back entrance, and since I'd never gone in that way, I didn't know what to expect. I approached it as silently as I could, concentrating on every sound, every scent, every stirring of the dense air. The night would mask my presence from any onlookers, but the Consortium was also likely to be busy.

The door was locked. I sucked in a breath as I held my hand to the palm scanner that jutted out from the wall. At the click of the door opening, I blew out a long sigh. At least I was in.

"In" was a corridor that made a perpendicular turn ten feet away. I made my footsteps slow and measured, despite my pounding pulse. At a bend in the hall, I paused and listened carefully for any sign of movement. All I heard were the slow, alternating beeps of several heart monitors, distant and muffled. I never would have heard them at all had I not been what I was.

I took off toward the sound but nearly blew my cover when a door, ten feet ahead and to my right, opened. Swiftly, I ducked back behind the bend, hoping that whoever had come out wasn't trying to leave the building. For one breath-stealing moment, I thought I would be discovered, but the rhythmic treads grew softer rather than louder. I let out my breath in a relieved sigh and cautiously looked around the corner. A flash of long, dark hair and the swirl of a white lab coat was all I saw before the individual disappeared behind a door at the end of the hall. From the sound of her steps afterward, it led to a stairwell.

I counted to thirty before following her and paused to try the knob at the windowless door from which she'd emerged. Locked. When I twisted harder, I heard the metal groan. I could probably have forced it, but that might have given away my presence, and I wanted to see where she had gone.

The door to the stairwell swung open at a touch and I found myself on a landing with two choices: ascent or descent. Closing my eyes, I listened for the beeping of the monitors. It was a little louder now, and seemed to be coming from below me, though I couldn't be sure as echoes bounced off the concrete walls. Down first, then I could always go up later, if I was mistaken.

I wasn't. The stairwell opened into an antechamber that seemed to be some kind of observation facility. Several chairs were lined up to face a large window cut into the far wall overlooking a larger room in which at least a dozen beds had been arranged in dormitory-style rows. Half of them were curtained off, the other half empty. As I watched, the woman in the lab coat picked a file out of a cabinet against one wall and drew back the curtain on the closest bed. I had the briefest glimpse of the patient's face—covered in heavy stubble and shining with sweat— before the woman's body obscured my vision.

I cursed, eyeing the scanner next to the sliding door that separated me from the room. I doubted this one would accept my palm.

Too late, I heard the snick of a lock catching behind me. I whirled to find Harold Clavier, dressed in deep red scrubs, stepping away from a small door next to the staircase that I had overlooked in my eagerness to discover what was going on in the makeshift hospital. A stream of cold air wafted past my face. In the midst of struggling to gather my thoughts, I absurdly wondered whether he had stepped out of a refrigerator. And then I realized that he had. A morgue. Gwendolyn's body was probably back there.

"You have no business here, Valentine." Clavier's voice was devoid of inflection. I wondered if the mannerism was studied, or if he really felt nothing.

"Yes, I do." The surge of adrenaline at being caught made me sound a little shaky. "A woman died tonight, displaying the same symptoms as the man at Luna a week ago and the woman in Tribeca a few days back." I searched his eyes for any sign of sympathy, of empathy. Had the parasite stolen every human impulse from him? "Something is killing shifters. Alexa is coming home soon. I need her to be safe."

"We are already investigating these incidents," he said, using the same tone of voice that a father might use for his recalcitrant child. "I can't tell you anything further."

"Let me help, damn it!" I couldn't keep from raising my voice. "I have skills you can use. My training is excellent. Put me to work. Please."

Clavier tilted his head to look at me over the tops of his glasses. "You can stop your snooping and allow me and my staff to do our jobs. We have this under control." He walked to the sliding doors, pressed his hand to the scanner, and stepped over the threshold. He was taunting me. Mocking me. As the doors hissed shut behind him, I clenched my fists hard enough to break the skin of my own palms.

"No," I said to the glass that separated me from the truth. "I don't think you do."

CHAPTER SEVEN

*T*he rough stone of the balustrade chafed my palms as I leaned forward in search of clean air. Across the boulevard, the walls of the library burned, even the stone catching flame in the impossible heat of the conflagration. Hoarse screams rose from the streets below as smoke reached down my throat to claw at my lungs. I was going to die. We all were. I could feel the lives being extinguished around me like so many flickering candles. How had I not seen this coming?

Breathing shallowly, I tugged hard at the rope I had knotted around one of the balusters. It would not extend to the ground. I could only pray that it would reach close enough. I didn't have much time—the floor was growing warmer. Soon, the four walls of this chamber would also be wreathed in flame.

One of us had to survive. If the clan line did not persist, the Order of Mithras itself would be jeopardized. I grasped the rope and swung my legs over the edge, then eased my grip enough to descend into the billowing haze. All too soon, I found myself dangling at its end, thick smoke obscuring the length of the drop. I flexed my knees, clenched my jaw, and let my hands fall away.

The impact sent streaks of pain shooting through my legs and up along my spine. My right foot twisted under me, and I felt my anklebone snap as I collapsed against the flagstones. They burned my palms. Closing my lips around an agonized moan, I tried to stand and failed. My eyes watered, tears tracking through the grime that covered my face as I slowly pushed myself forward, condemned to slide on my belly like the serpent in Paradise.

There was nowhere for me to go, but I had to carry on. Perhaps all *was not lost—perhaps the invaders would leave me for dead. So long as there was the slimmest chance of survival, I would not yield. And then, instead of heated rock, my hand touched smooth, cool leather. I looked up, and my hopes died.*

"You," I said, the pain in my leg eclipsed by the agonizing knowledge that I had failed.

Balthasar Brenner laughed, his wild hair dusted with glowing sparks. "Who else were you expecting, René?"

"This is madness," I said hoarsely. "You are declaring war on the vampires. Do you want the world to bathe in blood yet again?"

Brenner crouched and fisted my hair, baring my throat. I swallowed convulsively. "You know as well as I do that your kind started this war by engineering a plague against us." His lips drew back from his teeth and he snarled into my face. "The Alliance will be dissolved. Die certain of that."

Surprise. Bewilderment. They were sensations I had not felt in over three hundred years. As Balthasar Brenner's body blurred smoothly into that of a large, white wolf, I knew they would be my last.

I woke to the ominous sound of a stirring beehive. As I blinked my way into consciousness, I realized three things: my throat was throbbing more insistently than it had since I'd been turned, my left arm had fallen asleep, and the beehive was my cell phone vibrating against the coffee table. *Alexa.* I scooped it up and muttered a hasty hello, but the call had already gone to voicemail. Sebastian.

I set the phone down and shook the needling sensation out of my left arm, then swung my legs over the side of the couch and stared around my apartment. Twilight filtered through the window. A rerun of some crime show played on the television. I remembered getting home from the lab around six and collapsing into the soft embrace of the couch, silently vowing that I would only close my eyes for a second. So much for that plan.

The scent of char was still so strong in my nose that I got up to check the kitchen. Nothing burning—I hadn't used the pots all week. The odor was entirely a product of my crazy dream. It had felt so real— the sharp pain of my cracking ankle, the billowing smoke and panicked dread that had been choking me by turns. No, not me. René. But who was he? The name sounded familiar…

And then I remembered the annoying, holier-than-thou vampire who had so imperiously given me orders in Helen's office. He'd mentioned a René. "René Valois," he had said, "Blood Prime of the Clan of the Missionary, has summoned you to Sybaris." What a strange and vivid dream to have about someone I'd never met, never seen— someone I'd heard of only once. My pulse was still elevated from my dream-self's desperation, and thirst flared with every heartbeat.

To take my mind off the craving, I called Sebastian back. "Sorry I missed you," I said. "Fell asleep by accident. What's going on?"

"I have an address for you. Of the woman with the whip." I grabbed a pen and a crumpled pizza receipt from the table as he rattled off a street and apartment number in the Bronx.

"Thanks," I said, padding into the kitchen. For a long moment, I deliberated between the tap and a bottle of red wine. The choice was easy: the viscous wine sometimes fooled my throat for an instant. "I'll head out in a few minutes."

"I'm coming with you."

"Hell no, you're not!" My hand shook, and I cursed under my breath as the rich Shiraz splashed onto my white tank top. "If there's some kind of pathogen out there, then vampires don't seem to be susceptible. I'll be safe. You'd be in danger."

"If there's some kind of pathogen out there," he said, "then I've probably already been exposed."

However likely that was, I refused to believe it. I didn't want to think of Sebastian that way, convulsing helplessly in the thrall of some power he could not defeat. "Still, there's a chance you haven't been. And we should try to keep it that way."

He was quiet for a moment. The red wine sluiced down my throat, thick and fragrant but nothing like what I needed. Alexa was supposed to come home tomorrow. I would go to the airport, even though I suspected she would not be stepping off the plane. Grimacing, I threw the rest of the glass back in one swallow.

"Call on the land line. Hang on a second." Sebastian's murmur was followed by the sound of him setting down his cell phone. "Brenner," I heard distantly.

Brenner. The dream returned in a rush: the taste of smoke coating my mouth, the sharp tug of Brenner's fingers in my hair, the despair pressing behind my eyes as I realized my fate was sealed. *Balthasar*

Brenner. The memory of the snarling white wolf made my skin prickle. It had felt so real.

"Back," Sebastian said. "Now where—"

"Is your father named Balthasar?"

Silence greeted my question. "Yes," he said finally, his voice flat. "Why?"

"I had...a dream." I paused, the words sounding ridiculous as I said them.

"About my father?"

"Yes. It was very vivid. He turned into a white wolf."

"He has been known to do that," Sebastian said dryly.

"I'm sure there's a logical explanation," I said, even though I wasn't. Had Sebastian ever mentioned the kind of wolf into which his father transformed? I didn't think he had. So how had my imagination manufactured the correct details?

I was no stranger to nightmares, but this one had been different. "Just random neurons firing," I told him and myself. "Probably inspired by our conversation last week."

"If I contributed to his invading your dreams, then believe me, I apologize."

"Invading," I said slowly, remembering how my hope had been extinguished when I'd found myself in Brenner's hands. "In my dream, he was invading a city."

Sebastian barked out a laugh. "Your random neurons seem to have generated a very accurate picture. I have no doubt that he would like to invade several cities, if he could."

As he spoke, I upended the bottle of wine and frowned when only a few drops dribbled out. My throat was pulsing now, and my head was starting to ache. Sighing, I reached for the bottle of painkillers next to the sink and shook three into my palm. At least I could do something about my head.

"Val? You still with me?"

I blinked hard, realizing that in a matter of seconds I had zoned out. What the hell was going on? "Uh, yeah. Sorry. Distracted." Distracted, yet in dire need of a distraction. I pushed off the counter and headed toward the bedroom, putting the phone on speaker while I shucked off my stained tank and ran it under the bathroom tap. "I'm going out. Did you get a name to go with that address?"

"Shade."

"Anything else?"

"That's it." Sebastian's voice was laced with frustration again. "You'll call me as soon as you find anything."

It wasn't a request, but I didn't take umbrage. I couldn't stand feeling helpless either. And this was particularly difficult for him, I knew, since he was being forced to rely not on another Were, but on a vampire.

"I'll call." I pulled on a T-shirt and examined myself in the mirror: too thin, too pale, my eyes bloodshot. I looked haggard. Ill. On the edge of sanity.

❖

Sebastian's address led me to a run-down brick building in Mott Haven. The alley next to it smelled of decay and urine, and I focused on breathing through my mouth. It reminded me of the site of my attack at the hands of the Missionary, and I struggled to tamp down the surge of fear that accompanied the hazy memories. Concentrating instead on the door, which was almost hanging off its hinges, I knocked gingerly at first and then harder a few moments later.

At the sound of soft footsteps scuffing over floorboards, I rested my hand on my gun. The woman who opened the door bore only a slight resemblance to the dominatrix who ruled the Red Circuit's weekly stage. Without her heeled black boots she was of less than average height, and the long, dark hair that usually flowed down over her shoulders from beneath the mask was pulled back into a ponytail. Her eyes were a little puffy around the edges, as though she had been crying. This close, I caught the faint but distinctive musky scent that clung to her skin and marked her as a shifter.

"You're the one with the whip," I said, edging one toe between the door and the frame so she couldn't shut me out.

She took a step backward in alarm, eyes flickering between my face and the gun at my side. "Who are you? How did you find me?"

"It wasn't easy." I held up both hands, knowing that I risked her transforming if she became too frightened or upset. But instead of shivering into her animal form, she braced one hand on the wall and coughed hard into her elbow. Suddenly, her puffy eyes took on an entirely different meaning. The skin around her nose was red and a little raw, too.

"You're sick," I said. "Like Gwendolyn was."

She raised her head and I watched the apprehension on her face turn to despair. "Come in," she said, and I entered into a clean but Spartan apartment. Her asceticism confused me; surely Sebastian paid her handsomely for the services she rendered to the Circuit. But there was no evidence of money here.

"Who are you?" she said again, once the door had shut.

"My name is Valentine Darrow. I'm—"

"A vampire. I've heard of you." When she arched one thin eyebrow, I felt a brief echo of the aura of power that always surrounded the dominatrix. "Your girlfriend is infamous."

"She's saving my soul," I said quietly.

Shade scoffed. "Saving? You look about as good as I feel." She gestured to a worn armchair and perched on the edge of the futon across from it. "You're not here at the behest of Lambros, or I'd be in the back of a van right now. So, why?"

"What if I had been?" I countered. "If that's what you're afraid of, why did you open the door?"

She laughed. "Lambros wouldn't have knocked."

I rested my elbows on my knees. "I've seen two Weres die now with similar symptoms, and I've heard of a third. The Consortium is stonewalling me. Alexa is supposed to come home tomorrow, and I can't reach her. I need to figure out what's happening. To protect her. Please, will you tell me whatever it is that you know? If I can help you, I will."

Shade met my eyes for several seconds. Whatever she saw in my entreating gaze must have been convincing, because she nodded. "Gwen was my lover. A little over a week ago, she came down with a random nosebleed that wouldn't quit for the longest time. A few days later, she felt feverish. As though she had the flu. I tried to convince her not to go for the Record on Friday, but she insisted that she was starting to feel better." The ghost of a smile twisted her lips. "Always so stubborn, my Gwen."

"I'm sorry," I said, wishing that I had more to offer than the platitude. "When did you start showing symptoms?"

Shade closed her eyes as she tried to remember. "I got the nosebleed

<tt>NEVERMORE</tt>

three, maybe four days after she did. But I haven't really felt sick until yesterday." She paused to wipe her eyes, and I wondered whether grief or illness was responsible for the new moisture. "After she...after she died, I was afraid that I would be rounded up as a part of some kind of investigation. I heard what happened to that shifter in Luna—that no one has heard from him since." Another fit of coughing took her then, and she grimaced when she finally caught her breath. A light wheeze persisted in her lungs.

"Do you have any idea how she might have gotten sick?" I asked.

Shade looked uncomfortable. Her hands knotted together in her lap, and she glanced toward the kitchen before resolutely meeting my eyes again. "I don't know for sure. But I suspect the drugs."

"The drugs." I kept my voice even, not wanting her to think that I was being judgmental. Because I wasn't. I had been with Alexa for almost every minute of her early days as a shifter, and had seen firsthand how the panther had ravaged her psyche.

"Most recently, we've been taking an antipsychotic that's also a powerful sedative. It helps with the days just before the moon."

"How do you get it?"

"I'm not going to tell you that." Her voice was calm, but I heard the steel in it. Regardless, I was about to protest when she stood. "But you can have the rest if you want to...test it, or something."

"Thank you," I said as she went into the kitchen. When she returned with a film container, I cracked the top to find it two-thirds full of round, dusky pink pills. I stared at them for several seconds, wishing that I had the power to see deep inside them.

Fortunately, I did, in a manner of speaking. Thanks to my internship at NYU's hospital. "Would you mind if I came back tomorrow?" I asked Shade as I pocketed the container. "To get a blood sample from you? It would be useful to compare with the—"

"Take it now."

"But I don't have the proper equipment."

"I have everything you'll need. In here." And she led me into the bedroom.

The bed frame was simple but made of thick, solid-looking wood. As Shade pulled open the top drawer of the nightstand next to the bed, I wondered how much of the BDSM dynamic of the Circuit had extended

<tt>• 79 •</tt>

NELL STARK AND TRINITY TAM

to her relationship with Gwendolyn. Had Gwendolyn practiced her resistance to the whip here, bound to the bed under Shade's teasing, torturous hand? Or had the tables been turned? Did Shade shift into a submissive behind closed doors, submitting to Gwendolyn's highly honed control?

I closed my eyes as a lightning flash of arousal streaked down my spine. Oh, God, I didn't want to feel this. I didn't want the vision of Shade's supple, naked body stretched out like an offering upon the twisted sheets, her heels digging into the mattress as Gwendolyn drove her higher and higher with tongue and teeth and fingers...

When Shade laid a hand on my arm, I gasped and pulled away.

"Are you all right?" Shade was looking at me with a mixture of curiosity and concern. She was too thin. I could see the pulse in her neck. The pulse. So much blood, just beneath the surface, hot and rich and—

"Fine," I said hoarsely. "I'm fine."

She held out her hands, displaying a tourniquet and syringe. I suspected she used them to inject other kinds of drugs. "These need to be sterilized first."

"After you," I said, following her into the kitchen. I leaned against the door frame as she set a small pot on the stove to boil, careful to keep my distance. When everything was ready, she sat at her small table and offered up her arm.

I breathed through my mouth as I pierced her vein with the hypodermic, not trusting myself to keep it together in the split second when the aroma of her blood would infuse the air. Focusing hard on my technique, I offered up a silent apology for my own weakness.

I'm sorry, Alexa. Please, come home. I need you. Please.

CHAPTER EIGHT

I left Shade's apartment with the pills in my left pocket and a vial of her blood in my right. I lacked the expertise to run the necessary tests on either sample by myself, but my friend Sean at Tisch Hospital would know exactly what to do. If I concocted a story about a delinquent cousin who was into drugs, he'd help me out without asking many questions. Mind racing, I turned toward the nearest subway station...and stopped in my tracks when I heard a soft rustling noise in the nearby alley.

I rose to the balls of my feet, heart thundering against my ribs, and took three steps. As I flattened myself against the rough brick of Shade's building, I drew my gun. The stubbled grip felt comforting in my palm. One deep breath and then another. There was no sound from the alley now, but I knew what I had heard. Someone was down there, and I wasn't going to let them get the jump on me. Not this time.

I heard again the crunch of the gravel beneath my shoes as I took off in a sprint, felt again the spear of agony that lanced up my thigh as the knife landed in my calf. Saw again the slithering tattoo across his clenched fist...

No. Swallowing hard, I wrenched myself back to the present. I was not back there. I was right here, and I was armed, and I was never, ever going to be a victim again. I thumbed off the safety, raised my gun, stepped around the corner, and pointed it with a steady hand.

Squarely at the chest of Olivia Wentworth Lloyd.

My gaze dropped from her face to the gleaming barrel of the pistol she held. Wearing a navy blouse and dark jeans, she blended well into the shadows.

"Valentine?" Her voice was shrill, and I felt a rush of confidence in the knowledge that she was nervous. I was willing to bet she'd never fired her gun outside of a range.

"Olivia. What the hell is going on?"

"Lower your weapon," she said.

"Let's both do it. At the same time." Under normal circumstances, I would have trusted her. But meeting her here was too much of a coincidence for me to take her at her word.

"Are you kidding me?" I watched Olivia's grasp tighten. "I'm an assistant district attorney, Valentine. Drop your fucking gun."

I hesitated before I obliged, just to prove that I wasn't going to let her order me around. I crouched to deposit the gun on the ground, but kept my eyes focused on her trigger finger. If she so much as twitched, I would use every one of my reflexes, weakened though they were, in my own defense.

"Tell me," I said, drawing myself back up to my full height. "If I called the DA's office, would they be surprised to hear you're prowling the streets of the South Bronx in the middle of the night?" When her jaw tightened, I laughed. "This isn't lawyer work, Olivia, so cut the crap. And stop pointing your goddamn pistol at my head."

Olivia lowered her weapon slowly. "Tell me you have a permit for that gun, Val."

"I have a permit for this gun, Olivia," I said, unable to keep myself from getting snarky. "I've been carrying it—legally—since shortly after I was attacked."

She nodded, and I hoped I'd won some sympathy points. "What are you doing out here?" she asked as she holstered her pistol. Knowing it would freak her out if I reclaimed my own weapon, I left it lying at my feet and leaned against the wall of the alley.

"I came to visit a friend," I said, trying to stay as close to the truth as I could. "She's sick."

"Does this friend have a name?"

I thought fast, not wanting to give up Shade's name. "Gwen." Before Olivia could ask another question, I went on the offensive. "Why the interrogation? What are you doing out here?"

"Investigating."

"Investigating? You're a detective now, too?"

I watched her body language closely. She didn't betray much—she had plenty of experience at maintaining an impassive façade in court, after all—but the corners of her mouth tightened a little. "The case I'm working has our detectives swamped. I thought I'd help out."

I didn't buy that answer for a second. "By snooping around up here with no backup?"

Olivia's eyes narrowed and she crossed her arms beneath her breasts. "You're the one who barged into a dark alley like some kind of vigilante."

"I'm the vigilante? You don't have a badge either." I frowned. "Is this still about what happened to us? Are you going after him solo?"

"What? No. That trail has gone cold."

"So then what's this all about? Why the cloak and dagger?"

Olivia took a few steps closer and lowered her voice. "I think I'm on to something. And it's really big."

Deep in my brain, the alarm bells grew louder. Something really big. What if Olivia wasn't being tipped off about Sebastian's questionable business practices or the Consortium's shady legal dealings, but about the very existence of Weres and vampires?

"What kind of 'something'?" I asked, trying to sound skeptical.

Olivia shrugged. "I'm not exactly sure. But it seems like some kind of very large, and very secret, crime syndicate."

"Like the mafia?"

At that, Olivia's stubbornness kicked in. "That's all I'm going to say, Val, okay? This is part of an ongoing investigation."

"Sure, okay," I said, trying to placate her. My internal alarm had quieted; while Olivia appeared to be aware that the Consortium constituted some kind of corporate entity, she hadn't yet put all the pieces together. The secret was still safe. For now.

"Do you know anything about this?" Olivia abruptly switched back to her interrogator mode. Maybe she was trying to throw me off guard.

I laughed. "You think I have ties to some crime syndicate?" But when her expression grew stony, I held up both hands in a gesture of surrender. "Look, you're aware that I'm friends with Sebastian. But as far as I know, he's just another high roller with a business that caters to the elite. He's a playboy and a hedonist, but not a criminal mastermind."

I took a gamble then, and pointed to the building I'd just left.

"Gwen, who lives here, is one of the techs in my lab. She's got a nasty flu and doesn't have anyone to take care of her, so I brought over some soup." Crossing my arms, I tried to look indignant. It was an easy expression to muster in Olivia's presence. "Happy?"

Looking slightly deflated, Olivia rubbed at her eyes in an uncharacteristic show of fatigue. "Yes." Her smile was rueful. "Sorry, Val. I'm letting this one get to me."

"Well, hang in there. And be careful." When she nodded, I tried out a tired grin. "So, Counselor, are you going to charge me with something? Or can I head back downtown?"

At my banter, Olivia squared her shoulders and even managed to roll her eyes at me. "Of course. Go home. What a bizarre coincidence, huh?"

"Yeah," I said, willing to bet that deep down, neither of us actually believed that. Shade suspected her drugs of infecting Weres with whatever it was that had killed Gwendolyn and Martine. Olivia was being fed information by some elusive source that kept leading her back to Weres and vampires. And Alexa was missing in action.

No, I thought fiercely as pain seared behind my eyes at the thought. Alexa was fine. She hadn't been near whatever danger had infiltrated New York. She was going to come home tomorrow, and when I had to convince her to go away again for a while, she wouldn't be pleased but she would understand.

"See you around, Val," Olivia said, jolting me from my descent into panic.

"Yeah," I replied, willing the words not to tremble. "Take care."

I waited until she was out of sight to pick up my gun. As I stood, I patted my pockets, just to reassure myself that both the pills and Shade's blood were still safely where they belonged. I would go home and catch a few hours of sleep before heading to work early in the hopes of catching Sean before our boss arrived.

And later, finally, I would leave work to catch the train that would take me out to JFK in time to meet Alexa's flight. Tomorrow, I would hold her. Tomorrow, I would kiss her. Tomorrow, I would make love to her and feel her fragrant blood filling me up, making me strong once again.

Tomorrow. I had to believe it.

❖

A pounding at my door shattered the fitful doze I'd lapsed into after returning home. I swung my legs over the side of the bed and blinked hard in the dim light of the pre-dawn. Again, my door rattled, and this time Karma's voice accompanied the insistent knocking.

"Val! It's me."

I forgot about my exhaustion. Karma wouldn't have shown up like this if she didn't have some kind of news. I threw on a T-shirt and shorts, raced to the door, and threw back the deadbolt.

"What's going on?"

Karma was dressed as immaculately as always, but her eyes were wild as she stepped inside my apartment. "It's Telassar," she said with no preamble. "The city has fallen."

"Fallen?" My heart leapt into overdrive, and I clutched at a nearby bookshelf as the world seemed to tilt. "What—what does that mean?"

Karma's hand closed around my forearm. Her touch was warm, and my throat began to burn at the sensation of her pulse fluttering lightly against my skin. "The city has been besieged for a week. Yesterday, the invading force broke through Constantine's defenses. A few escaped, one a contact of Malcolm's."

"Alexa?" My voice sounded strangled to my own ears. With my free hand, I pressed hard against my chest, over my galloping heart.

Karma shook her head. "Malcolm's source said that she left the city with Constantine two days ago." When she hesitated, I shook off her hand.

"What? What, aren't you telling me, Karma?" My breaths were coming in quick gasps, and I was starting to feel dizzy. Hyperventilating. I couldn't stop.

"My source claims that Brenner was after Constantine and Alexa specifically."

My entire body jerked at the name. "Balthasar Brenner?"

Surprise flashed across Karma's delicate features. "Yes, how do you—"

"A dream." I stumbled to the futon and sat, holding my head in my hands, trying to tamp down the panic long enough to think. She had escaped. With Constantine. She wasn't dead—or at least, she hadn't been, a few days ago. A groan escaped my lips at the thought.

"Oh, Val." Karma sat beside me and wrapped an arm around my shoulder. Warm. So warm, the aroma of night-blooming jasmine rising fragrantly off her smooth, dusky skin... Saliva flooded my mouth as my jaw began to ache. So thirsty.

"She'll make it through this," Karma said. "Constantine is wily, and the lands around Telassar have been his for generations. He will know how to keep her safe." When she began to rub the back of my neck with gentle pressure, a spark of arousal burst in my gut to flood my body with swollen heat. "Now, what were you saying about a dream?"

I took a deep, shuddering breath, desperately trying to focus on her words instead of the delicious promise of the delicate blue vein that ran just above her collarbone. "He was in my dream, two nights back. Sebastian's father. Burning a city, but not of Weres. Of vampires."

Karma's hand stilled. "You had a dream about the razing of Sybaris?"

"It was just a dream," I panted, shaking with the effort of holding myself in check. The impulse to feed was growing stronger by the second, and I had no idea how long I could hang on before it overpowered me.

Karma frowned. "No. It wasn't. Because Sybaris was razed to the ground by Brenner's elite forces a few days before he besieged Telassar. Our source fled there after he escaped Telassar, because Sybaris is the nearest Consortium outpost. But he found it in ruins."

"Weres and vampires fighting." Was this the beginning of a war, like the ones to which Helen had alluded several times? "What will this do to the Consortium? To you and me? Oh God, to me and Alexa—"

"Val, stop." Karma tugged hard on the short hairs at the back of my neck. Alexa had done that sometimes when she was seducing me, taking control of the moment, using her sensual force to compel me to surrender. *Surrender*...

"Constantine and Helen are allies," Karma was saying. I watched her full lips form the words and licked my own. "This isn't a matter of Weres and vampires fighting. This is Balthasar Brenner and his cronies lashing out against the Consortium itself. Against our alliance."

In the pit of my belly, Thirst finally broke its chains. I wondered whether this was how Alexa felt, in the moment when her panther overwhelmed her consciousness.

"Karma," I whispered, barely clinging to lucidity. "Oh God, something's—please, will you just—it's not safe, please, *go*."

Something in my tone must have alerted her jackal, because in the span between two of my breaths, she was off the couch and her hand was closed around the doorknob. She faced away from me, head bowed, suddenly struggling with her inner beast for control.

I should have been afraid, but I wasn't. The rush in my ears was the thunder of her blood—hot and fresh and mine, mine, *mine* for the taking. My vision telescoped until all was darkness save for the buttery swath of skin where her neck met her shoulder. Reason fled.

Yes.

I rose and lunged for her in the same fluid movement, a cobra striking its prey. In the split second before my sharpened teeth sank into the smooth expanse of her skin, she whirled, snarling deep in her throat—an inhuman noise.

Darkness descended, mercifully swift.

I woke to the steady beeping of a heart monitor. Blinded by the harsh fluorescent lights, I blinked until my vision cleared enough for me to distinguish my surroundings. A small room, its windows swathed by blackout curtains. The acrid scent of antiseptic. A dull ache in my left arm.

Hospital. No. Not again!

I sat bolt upright, clawing back the thin sheet that covered me. The metronome of the monitor leapt into hyperdrive, but my gaze skidded to a halt at the bag of blood hanging to my left, connected to the line that was buried into the crook of my elbow. I swallowed back a surge of bile as I realized what was happening. A transfusion. Someone else's blood, not Alexa's, flowing into my body.

I was reaching to yank the IV out of my arm when the door to my room opened and Harold Clavier stepped inside, his tinted glasses perched atop the line of cropped dark hair that framed his thin face.

"Don't, Valentine."

"What have you done?" I spat, my voice cracking as a wave of fury burst over me. "You've fucking violated me! I drink only from Alexa. You know that, you bas—"

Clavier moved to my side and loomed over me. "Be quiet," he said disdainfully. "Hysterics will accomplish nothing."

I glared up at him, trembling in my rage. "Why have you done this to me?"

He stared at me for several seconds before turning to examine the monitor's printout. "You brought this on yourself by denying your own needs."

I squeezed my eyes shut, trying to regain my equilibrium. How long had I been here? The last thing I could remember was sitting on my couch with my head in my hands, fighting off panic as Karma told me about Telassar and Sybaris and... All in a rush, the memories returned: the call of her blood, my rising thirst, the jarring sensation deep in my brain as parasitic instinct replaced human superego.

"Oh God, Karma—is she all right?"

Clavier's lips tightened. "Is *she* all right?" He laughed, but the sound carried no humor. "She brought you here, after putting you down like a whelp. If she didn't have excellent control, your remains would be strewn all over your own apartment."

"I don't understand. I've gone almost this long in the past without Alexa's blood. It's difficult, but I've never even been close to losing control before now."

He looked toward the door a moment before it opened. "Your situation has changed," he said, stepping away from my bed to make way for my new visitor. Helen. Her pantsuit was the same deep blue as her glinting eyes, and her dark, wavy hair brushed against her shoulders as she moved into the room.

"Valentine, hello." When she reached my bedside, she stooped gracefully and swept a light kiss across my cheek. "I wish I could say you look well."

"Helen." I glanced between her and Clavier and decided that small talk was out of the question. "Get this thing out of my arm. Now."

Unmoved by my brusque demeanor, Helen sank into the empty chair to my right and crossed one leg over the other. "If you promise to hear me out."

My skin crawled with the knowledge that someone else's blood was mingling with mine. How would this affect the chemistry Alexa's blood shared with my own? I needed that IV out, now.

"Fine." At Helen's nod, I removed the needle myself, welcoming the twinge of pain. Clavier taped a small square of gauze to the insertion point, and I focused on breathing deeply, willing my stomach to settle.

Helen waited in silence until my heartbeats were steady again. "Karma Rao told us that she informed you of the attack on Telassar."

"Yes," I said, my throat tightening as I thought of Alexa in peril. "Has there been any word?"

"Constantine will reach me when he can," Helen said, and I took a small measure of comfort in her confidence. "And we will help him to wrest control of the city back from Balthasar Brenner. But I have come to talk with you today about Sybaris."

"The vampire city." I shuddered at the dream-memory of ash coating my tongue and filling my lungs.

"One of the seven great fortifications of our kind." Helen pulled her chair closer. "The city traditionally inhabited by your clan."

"Karma said the two are related—that Brenner destroyed Sybaris first before invading Telassar."

"That is correct." Helen grimaced, and I wondered why she was taking the time to sit here and hold my hand when one of the "seven great fortifications" had just been razed. "Brenner has harbored a strong resentment toward Sybaris for many years, because its army drove him out of Telassar many years ago."

"So he was taking revenge."

"Yes. But he timed his vengeance to coincide with the election of the new Missionary."

Comprehension dawned as I recalled Henri's words aloud. "All members must be present."

"Precisely." Her lips thinned and I watched her eyes grow several shades darker. This quiet, unexpressed rage was even more frightening than the moments when I'd seen her lash out. "Balthasar Brenner has succeeded in almost completely eradicating one of the seven great vampire clans—the clan, remember, whose parasite may in fact be the original species from which all others derive. Your clan."

Her emphasis on "your" roused my apprehension. "What are you trying to say?"

She took my hand and held it tightly. "You are the sole survivor of your clan, Valentine. The blood prime. And as such, your parasite's cravings are exacerbated. As you can imagine, each blood prime feels a significant evolutionary imperative to increase the numbers of their clan."

I stared at her numbly. I had been the newest member only a few days ago, and now I was the blood prime? And that fact was the trigger for the intensification of my thirst? "So I attacked Karma because my parasite wants to…reproduce?"

"An oversimplification, but yes. As soon as you became blood prime, your urge to feed became magnified."

I shook my head. "This is impossible. There's no scientific basis for what you're proposing. How could my parasite suddenly 'know' that it's the only one left? That's…that's mystical!"

Helen looked as though she'd swallowed something unpleasant. "Really, Valentine," she snapped. "You, who are studying to be a doctor—you, who have experienced firsthand the effects of the vampire parasite and witnessed the transformation caused by the Were virus— you are going to protest that something which appears miraculous *cannot* be explained by science?"

I raised my hands in surrender. She did have a point. "Fine. It's true that my appetite has been much sharper than usual for the past few days."

"What you also must realize about your new condition," she said, "is that not only are you the blood prime, but you are also the Missionary. The office is yours by default, and as such, you will sit on the ruling counsel of the vampires known as the Order of Mithras."

I couldn't believe what I was hearing. I had gone from a relative nobody in the Consortium ranks—a newly turned vampire struggling to control her appetites and find her place in a new world order—to a subspecies on the verge of extinction? I hadn't even known that I was part of a clan before two weeks ago! And to pile on the lunacy, I was now expected to take an active role on the council that ruled all vampires, everywhere?

"This is insane," was all I could say.

Helen stroked my hair back from my forehead. The simple touch felt so good, just as Karma's had earlier, and I had to struggle not to lean into her hand. My body was starving and my bloodstream parched.

"I'm sure you're feeling overwhelmed, especially given the news from Telassar. But don't worry. I will do everything I can to help you ease into these new responsibilities."

"Responsibilities?" Suspicion suddenly trumped my surprise, and I balled my hands into fists. "Are you talking about turning people?" Clavier's violation of my blood notwithstanding, I was faithful to Alexa and always would be. Besides, I had been turned against my will. I never would have wished this life for myself, and I certainly didn't wish it on anyone else.

She seemed unfazed by the edge in my voice. "It will be important to grow Sybaris's numbers, yes." When I opened my mouth, she cut me off. "Don't be hasty, Valentine. We will discuss the specifics later. The other members of the Order are eager to meet you, but given the present political unrest, we will have to delay a convention."

I nodded, not trusting myself to speak. No good would come out of getting into a blowout argument with her right now. I would have to bide my time and remain firm in my convictions. No matter how hard the parasite rode me.

"In the meantime," she said, "I've asked the staff to prepare a room for you here."

"But—"

"Make no mistake, Valentine—Balthasar Brenner knows that you are alive. And as long as that is the case, his plan to eradicate an entire clan of the Order has failed. You are under my protection now, and I insist that you not leave this facility without my knowledge and a bodyguard."

I blinked at her, probably looking like an idiot. Sebastian's father had a price on my head? "All right," I said, still battling my disbelief.

Only after she left did the exhaustion slam home. In the wake of the adrenaline surge, it settled over me like a dense fog. Alexa was missing. I was the Missionary. A shifter plague had broken out in New York and Sebastian and I seemed to be the only ones who cared. Balthasar Brenner wanted to kill me. And all I wanted to do was sleep.

But beneath my fatigue, anger simmered. I didn't care who or what I had become in the past two days. If Helen thought that I was going to run around creating new vampires just to repopulate a clan, she was sadly fucking mistaken. I slid out from under the thin sheets and stood naked in the empty room. Helen had put me under house arrest, but I wasn't going to let that stall me. At least I had a legitimate reason to be lurking around the Consortium's medical facilities. I wasn't going to stop until I finally got some answers about the disease.

Alexa would find her way home. I had to believe it. My job, in the meantime, was to focus on making "home" a safe place again.

alexa

CHAPTER NINE

I ran. The whispered drumbeat of my paws on dry earth mingled with the throaty call of a nearby ibis and the rustle of wind through cedar leaves. The air was redolent with the musky aroma of macaque, but still satiated from my morning hunt, I did not slow. As the cedar canopy began to thin, the spires of Telassar became visible to my trained eye. Nestled in the shadow of Jbel Toubkal, the highest mountain in Morocco, the city's precise location was a secret jealously guarded by the Were community. Shifters patrolled its borders unceasingly, keeping tourists, explorers, and enemies at bay. Its remoteness made it an ideal place for Weres who wished to embrace their animal halves in a more sustained way than was possible in the midst of human civilizations. Many Weres thought of it as their one true home, but mine would always be with Valentine. Nonetheless, Telassar was a welcome sanctuary and training ground.

I broke out of the grove and began to make my ascent to the citadel. Rocky debris trailed in my wake as I leapt nimbly up a scree slope that would have been impossible for a human to climb. I loved this body—the powerful surge of my haunches, my impeccable balance, the panorama of sounds and scents accessible to me. It felt good to be strong.

The guards stationed at regular intervals along every possible route into the city paid me no mind; they knew my scent well. On my first foray into Telassar, by contrast, they had surrounded me moments after I had crossed over the invisible border of the shifter enclave. Menaced on all sides by a variety of snarling beasts, I was ungraciously herded into the presence of their alpha, despite having been expected. Constantine

Bellande placed the highest possible premium on the continued secrecy and safety of his kingdom.

The narrow, winding path—little more than a goat track by human standards—broadened as the front gate came into view. Only after darting beneath the menacing portcullis did I slow my pace. Silently, I urged my muscles to flow in, in and up, up into my two-legged form, until I felt the warm, packed earth of the courtyard slide between toes instead of claws.

A familiar figure stepped out of the building to my right, holding my robe. Weres in Telassar rarely bothered with conventional clothing—in a community such as this, it was sensible to dress in garments that could be easily shed for transformation. I had chosen a soft blue fabric for my robe, a royal blue that matched the shade of Valentine's eyes. It had been over a week since I'd last seen her, and two more would pass before we were reunited. Every reminder of her was equal parts pain and pleasure, and I sent up a silent prayer that this, our last and longest separation, would pass quickly.

Unmindful of my nakedness—another byproduct of having spent two months in Telassar—I took the robe from Delacourte's hands and wrapped it around me, then tightened the white sash emblazoned with Constantine's crimson crest. Delacourte was Constantine's chief medic. The former army surgeon from the French and Indian War was dark-haired and bearded, his muscular, heavy-set body hinting at the *Morphoviridae ursus* that gave rise to a massive and fearsome Kodiak on the night of each full moon. His size belied his gentility. Highly educated and cultured, he was one of the few Weres in Telassar who didn't pointedly ignore me. My arrangement with Valentine was distasteful at best to most shifters. In my first days at the walled city, racked with homesickness for Val and burned by the caustic reception of my peers, it was Delacourte who had taken me in and filled my nights with conversations about history and literature.

"How did you—"

"The guards saw you coming," Delacourte said. "I was walking along the parapet and heard them conversing."

I wondered what exactly they had said about me. Nothing complimentary, I was sure. Tamping down a surge of bitterness, I smiled my thanks at Delacourte for his kindness in coming to greet me. Old prejudices died hard; I knew that already. My true friends, like Karma and now Delacourte, understood exactly why I had chosen to be infected with *Morphoviridae pardus* and had so readily accepted my role as Valentine's sustenance. I got the sense that Constantine understood as well, but he was so preoccupied with the governance of Telassar that we rarely had a chance to speak. Hopefully that would change tonight, when I finally had the opportunity to share a meal with him.

Delacourte offered me his arm, and we proceeded across the courtyard toward the avenue that would lead us deeper into the city.

"Would you care to dine with me this evening?" he asked.

"I'd like to very much, but Constantine has invited me."

"Ah. You haven't heard." Delacourte's expression turned sympathetic. "He and Katya left the city a few hours ago. They're not expected back until late tonight, perhaps even tomorrow."

Disappointed, I suppressed a sigh. "Do you know why they left?"

The brief hesitation before Delacourte shook his head was a sure sign that he knew more than he was letting on, but I knew better than to push him. He patted my hand. "Will I have your company, then?"

"Of course."

Delacourte's apartments were adjacent to the infirmary, one of the buildings in the inner sanctum of the city. We walked at a leisurely pace through the sinuous streets, enjoying the crisp breeze blowing down the valley from Toubkal's summit. When I had first arrived, Telassar's labyrinthine corridors had confounded my geometric sense of direction ingrained from years of living in the perpendicular orderliness of Manhattan. The six-and-a-half-acre city comprised concentric rings of stone buildings connected by passageways, tunnels, and blind alleys. Narrow streets separated each structural layer, and broader avenues intersected the circles and provided throughway to the city center. At the heart of the city sat a one-acre park, bisected by a brisk stream and densely studded with tall evergreen trees. From the center of the park, one could see the clay-tiled rooftops of the innermost band of buildings, a fusion of civilization and wilderness that made me homesick for Central Park.

As we drew closer to the city center, we passed beneath an archway more ornate than the others. The walls in this section had a hint of green to them and were subtly embellished by engraved patterns. Weather and time had worn away the fine detail; if they were symbols, I had no idea what they meant. But Delacourte might.

"The architecture here is different from the rest of the city," I said. "And the stone—it has a greenish tinge. Do you know why?"

"This is the oldest part of Telassar, built in the late seventeenth century. I believe the green comes from traces of fluorite within the marble." Delacourte paused to run his hand over the delicate etchings that veined the white stone. "Building the keep was a massive undertaking, especially since Balthasar Brenner demanded that the marble be transported from a quarry in what is now Namibia."

"Balthasar Brenner?" The name brought me up short. "Who was he?"

Delacourte grimaced. "Not was, *is*. He is a powerful wolf Weremaster and, among other things, the founder of Telassar."

"Does he have a son named Sebastian?" I asked, unable to shrug off the surge of anxiety I felt whenever I thought of Sebastian Brenner and his fixation on Valentine. The panther snarled in response to my unease.

Delacourte scoffed. "Probably. He takes great pride in spawning whelps all over the world."

We walked the rest of the way in silence. For Balthasar Brenner to have founded Telassar in the late seventeenth century meant that he had to be over four hundred years old. The oldest shifter I had met was Malcolm Blakeslee, Weremaster of New York, who was in his two-hundreds. What must life look like, to a person who had seen four entire centuries pass? Both man and beast must have evolved in ways I could barely fathom.

And then there was Delacourte's tone of voice when he spoke of Brenner. Distaste. Fear. Perhaps even some grudging admiration—it was difficult to tell. But whatever the exact nature of Delacourte's feelings, they were complicated.

"I'm intrigued by this Balthasar Brenner," I said as we entered Delacourte's lodgings—a set of chambers spanning two floors, the west wall of which abutted the infirmary. A rich tapestry depicting some long-ago maritime battle hung over the fireplace, its colors complemented by the lush rug that covered the floor. Aside from those two splashes of color, the furnishings were wooden and unadorned, as was the prevailing style of interior décor in Telassar. Possessions had little meaning here, where residents were encouraged to give up the props that had defined them as humans and seek harmony with their inner beasts.

"He is a fascinating man," Delacourte said after a moment, choosing his words carefully. "And dangerous. I will tell you what I know of him over our meal, if you wish."

I nodded, and while Delacourte went to the pantry, I lit the candles on the mantel and around the room. He returned carrying a large platter laden with fruit, bread, cheese, and a bottle of wine. The Weres of Telassar, I had quickly learned, rarely ate meat while in human form. While I understood the rationale—when nearly every day involved a hunt, there was no point in further depleting the wildlife resources around Toubkal—my very human self hungered for a juicy ribeye. I smiled as I thought of how eager Val would be to take me out for a celebratory steak dinner upon my return to New York. She would probably insist on Smith and Wollensky.

Delacourte set the tray down in the center of the rug and we sat across from each other. I poured the wine while he broke the bread, and when our glasses were full, we raised them in a silent toast.

"I would start from the beginning," he said, deftly slicing an apple with precision learned on the battlefield, "if I knew it. But Brenner's origins his family and childhood—are remembered only by him. He is reputed to have served as a member of the Habsburg forces during the Thirty Years' War, but his meteoric rise to power happened a few decades later, as an officer in the Holy Roman Emperor's offensive against the Ottoman Turks. He funneled the personal wealth he gained in battle into seeking out and gathering together Weres living throughout Europe. He established a sanctuary deep in the Basque mountains and mustered them there."

I could only imagine what it must have been like to be a Were before the advent of modern medicine—before the mechanism of infection was known and most of its effects understood. To be alone during that transitional period, confused and overwhelmed by powerful and conflicting impulses, must have spelled death for so very many shifters. Without Karma's Web site and Darren's example, not to mention Val's unflagging faith and love, I would have been lost. The Consortium, despite its many faults, had saved many lives.

"All of this was before the founding of the Consortium?" I asked. "The vampires built their own network much earlier," said Delacourte. "But there was no collaboration between the species, and often open hostility. No one had ever succeeded—perhaps had never even tried—to gather more than a small pack of Weres together at a time. Brenner's charisma was the force that brought and held them together, even when they might have turned on one another."

I nodded. Sebastian had inherited that kind of charisma, and it was reflected by his success as a businessman. "So if Brenner formed an enclave in the Basques, what led him to found Telassar?" At Delacourte's shrug, I considered what I knew of the Basque Country, a small area in the Pyrenees that straddled the border between modern-day France and Spain. "Maybe he wanted more space?"

"Perhaps. In any case, Brenner led his band of Weres here, drove out the local tribes, and founded Telassar. He ruled the city for nearly a hundred years before the newly formed Consortium ousted him."

Startled, I leaned forward, the food forgotten. "Why? And how did they do it? I thought this place was impregnable."

Delacourte's smile was bemused. "You have been…what is the American expression? Drinking the…"

I felt myself blush. "The Kool-Aid. You're saying I'm naïve."

"How could you not be? It was not an accusation, merely an observation." He refilled my wine. "But Telassar inspires legends, and most are half true at best. This city has been invaded many times. The Consortium used the vampire stronghold of Sybaris, only two days' journey from here by horseback, as a staging ground for their assault against Brenner. They besieged the keep for months before finally breaking through its defenses. Many of his followers were killed. A few surrendered. A small, elite group escaped with him."

It was difficult for me to imagine the thick walls being overrun by any host, even an army of blood-drunk vampires. "He must hate the Consortium."

Delacourte murmured his agreement. "He has tried to retake the city several times over the past two centuries. But he has never succeeded."

I twirled the stem of my goblet between my fingers and gazed into the deep red liquid. Delacourte's knowledge was formidable. I had been focusing my attention inward, in an effort to understand and embrace the panther's needs and desires. But maybe it was time I paid closer attention to the external world as well—to the history of my people. The political tensions had to run deep in a community with such a long living memory, and if Val and I were going to thrive within the Consortium, we would need to know the big picture.

"You've made me curious," I said. "Are there some books in the library that you might recomm—"

Delacourte's head snapped up a split second before Constantine himself burst through the door. His ebony skin gleamed as dark as the panther that lurked on the other side of his moon, and he moved with the athletic grace of a world-class sprinter. But his eyes were wild and his expression grim. My panther made a bid for control as she sensed the distress of her sire and alpha, and I was hard-pressed to rein her in. Wine sloshed over the rim of my goblet, and breathing deeply through my teeth, I set it onto the tray with a trembling hand. I caught Constantine watching me closely.

"Should I leave?" I asked as calmly as I could manage.

"No. I'm glad you're here, and you must stay close to either Delacourte or me from now on." He paused for a moment, and only then did I realize that he, too, was fighting for control. "We have spies among us."

CHAPTER TEN

We had him cornered and outnumbered but he wasn't going down without a fight. The dusky brown wolf before us was snarling and snapping whenever one of us got close. We had sent for help in the form of a tranquilizer gun but it hadn't yet arrived. In the meantime, Constantine and I were holding heavy wooden chairs in front of us like lion tamers at a circus, but this beast refused to yield. Blood streamed down my forearm from a bite I had sustained while pulling the wolf off Constantine when he had first attacked. It had taken all of my control not to shift in response to the pain. Ordinarily, an animal loose in the castle was a commonplace occurrence easily remedied by flushing the beast outside and into the woodlands beyond the city walls. But Telassar had been under siege for the past week by a rival army of shifters and none of the Weres who left the city, for scouting or escape, had managed to make it back.

The wolf snapped viciously at Constantine, slicing through one of the rungs on his chair. If he had taken that kind of bite out of me, I never would have been able to hold back my panther. Her growl reverberated through my head, and part of me wanted to let her loose—to meet the traitor wolf head-on in battle. We had caught Anders while he was in human form, rifling through files in Constantine's study. His capture had been a stroke of pure luck; Constantine had been in the midst of an emergency briefing when he remembered he had left an important map in his desk. I had been in the middle of expressing my opinion that we needed to shift our defensive strategy to one of escape when he abruptly stood and left the conference. I followed him back to his study, all the while arguing my case. We had stumbled right into Anders as he was tucking folders into a bag. The ensuing struggle had spilled into the vestibule outside Constantine's study and triggered Anders's defensive shift into wolf form. Once transformed, Anders abandoned all thought of escape and instead turned on us instinctively as easy prey.

The sound of footsteps slapping against flagstone echoed through the chamber. I glanced over my shoulder to see reinforcements pouring into the room. Katya, the head of Telassar's security detail, raised the trank gun, a long-muzzled pistol with a Day-Glo orange grip, and fired two silent darts into the charging wolf, felling him before he could hurl himself at us again.

"Take him to the pens." Constantine threw his chair disgustedly against the far wall where it shattered into splinters. He rounded on me. "When you go to the infirmary to take care of that scratch, inform Delacourte that his services are needed. I want Anders back in human form as soon as possible." He turned back to the small security detail. "And I want to be alerted as soon as he gains consciousness. He's not to be touched. If I hear that he has come to harm, I'll assume the transgressor is an accomplice trying to shut him up."

Katya snapped her fingers and two muscular guards stepped forth. The men carefully lifted the body and carried it out of the room with Katya close behind them.

"Katya." Constantine's command stopped the woman mid-stride. She pivoted crisply. "Where there is one traitor, there are likely others. I want you to assign an extra security detail to patrol all tactical nodes."

Katya saluted and then hurried after her men, leaving Constantine and I alone once more. I gave his tall, lean frame a once-over, checking for injury. He appeared to be favoring his left arm, and a diagonal gash ran red with blood and sweat along his forehead and halfway across the mahogany dome of his clean-shaven scalp. Our wounds were relatively minor, superficial, easily healed by shifting into our animal forms. Though the panther inside me howled with every beat of pain that thrummed through my body, I held fast, preventing the change that needed and wanted to come. Constantine, as a Weremaster, had fully integrated his feline and human psyches. I was still a long way from that kind of control; if I were to relinquish my body to the panther in this moment, I would be little more than a backseat driver—sometimes able to influence her actions, but not always.

Constantine picked up Anders's bag and rifled through the files, cataloguing what had been taken. Stopping at one page, he frowned as he studied the information, then cursed under his breath.

"What was he after?" I wanted to cross the room and examine the documents with him, but the stiff set of his stance and the sharp relief of the tendons straining in his neck as he clenched his jaw in anger cautioned me to keep my distance.

"The hydraulic and sewage plans for the city. They're either trying to break their way in, or they plan on poisoning us."

Poison. My mind reeled. In a way, we were lucky—there were fewer than two hundred Weres living in Telassar at the moment. The numbers swelled to over a thousand in the winters when prey was sparse and Weres preferred the seclusion of the surrounding woods where they could hunt at their leisure. Thankfully, the summer season meant fewer bodies to organize and evacuate.

"That's good news." Constantine's head jerked unconsciously in my direction at the apparent non sequitur. "If they're trying to sneak in or poison us, that means they don't have enough resources to take the city by force. We can still get away."

Constantine remained silent, but his outrage at my suggestion was palpable. It fueled my beast, waves of anger pummeling and suffocating me in this cramped room, stirring up an alien, claustrophobic anxiety. He was alpha, I reminded myself. Running away, abandoning his territory, was anathema. I took an unconscious step toward the exit and drew his attention.

"I thought I told you to go to the infirmary." His obsidian eyes dropped to my bleeding forearm. "Our medical supplies are running low. You can't afford to get an infection."

"I'll walk with you," I said. "You should get that cut stitched up."

Constantine spun away from me and strode toward the stairwell, in the opposite direction from the infirmary. Four parallel gouges perforated the white linen across his blood-soaked back.

"Your back—" The rest of the sentence died on my tongue as he disappeared around a bend in the stairs. I swallowed the growl that crawled up from my belly, uncertain whether it came from the panther or from my own frustrations. Constantine, I was learning, could be even more stubborn than Valentine. I made my way gingerly down the stairs and out into the street. A lone squirrel darted for cover as I cut diagonally across the northern corner of the park toward the monolithic granite building that served as the infirmary and quartermaster suite. Gamesmen typically kept the park well stocked with small animals that were easy to hunt for Weres who needed to blow off steam quickly and didn't feel like venturing into the woods beyond the city walls. In the ten days of the siege so far, the critter population had dwindled to near extinction. I made a note to check with the quartermaster on how human provisions were doing. At some point, necessity was going to force our hand into fight or flight.

The infirmary took up two-thirds of the stone structure we referred to as the Union. It was made from large blocks of hand-hewn sandstone in a vibrant shade of ochre. Decorative turrets framed each corner and massive windows plated with thick safety glass reinforced with wire webbing punctuated each wall at even intervals. It was the most modern facility in the city, which wasn't saying much. Because the purpose of Telassar was to exist under the radar of humanity, literally and figuratively, all technological implements were banned. There was no electricity, fuel-powered machinery, cellular or satellite phones of any kind. The restrictions served two purposes. First, it guaranteed that satellites orbiting the earth would not be able to detect the existence of the city. Second, shifters who came here for sanctuary were forced to live in a natural, wild environment conducive to bonding with their animal halves.

The only exception to the technology blackout was the armory. Access to the armory was restricted to Constantine, Katya, and her lieutenants. Today's incident with Anders was the only time in my sojourn here where the armory had been accessed, and I wondered if there were enough weapons for us to shoot our way out against the invading host.

The main room of the infirmary was a large vaulted chamber divided into a dozen curtained treatment pods. On the east and west ends of the room, natural sunlight streamed in through long windows that stretched from floor to ceiling. On the wall opposite the doorway where I stood, half a dozen heavy wooden doors marked the individual treatment rooms. I found Delacourte adjusting the intravenous drip on an unconscious teenager strapped down in one of the curtained cots. Since Weres could heal themselves by shifting into animal form, the infirmary was usually a deserted place. The types of cases that made it here tended to be new Weres who were having a hard time adjusting to the change and those who had injured themselves so severely while in animal form that they couldn't hunt to shift back. A wash of sympathy suffused me as I regarded the patient in Delacourte's care. Barely six months had passed since my own difficult transition, and the sight of the young man, sedated and restrained, brought back terrifying memories of wrestling with my panther every time Valentine tried to feed. Delacourte turned, finally satisfied with his adjustments.

"Alexa!" His smile of welcome melted into concern as he caught sight of my injury. He hurried over and examined my arm, turning it and probing gently. "This is a bite. Wolf, from the looks of it."

"Anders." I winced as his fingers skated over the broken skin. The panther flared briefly in response to the pain and then retreated into the silence of my subconscious. "He's a spy. We caught him searching through Constantine's files. Katya is holding him in the pens now."

"Does he require treatment as well?" Delacourte led me to an empty cot and retrieved his medic bag. He doused a gauze pad with antiseptic and carefully cleaned my wound.

"Constantine wants him back in human form. He seemed to indicate that you have some way of getting him to make the change?"

Delacourte didn't answer right away. He palpated the skin around my wound, shaking his head. "Weres fighting Weres. It's not natural."

"But animals fight all the time in nature…"

"Not over philosophy. Not over imperialism. This dispute, this siege, is very human." He covered my forearm with more gauze pads and wrapped it with first aid tape.

"But you yourself told me that Weres battle over Telassar all the time. This is a turf war just like any other, isn't it?"

Delacourte shook his head again but didn't continue the debate. Instead, he walked to the far side of the room and unlocked a cabinet. He pulled out two clear plastic bags filled with some kind of fluid and brought them back to me, then opened one of his desk drawers and withdrew a syringe. When he began to fill it from a vial of pastel blue liquid, I grew curious.

"What's that?"

"Diluted wolfsbane." He capped off the syringe and handed it to me carefully. "Have someone inject this into his scruff after you've hooked him up to the IV. Combined with the glucose in the bag, this will force him to change back. Having this in his system will make it much harder than normal for him to return to wolf form, even if his metabolism could handle it."

"That's amazing," I said. "This blocks the change to animal form? Why has no one told me about it before?"

"Nothing blocks the change," Delacourte corrected me. "This herb simply delays it. But it is quite toxic, and dangerous if used frequently." He washed his hands and returned to the bedside of his unconscious patient.

"Make sure Constantine and Katya check with me before they raid my IV supplies again. We're going to have to watch our resources if they plan on waiting out this...turf war."

Clearly dismissed, I headed back toward the barracks in search of the imprisoned Anders. While the Union stood out in size and architecture from its surrounding buildings, to the casual observer, the barracks compound appeared unremarkable. The compound comprised two squat brick buildings covered so thickly in ivy, they gave the impression of being swallowed by nature. The larger structure housed the administrative offices of the security detail and the prison pens. The smaller building served as the armory. I walked into the former and headed for the conference room in the back. These days, it served as a defense headquarters. There was a guard stationed in front of the door and I held up the supplies to show my purpose. For a second it looked like he was going to harass me anyway, but angry voices from the conference room gave him pause. Instead, he flashed me a feral grin that said "better you than me" and waved me in.

Thin shafts of late-afternoon sunshine slanted in through the slitted windows, casting long, tapering fingers of light against the pine-planked flooring. A high oak table dominated the center of the room just barely out of reach of the late afternoon sunlight. Seven men stood at attention against one wall while Katya paced menacingly before them. Constantine sat in a corner, arms crossed and face impassive.

"There were two patrols assigned to that building. How could Anders break into the office and have time to go through half of the files without anybody noticing?"

The men shifted their feet and glanced at each other but remained quiet. I noted the uneven spacing of their formation and the nervous fidgeting and clenching of hands hanging loosely at their sides. These were not soldiers or even security guards. These were men pressed into service under urgent circumstances. With the dearth of military aptitude currently within the walls, it was a testament to the construction and fortitude of Telassar that the invaders hadn't yet taken the whole city.

"We're going to double our shifts. If any more spies gain access to our sensitive materials, I'm throwing you all in the brig with Anders. Dismissed."

The men hurried out of the room without daring eye contact as they edged by me in the doorway. Katya waited an extra moment for additional instruction from Constantine and when none came, she followed her men out of the barracks. The door closed heavily behind her. I placed the two bags and the syringe on the table.

"Glucose and wolfsbane from Delacourte. He says you'll need to consult him if you want any more IV supplies. He's rationing what we have left."

Constantine continued to stare impassively out the window. Perhaps he expected I too would take his silence for dismissal, but instead, I stood and waited. Eventually, I was rewarded with a glance, a token gesture of acknowledgment.

"When I took Telassar eighty years ago, the barbarians who held it were halfway feral. It only took a dozen of us to storm the gates and put down the dogs that were turning this haven into Hell." Constantine turned his gaze back to the window. "Telassar had always been a place for Weres to explore their animal natures away from the dangers of humanity. But those Weres took it too far. They indulged in violence and mindless bloodshed. When hunting prey lost its excitement, they turned on each other and slaughtered their own kin by the hundreds."

"My God." An image of a large black wolf devouring the still-beating heart of his opponent flashed through my thoughts. Helen had called the Red Circuit a necessary evil, and at the time, I resented her dismissive attitude. But hundreds slaughtered for sport? My mind reeled at the idea that Helen might have been right.

"Telassar has been attacked under my watch before. We have always prevailed."

"Do you know who is behind this? Do you know what they want?"

Constantine rose from his seat in one fluid motion. He picked up both bags and weighed the syringe in his palm as if assessing the value of an apple at a street fair. "Perhaps it is time we found out."

CHAPTER ELEVEN

A nders came to naked and choking against the iron collar padlocked around his neck. Once Constantine had administered the wolfsbane, Anders had returned to his human form within minutes. Now I saw that only one of the bags that Delacourte had given me was for feeding. The second hung from a hook on the wall and was now flooding his bloodstream with sedatives. I doubted the contents of one bag gave Anders enough energy to shift even without the drugs and the wolfsbane, but the precaution gave me a sickening insight into intended interrogation methods. Katya grabbed a handful of Anders's shaggy brown hair and yanked him forward so that the collar pulled even more tightly against his windpipe. He flailed, his eyes bulging in panic. Constantine stepped forward, filling his line of sight.

"Who are you taking orders from?"

Anders clamped his jaw shut. I could still smell the fear rolling off him, but outwardly, his defiance was resolute. Katya released his hair, grabbed the arm without the IV port and twisted it roughly behind his back. He cried out but didn't capitulate. Constantine backhanded him twice, snapping Anders's head first to the left and then to the right. The momentum of the last blow jerked his body so hard, his shoulder dislocated with a pop in Katya's grip. Anders screamed in pain. Despite being prepared for violence, the quickness with which Constantine devolved into brutality shocked me. I opened my mouth to protest but swallowed my words at the stern look Constantine shot in my direction. He was alpha, and the panther inside jerked me back in line.

He returned his attention to the inquisition. "Whoever it is will make himself known eventually. Why suffer any more?"

Katya shook Anders by the arm and he whimpered in pain. Anders was a small man, his body pale and soft, at least for a Were. He was the type of man who hid among the humans by working all day in front of a computer or on a telephone fielding customer service calls. I had never really noticed him during my time here. That was probably how he had escaped scrutiny for so long.

Constantine flexed his fingers, cracking his knuckles loudly, each pop like a gunshot that ratcheted up Anders's pulse. When Constantine raised his hand, Anders finally broke.

"Stop, please stop!" He was sobbing now, snot dribbling out of his nose and mixing with the blood-tinged spittle that leaked from the corner of his mouth.

"Who is it?" Constantine demanded.

Anders closed his eyes and swallowed, his large Adam's apple bobbing dramatically. He was quiet for so long, I thought he might have changed his mind. Then he opened his eyes and spoke. His voice was low and deferential. "Brenner. Balthasar Brenner."

With a snarl, Constantine backhanded Anders again, this time knocking him out cold. He nodded curtly to Katya, who unlocked his collar and grabbed his injured arm with one hand and braced herself against his shoulder with the other. Satisfied that the prisoner would be taken care of, Constantine exited the interrogation room as Katya jerked Anders's shoulder back into place with a sickening pop. Constantine crossed the threshold just as Anders came to in a horrific wail of pain that echoed lingeringly in the empty stillness of the brig.

I hurried after Constantine. "Delacourte was just telling me about Balthasar Brenner last night. He's trying to regain control of the city again, isn't he?"

"Most likely." Constantine's voice was calm, his gait fluid and steady. Considering the circumstances, he seemed remarkably unperturbed about Anders's revelation.

"You seem relieved to hear it's Brenner."

He shrugged. "The Consortium tracks his whereabouts. It won't be long before reinforcements arrive. They won't let him have Telassar."

Just then, a commotion from down the hall stopped us. A split second later, one of Katya's guards careened around the corner, almost running into us. He pulled up just in time and sketched a quick salute at Constantine. "Sir. It's Brenner." He was out of breath, and rivulets of perspiration cascaded from his hairline down his face.

"I know. Anders told me." Constantine answered curtly, his surprise giving way to annoyance.

"No, sir. I mean, Brenner is at the gates. He wants to talk to you."

❖

Balthasar Brenner was enormous. He stood nearly six and a half feet tall with broad shoulders framing a thick, muscular body. His coarse black hair, which ran down to his waist, was streaked with white and partially braided to keep it from whipping into his face in the wind. Aside from the striking angular features of his face and the flat steel gray of his eyes, I had to strain to find any resemblance to Sebastian's refined gentility in Balthasar's rough, barbarian appearance. I was irrationally grateful for the twenty-foot-wide moat that separated me from the massive scimitar that hung from his belt. That and the fact that Constantine, Katya, and I were able to look down upon Brenner and his coterie of guards from the relative safety of a high, crenellated parapet. We were flanked by security with machine guns at the ready. Brenner's guards, in turn, had their semi-automatic weapons trained on us. Instinctively, I edged sideways out of line of sight of the guns. His sword should have seemed anachronistic and pathetic in light of all the modern firepower. Instead, it highlighted the fact that if Balthasar Brenner chose to take your life, he would do so up close and with the strength of his own hands.

One bullet could end this now, I thought and quickly dismissed the monstrous impulse. *Vampires lose their souls, not Weres*, I chided myself.

"Constantine Bellande, surrender yourself and that vampire whore and I might show mercy on your pathetic brood."

I frowned. Was he talking about me? Anger at his words warred with surprise that he would even know of Valentine's and my relationship at all. I moved even closer to the edge so I could watch his movements, curiosity winning out over caution.

Despite his indelicate words, the lilting cadence of his speech and the measured delivery of each syllable belied his sophistication. Balthasar Brenner appeared to be a highly educated man and more like his son than the obvious crudeness of his façade would suggest. I was intrigued, but the panther stirred inside me, agitated by the threat in his demand.

"Balthasar." Constantine remained fully visible between a low gap in the wall, as if daring Brenner's men to shoot. "Leave this valley now and the Consortium may not catch you."

Brenner grinned, a cruel mirror of Sebastian's charismatic smirk. "The Consortium is busy dealing with some vampire casualties. You know their priorities as well as I, Bellande. I could exterminate an entire continent of Weres while they wring their hands over a bloodsucker with a migraine."

Vampire casualties? My thoughts flew to Valentine. I hadn't talked to her in ten days, since before the siege began. Before this summer, Val and I had never spent any significant length of time apart from each other in the year and a half since we'd started dating. We had spent time together almost every day, even when we had each been holed up in the Consortium medical facilities dealing with our transitions. The longest we'd been apart before this summer had been those three terrifying days after the Missionary's attack on Val, when her mother had prevented me from visiting her in the hospital. Even then, I had camped out in the lobby the entire time, wanting to be as close as possible. During my stay here in Telassar, Val and I had made the best of our time apart, arranging to talk by phone at least twice a week from the small village of Tinmel, over two hours' run to the east in panther form. This protracted separation was highly unnatural for me, and even the panther was uneasy whenever thoughts of Valentine made my heart seize with longing.

Constantine remained standing in plain sight of the guns. If Brenner's words affected him, he was doing a damn fine job of covering it up. "You overreach yet again. You will not take Telassar, Brenner. Not under my watch."

Brenner turned away, a nonchalant gesture. "You have until noon tomorrow to surrender," he called back over his shoulder. "Otherwise, I will burn you all alive in that city."

❖

I found Constantine and Katya huddled over a large terrain map of the area surrounding Telassar. She was pointing to a mountain range due north of the city and he was shaking his head violently.

"This pass is the most direct route to the closest Berber settlement. We can call for reinforcements when we get there." Her voice was calm and level, but her tension was betrayed by the clipped, guttural intonations of her Slavic accent.

"It's too narrow and there are no escape options if they intercept us." He pointed to the woods. "They can't cover the entire forest. We'll stay off the main paths and head for Asni or Igoudar. We'll have more cities to choose from so they won't know where to station their guards."

I cleared my throat to get their attention. "I thought we were staying put until the Consortium came to rescue us."

Constantine looked up from the map just long enough to scowl. "Plans have changed."

"But you told Brenner—"

"I told Balthasar what was necessary in order to buy us the time and space to plan our escape." He shook his head again when Katya pointed to another spot on the map. "He is bold and arrogant. Threats are not his usual style. When he wants something, he takes it, whether by force or by guile."

Katya nodded in agreement. "He miscalculated by threatening to burn the city. The fact that he hasn't yet either means that he can't or he doesn't want to. Something is going to happen by tomorrow noon. We're guessing that his reinforcements arrive. If that's the case, our best chance for escape is tonight."

Something didn't add up. "We have been under siege for ten days. Why is he just making himself known right now?"

"Because he just got here." I frowned at the surety in Constantine's response. He replied before I could ask for clarification. "The tower scouts have reported new patrol patterns among the invader ranks. They've sharpened their performance now that the boss is here. Besides, the news about the vampire casualties was delivered with conviction. He had a part in that, I'm sure, and I'd wager he's just getting here from wherever that occurred."

"Why does he want us in particular?" I didn't know Balthasar

Brenner well enough to psychoanalyze his behavior but I certainly hadn't expected him to single me out.

The dead silence that greeted my question confirmed my suspicion that Constantine and Katya were as in the dark as I was on Balthasar's agenda. While they seemed to have a solid understanding of his motivations and his history, this particular demand baffled even them. Constantine, at least, was Master of Telassar, a position of some import. If Brenner's goal was to take Telassar and send some kind of dominance message to the shifter community, holding Constantine prisoner made sense. I, on the other hand, was nobody in the Were pecking order—a fact that Helen slapped across my face at every opportunity. But the fact that Constantine's and Katya's current plans were a complete about face from their stance that morning signaled a clear respect for Brenner's ability to carry through on his plan, whatever it might be. The memory of his scimitar glinting cruelly in the late-morning sun flashed through my mind, and I shuddered.

I stepped closer to the table so I could see the map they were working from. We had almost two hundred shifters to evacuate, and Telassar's remote location surrounded by mountains and forests provided limited options. We had to get to a human settlement with cable or satellite service to send a message to the Consortium. Based on all of the crossed-out portions of the map, it looked as if our sparse options were even further diminished strategically. The benefits of Telassar as a Were haven—remoteness, isolation—were working against us in this situation. Not for the first time, I wished I had listened to Val when she suggested I sneak a satellite phone into the walled city. At the time, I had been trying to be respectful of the policies and traditions of Telassar. Now I realized just how dangerous the technological quarantine could be.

"We have to assume Brenner has taken control of the safehouses and waypoints in Tinmel, Tazalt, and Areg." Katya circled each city in red. "Perhaps the villages to the north?" She gestured at a smattering of dots too small to even be labeled on the map.

Constantine considered the suggestion for a moment, then grunted his assent. "We'll split up into small groups. No more than six in each. Send some north and some to the west." He pointed to some additional unnamed dots a distance away from Telassar. "These villages are too small. If we all show up at once, Balthasar will catch wind of it. Better to split up and stagger our escape."

"We'll put you and Alexa in different groups—"

"No. Alexa stays with me."

Katya's head jerked up in surprise. "Brenner specifically asked for you two by name. I think it's better if we separate you. That way he'll have to split his forces if he wants to go after you both."

Constantine shook his head emphatically. "He wants us alive. I gave his men every opportunity to gun me down today and they didn't. I'm not so sure he cares about the other Weres in this city. He may let them go without a care; he may find them a liability. We endanger fewer people if we go together. Alexa is my responsibility. I owe it to Helen to make sure she gets back to New York safely."

It was interesting to hear Constantine talk about Helen; he spoke her name with both familiarity and deference. He seemed to know her on a personal level, not only as the Master vampire of New York City. The few in-depth conversations I'd had with Constantine had never broached Consortium politics—when he could give me the time, we always discussed methods of cultivating a stronger integrated relationship with our feline halves. Now I wished I had pressed him on his own story, and his reasons for inviting me to Telassar through Helen.

He turned to Katya with an air of confidence that made me feel reassured despite the fraught situation. "Draw up the groups as you see fit, but Alexa stays with me. Report back to me in half an hour. We deploy at nightfall."

CHAPTER TWELVE

Night unfurled before me like a riddle, revealing itself gradually with each beat of my paws. Ahead of me and to my right, Constantine set the pace, a flowing stride that favored stealth over speed. Seeking to divide Brenner's forces as much as possible, we had parted ways with Katya and Delacourte as soon as we were clear of the perimeter of Telassar. The plan was to meet up, in human form, just outside of Aguerda, a small town on the southwestern edge of the Toubkal National Park. From there we hoped to reach the Consortium to arrange our evacuation.

The hardest part had been picking the Weres to join us in the escape. Neither Constantine nor Katya trusted anyone implicitly, especially the wolves. In the end, fewer than twenty of the more than two hundred Weres in Telassar were included in our escape plans. Constantine and Katya had assembled the select group in the map room above the brig. Besides Delacourte, I recognized a few of Katya's armed guards, but the other escapees were strangers to me. There were neither questions nor debate when the plan was unveiled and I wondered if they had been chosen as much for obedience as trustworthiness. The exclusivity bothered me. I couldn't help but think that my freedom would be bought at the expense of the lives we left behind.

The plan was simple: we would leave Telassar in small, staggered groups through the city's labyrinthine network of underground waterways and drainage tunnels. The outer rings of the city had been built on wetlands resulting from the runoff of water from the surrounding mountain peaks. The drainage system formed the foundation of the expansion and continued to provide rudimentary plumbing and sewage facilities. It was unlikely that Brenner knew of the existence of these tunnels, and even if he did, the sheer complexity of the system and the number of outlets made guarding every exit point virtually impossible.

Constantine made a sharp turn at the next clearing, leaping over a fallen tree. I adjusted automatically and fell into stride behind him. My panther, oblivious to the potential danger all around us, luxuriated in the freedom of the run after spending the last several days stymied by Brenner's siege. Escaping through the tunnels had been especially bad. I had never been claustrophobic before, but hours of crawling through the choking stench of sewage and detritus in pitch darkness had nearly pushed my anxiety to the breaking point. Every inch had been a bargain with my sanity and a struggle with the panther. I had cried actual tears of relief when we finally tumbled, exhausted, into the forest a quarter mile south of the city's walls. My panther had come quickly, then, the tremors of my turn upon me before the final syllable of "Uje" passed my lips. Weary of my own racing thoughts, I had willingly surrendered the last threads of control to my animal half. She would follow Constantine, the established alpha, and her feline instincts were far better than my human ones to keep us alive. While I envied Constantine his connection with his beast, and sought to achieve my own someday, for now I took advantage of the respite from full control to rest my human psyche.

It was almost dawn before we stopped. Constantine had led us to a hiking way station, vacant and deserted in the off-hours. We tracked and killed a gazelle to turn back into human form and then broke a window to get into the station. Once inside, we were able to scavenge clothes from the staff closet and lost and found. In another time and place, without Brenner and his army in hot pursuit, the sight of Constantine in a Hard Rock T-shirt and baggy cargo shorts would have made a hilarious snapshot to share with Val. My heart clenched at the mental image of Val laughing out loud, an increasingly rare occurrence since our induction into the world of vampires and Weres. The urge to get home was overwhelming, and I forced myself to concentrate on my immediate surroundings to ground myself against the wave of nostalgia that threatened to paralyze me.

The way station was small and sparse. It served as little more than a rest stop for tourists. There was no phone or computer set-up, just a vintage-looking shortwave radio that Constantine examined extensively before declaring it unusable for our purposes. Over the entrance, a battered clock with a cracked dial matched the window we had just broken into. It said the time was just past four in the morning. A sign on the door indicated that the station would open at nine, so we had a few hours to spare. I perused the racks of pamphlets and maps and learned that we were approximately eight kilometers from Aguerda, our rendezvous point with Katya and Delacourte. I turned to Constantine to ask him when he wanted to head out and I was surprised to find him lying, with his eyes closed, on a bench against the far wall.

"We made good time and took the most direct route. It will be a while before the others catch up to us. You should rest now while you have the chance." Constantine's eyes remained closed as he answered my unspoken query.

I claimed the remaining bench and tried to make myself comfortable. I was physically and mentally exhausted, but my panther, exhilarated by the escape and the recent hunt, fidgeted anxiously just beneath the surface. I was bursting with questions. How were we going to get word out to the Consortium without Brenner knowing? Why did Brenner want me as a hostage? Question after question thwarted my attempts to rest.

"Why would Brenner declare war on his own kind?" I surprised myself by asking out loud. "If his rage is directed primarily at the vampires, then why bother with retaking Telassar at all? Is it because of his history as one of its founders?"

"In part, yes." Constantine remained still, looking up into the rafters of the way station. "I have no doubt that he regards Telassar as his sovereign territory still. But the city's symbolic value to our community cannot be underestimated. Whoever holds Telassar has an elevated status among the Weremasters of the world. It is our primary seat of power."

"Still, I think I'm starting to agree with Delacourte: Weres fighting their own kind only seems natural to a point, and Brenner's ongoing fight with the Consortium is far, far beyond that point."

"Don't forget," Constantine said, "that Brenner does not, in fact, consider us to be 'his kind.' He has few scruples."

"Not his kind? You mean, not wolves?"

"I mean not pureblood. Brenner is descended—or so he claims—

from a line of born werewolves and he is an outspoken advocate of pureblood superiority. He does not consider turned Weres, like us, to be his kind at all. He and his followers call themselves the Ferai."

"The Ferai? What language is that from?"

"It is not from any known language. That is why they use it. They refuse to use the term 'Were' because it is derived from the Old English word for 'man.' They consider themselves neither man nor animal but an evolutionary step above both." Constantine's voice bore no trace of vehemence, only exasperation, and I was glad he did not share Balthasar Brenner's bigoted contempt.

"So he's done this before? Attacked other Weres, I mean."

"Before the Consortium came into power, skirmishes broke out constantly between purebloods and turned shifters. Mostly they were territorial or interspecies disputes. Telassar has always been a haven for turned Weres to nurture their animal sides. As such, it has been attacked many times over the centuries. But most of the meaningless turf battles ended when the Consortium was formed."

I flashed back to an image of Helen glaring at me from across her wooden desk while explaining the "necessary evil" that was the Red Circuit. Violence was inevitable for our kind, she reasoned; better that she allowed it in a controlled setting than let it run rampant in the open. It didn't surprise me that Helen and her Consortium would find an effective method to neutralize millennia of Were in-fighting. "But what's changed? Why is Brenner attacking now?"

Constantine shifted restlessly on his bench. "I am not sure. He has been opposed to the Consortium from the very beginning. If there is one thing that Balthasar hates more than turned Weres, it is vampires. He chafes at the alliance because he believes that Weres have been subordinated to vampires in the agreement."

"But if he has contempt for turned Weres, why should he care who we consort with?" I heard the petulance in my own voice and hated myself for letting Brenner get under my skin. What Constantine had said about subordination pricked all my defensive instincts when it came to protecting and justifying my relationship with Valentine. "It seems like he's just a self-important egomaniac using his dubious celebrity to stir up trouble."

"I do not pretend to know Balthasar Brenner's motivations. But if there is one thing that you can count on, it is that his hatred runs deep. He has vowed, boldly and openly, to take the Consortium down. Perhaps he has lost his last shred of reason and decided to finally follow through."

"Do you think he can make good on that threat?"

"I do not know. Before last week, I would have said no. But he has managed to take Telassar with no intervention from the Consortium. It is imperative that we get through to Helen because she will need our help."

It did not escape me that despite our predicament, Constantine's primary concern would be for the Consortium. From our first meeting, I sensed that his loyalty to Helen seemed to run deeper than could be explained by politics or business. There was a story lurking beneath the surface. Where Helen Lambros was concerned, the reasons behind our acquaintances were often complicated and personal.

Constantine woke me a few hours before the way station was scheduled to open. I had managed to fall asleep for an hour. My back ached from the hard wooden bench, but resting had been a good idea. I felt more mentally alert. We tidied up, doing our best to cover our tracks, but the broken window was a glaring sign of our intrusion. I made a mental note to send an anonymous donation to the park's wildlife fund when I got back to New York.

We followed the trail toward the city, taking care to avoid the major paths. Even at this early hour, several tourists were already winding their way toward the park. Aguerda would be similarly busy. We decided to take a longer route that brought us in under the cover of the freight trucks and vendor caravans hauling in the day's market goods. From there, we would make our way through the side roads and alleys toward the café Katya had chosen for our rendezvous point.

Aguerda was a small city that doubled in population during the tourist season with hikers seeking to explore the mountain ranges in the national park. We slowed as we walked through the city to match the relaxed pace set by the locals. I saw a convenience store that had a hand-painted sign in the window advertising their satellite pay phones.

I pointed this out excitedly to Constantine and began to cross the street toward the store, but stopped abruptly as Constantine's hand closed on my shoulder and pulled me back.

"They are closed." He gestured toward another sign that I had not seen in my excitement. "And we are running late. We will come back once we have met up with Katya and Delacourte."

Every ounce of me wanted to rush to the store and beat down the door until the shopkeeper let us in, but I let Constantine lead me away and down the street. As we rounded the final corner toward our destination, he stopped and lifted his head slightly to both sides, scenting the air. Ahead of us was the café with a bench out front painted in a cheerful orange color. The street was narrow and deserted, unusual for this time of day. Constantine gestured for me to head back toward the main street. I turned around to see three rough-looking men approaching us with handguns visible. I spun back toward the café in time to see two additional men with guns step out of the door.

Fear and anger cascaded through me, bringing me to the balls of my feet. "It's a trap."

Next to me, Constantine vibrated with energy. His beast was near the surface and I could tell he was debating the benefits of staying or shifting. My own panther surged to life as she sensed the danger all around us. I focused my control on keeping her in check while waiting for Constantine's lead. The men were converging on our position quickly, and I felt, rather than saw, Constantine dip into a crouch beside me. He was going to make the change. I loosened my hold on the panther and felt her awareness flooding mine. Beneath the reek of cigarette smoke I could scent the particular metallic musk of wolves. I was just about to utter my summoning word when I picked up another scent, earthen and familiar, and looked up to see Katya emerging from the café. I had only a second to register surprise at the fact that the gunmen paid no attention to her, for in the next moment, another familiar figure stepped out into the street.

Chapter Thirteen

Balthasar Brenner strode out of the café dressed in military fatigues down to the heavy-soled, calf-high boots. His dark hair was gathered loosely at the nape of his neck in a rough braid. When he gestured for his men to fall in beside him, their guns disappeared back into pockets and waistbands. There was no need for firepower now that the master was here. Constantine straightened up from his crouch and let out a low growl. My panther thrashed inside me in agreement.

Brenner's minions began to herd us into the café, and Katya fell into step behind the group. She locked the door behind her. Brenner gestured for us to take a seat in a booth. The guns were out again now that we were out of sight of any locals. I slid onto the rough wooden bench beside Constantine, trying not to fidget as Brenner pulled up a chair and sat opposite us. My skin prickled and my muscles clenched involuntarily. The last time I had experienced this kind of proximity with a pureblood Were, I had been sitting across a table at a club with Sebastian. I had been uncomfortable then; his pureblood aura mixed with his clear alpha status had triggered an immediate fight-or-flight response in my panther. It had taken considerable force on my part to hold her in check so as not to give Sebastian the pleasure of provoking my turn. Balthasar's presence was even more intense. Whereas Sebastian channeled his energies into seduction and charisma, his father exuded overwhelming command and demand for obedience. The fact that the full moon was only two days away made assuaging my beast even more difficult. I ground my teeth harshly as Brenner leaned in, and unable to hold his eye contact, I focused on his powerful hands resting on the table. I was surprised at first to find them soft and delicate, more like the hands of a pianist than those of a warmonger. I reminded myself that he was pureblood; any calluses or scars he had sustained since his adolescence would have been erased with each subsequent transformation. His skin would never bear testament to his life of violence.

Brenner and Constantine stared each other down from across the table. Constantine spoke first. "Where is Delacourte?"

"You keep such learned company, Bellande. Dr. Delacourte is far too valuable to waste away in a cell. I have pressed him into a nobler service."

"Nobility is an outlier with the company you keep." Constantine shot a dangerous look at Katya. She had the decency to look ashamed for a moment before slamming down a mask of defiance. "I always thought of you as a survivor, Balthasar. Perhaps you have a death wish, bringing down the wrath of the Consortium on your pathetic brood."

"I have no fear of the Consortium."

"Then you are as stupid as you are rash."

Brenner laughed then, a deep, bellowing rumble that shook the room. "Ah, Constantine, I see you are still hiding behind the skirt of that vampire bitch. But look around you." He gestured broadly around the room. "You have no allies here and none are coming. I made sure of that."

"You overstep, Balthasar. The Consortium will intervene. Telassar will be returned to its rightful master."

"You really haven't learned, have you? Shifters are not the priority of the Consortium. We merely pad their numbers and provide the resources for the vampires to further their own agenda." Brenner turned and shot me a glare filled with hatred. "And yet those of you in their thrall manage to find new and perverted ways to insult our grand heritage. The Consortium will not come to your rescue because they have more important matters to attend to."

Constantine's confidence wavered, but he regained his composure quickly. "You will bring us all to the brink of war."

The windows of the café rattled as a large vehicle pulled up in front. A sharp horn cut through the silence once, then again. Brenner stood, pulling himself majestically to his full height. He gestured to two of his armed guards who dragged us to our feet.

"We have been at war for centuries. I will bring us victory."

❖

Brenner had us transported by cargo van to a location just outside of town. The ride lasted less than twenty minutes but our new surroundings were remote. It seemed to be some kind of compound with several stone huts arranged haphazardly around a clearing in the woods. Brenner and Katya, who had taken a different car, were nowhere to be seen. As the guards escorted us to one of the huts, I managed to catch sight of Delacourte through the doorway of the largest of the buildings. He was wrapping a splint around someone's arm. He looked up as we passed by but made no indication that he recognized me.

I had assumed we would be brought directly to Brenner for interrogation or torture, and was surprised when we were shoved into one of the smaller stone huts. The guard slammed the door shut behind us and locked it from the outside. I just barely stopped myself from retching as the acrid scent of urine and wet fur overwhelmed me. There were patches of soiled hay and loose rags scattered over the dirt and rock-strewn floor. Fractured beams of sunlight dappled the walls and floor through seams in the slat and thatched roof above. Constantine took three strides to cross the room. He peered through a thin slit in the wall that served as the only window.

"There are maybe a dozen but no more than twenty men here. Most of them are armed but there are not enough bodies for an invading force. Balthasar must have several of these camps spread throughout the park." He cocked his head and squinted into the light. "They appear to be...packing."

"Packing? But where would they go? The full moon is less than forty-eight hours away. They wouldn't get very far before having to disband for hunting."

"Not just packing," Constantine said after another minute of observation. "They are disassembling the camp."

A glimmer of hope sparked to life within me. "Perhaps the Consortium is on their way, after all."

"Perhaps. Whatever he is planning, they seem on pace to leave this location just after the full moon." But Constantine did not sound convinced, even of his own logic. He stepped away from the window and scanned the rest of the room. "I hope we fit into their plans."

"Why's that?"

Constantine ran his hand over the walls. "We may be able to break through the roof, but the stone is smooth. Even as panthers we will not be able to climb our way out. And we are close to the mountains, which means there is rock just under the topsoil. We will not be able to dig our way out, either."

The realization hit me with a wave of panic. "So when we transform with the full moon..." I trailed off as my imagination filled in the blanks.

"If we cannot hunt, we will turn on each other eventually."

Night finally came and banished the oppressive heat that had threatened to bake us alive in the hut. Nobody came to the door to bring us food or water, reinforcing my fear that we were being left here to die. I didn't want to admit that Balthasar's boasts were getting the best of me, but with each passing moment, the hope that the Consortium would ride in and rescue us grew dimmer and dimmer. Would Helen look out for my best interests if Valentine wasn't threatened? Constantine had been aloof and secretive throughout our captivity, understandably preoccupied by our predicament, and in that silent moment, my heart ached even more forcefully for Val. She was my tether to this community. I was honest enough with myself to recognize that the only reason most vampires or Weres took any notice of me at all was because of the unusual nature of our relationship. Other than Karma and Kyle, nobody else in the New York community acknowledged me as an individual. That knowledge had only fueled my desire to come to Telassar and capitalize on the special bond I had with my panther. To explore our vast potential. Val had recognized the strength of that desire and had graciously encouraged my trip, despite the physical strain it would put on her.

Perhaps I had been misguided. If only I had been content to remain at home with her... Not allowing myself to finish the thought, I shook off my despondence and looked over at Constantine, who had stretched himself out on the floor. I needed to take a lesson from his calm in the midst of so much chaos.

My eyes bored into his prone figure, attempting to dissect the motives that had made him the object of Balthasar Brenner's fury. Constantine was loyal to Helen, that much was obvious, but he didn't carry himself in the manner of an obsequious crony like Clavier or a dutiful lackey like Darren. There was respect in the way he spoke about her, and something else. I couldn't place it, but I was sure that whatever it was, it was the reason Brenner had taken such great delight in disabusing Constantine of the notion that we would be rescued.

Ironically, now that we were both captives, we finally had the time together that had eluded us all summer. I decided to take advantage of his presence. "Why did you allow me to spend this summer with you?"

Constantine was quiet for so long, I assumed he had either fallen asleep or was doing some kind of meditation. I was just about to give sleep another try when he spoke. "Helen asked if I might consider inviting you to Telassar and I was happy to oblige her."

I wondered why Helen had asked in the first place. She'd made it clear that she only cared about my well-being insofar as it impacted Valentine. Had she wanted to get me out of New York for some reason? The thought that she might have some kind of designs on Valentine made my blood boil, and I took a deep, steadying breath.

"You are the Weremaster of Telassar. Surely even Helen's significant power couldn't force you into anything you didn't want to do." I cringed inwardly at the childish note I heard in my own voice. As much as I resented being treated like a second-class citizen in the hierarchy of the Consortium, I didn't need to reinforce their disdain by acting like a brat.

Constantine frowned. "I was happy to take you in. You and I share many traits, including an unusually strong bond with our panthers. And we are similarly indebted to Helen Lambros. Although I choose to repay her with gratitude."

His rebuke hit me like a slap in the face. I almost missed the implication in his statement. "Helen orchestrated your infection with the Were virus? Why?"

"Why would she help me? Or why would I desire the transformation? I do not know why she helped me. I do know that there have been many others like us, who have chosen this existence. It is why I sought her out in the first place. She seems to have a sympathy toward people in our situation." Constantine hesitated, seeming loath to reveal too much personal information.

"Sympathy? More like she saw an opportunity to garner favors to further her own agenda." I bristled at the memory of Helen practically undressing Val with her eyes as I pled my case to receive the Were virus.

"I was nobody. There was no reason for her to covet my favors."

"But you became a Weremaster and the champion of Telassar. It looks like her investment paid off royally with you."

Constantine barked out a humorless laugh. "Alexa. Did nobody warn you of the risks before you became a panther? We are solitary animals. As such, our life expectancy as Weres is short. Helen was not making an investment in me. She was doing me a favor."

A short life expectancy and a solitary nature? I wondered if Helen had intentionally picked such a challenging animal for me. I gritted my teeth. It didn't matter. As long as I had Valentine, I would never be alone. "So it seems she doomed us both."

"No. I cannot say why she chose me to be your sire, but the panther form was of my choosing." Constantine paused again. When he continued, he sounded soft and distant. "I chose this life to take care of my brother. Fabian did not select his fate; an unlucky encounter on a full moon decided for him."

Regret and a profound sadness inflected Constantine's voice, along with an echo of the anger that he often wore like a coat of armor. Curiosity replaced the shock I felt at the fact that he had finally revealed a shred of his personal story. "What happened?"

"My brother contracted the virus but had a difficult time with the transition. He became violent and withdrawn. Most of my family abandoned him. But I could not. He was my only brother, and I was determined to discover what had changed him. For months, I followed him everywhere, and on one full moon, I witnessed his secret. When he changed back into human form, I confronted him."

"Oh my God. He had to do all of that alone?"

"No. Not alone. Fabian told me that the Were who accidentally attacked him had brought him into the community for treatment and training. It did not help. My brother could not handle his animal half."

I remembered one of the many conversations that Karma had

with me back when I was preparing for my infection. She had warned me of what could happen if I could not control my beast. "He became feral?"

"Yes."

I could not contain the small, involuntary cry that escaped me. Turning feral was a terrible fate. It meant permanently subordinating your humanity to the beast. A feral Were never regained human form.

"It did not happen right away. He fought it as long as he could. But it was obvious to me that he would lose the battle. I approached his sire and begged him to turn me too. He would not. The governing body of Weres at the time forbade it. So I began to frequent all the Were hunting grounds on the full moon, hoping to be attacked. That was how I caught Helen's attention. The Consortium did not exist then, but Helen was part of a fledgling alliance between vampires and Weres. She heard about the human with the death wish. When I explained Fabian's situation and my desires, she agreed to help, even though it was against the wishes of the Weremaster of Africa."

"How were you infected?"

"The techniques were not as advanced one hundred years ago. Helen had my brother's blood transfused directly into me. It was a highly dangerous procedure, because in order to get the active Werevirus into my system, my brother had to be in his feline form during the transfusion. Fabian was caged during the process, but the sight of his panther hurling himself against the bars will forever haunt me. He raged until he was bloody and continued until he was unconscious. There was hatred and murder in his eyes the entire time."

"I am so sorry." The process of infection was the most intense physical pain I had ever experienced. I couldn't imagine having to shoulder that degree of emotional pain as well.

"By the time I adjusted to my animal, it was too late. Fabian had lost his battle and could no longer change back into human form. I kept track of him the best that I could. Without the regenerative properties of transformation, he lived out the rest of his panther's life. When he died, I buried him with my own hands in the fields where we used to play as children."

As Constantine's story ended, I felt him withdraw and sever the connection we had so unexpectedly forged. So we did share a common bond beyond the biological. He, too, had chosen this life for a loved one. I wondered if Helen had kept that in mind when she asked him to be my sire.

As I stared through the slit window at the moon, waxing gibbous in the ebony sky, I wondered if I would ever have the chance to ask her.

CHAPTER FOURTEEN

As full moonrise drew near, it became impossible for me to sit still, and I began to pace the length of our narrow cell. Early that morning, one of Brenner's soldiers had tossed a canteen of water into the hut through the window, but they had continued to deprive us of food. My hunger, combined with the insistent push of my panther at the nearness of the full moon, conspired to fray my nerves. Constantine watched me from across the room, arms wrapped around his knees as he sat on the bare ground against the far wall.

"How do you do it?" I asked finally, exasperation snapping my voice.

A sympathetic smile flashed across his lips. "Many years of practice." He looked at the slivers of night sky visible through the gaps in the roof thatching. "My panther knows that he will be free soon enough, and he knows that I will not resist him. We are both content to wait for that moment."

"Whereas I'm still fighting her." I forced my frenetic feet to stop and focused on holding myself still. On the few occasions when his schedule had allowed us the time to meet, Constantine's message had been consistent: the key to full integration was to willingly allow the panther and human consciousnesses to bleed into one another—not just sometimes, but always. She would emerge when the moon rose, as was her nature. Any measure of unwillingness on my part was just unproductive human stubbornness. I had to let go of it.

Closing my eyes, I took one deep breath and then another. I could feel her thrashing at the doors of my brain, trying to assert her dominance in the face of my obstinance. The stress of being a captive, of my uncertain future, of being far from home and away from Val—all of it made me want to keep command of my own self. But right now, in the face of a full moon, none of it mattered. My panther would come and it was pointless for me to do anything but welcome her.

A subtle shift, an expectant pause. She was listening. I kept my breathing steady and thought of what would happen in a few minutes— of the glistening moon that would brighten the sky and bring her into the world. Her eagerness and anticipation were palpable. *Soon,* I thought. *Soon.* An image flashed behind my eyes, then: her, us, lying in wait, concealed among the deep grass of the savannah. Ready and alert, but no longer agitated. *Yes.* I smiled.

"Impressive." Constantine's rare praise brought me out of my own head, and as I opened my eyes, I realized that the needling sensation— as though I'd been about to crawl out of my own skin—had subsided.

"Thank you." I paused as the precariousness of our situation once again reasserted itself. When Brenner's men returned from their hunt, would they bring us prey so that we too could transform back? Or would they torture us, leaving us imprisoned and ravenous, until one turned on the other? I knew my panther would want to obey Constantine, her alpha and sire. But when her hunger reached fever pitch? Then what?

Sensing my growing unrest, Constantine stood. "Do not lose hope. Perhaps our feline halves will find a way to escape that we have overlooked."

I nodded. And then I felt it—a sense of gathering pressure in my mind, like the expectant hush before a summer storm.

"Ah," Constantine said. "It is time."

I looked up and saw the instant in which the pitch black of the sky brightened to a deep sapphire as the moon broke over the horizon. She called my panther, demanding the release of my animal self, and I obeyed.

"Uje," I whispered, dropping to my knees.

But I never hit the floor. She was upon me in an instant, the wrenching transition giving way to a new, sharper reality. Balancing lightly on the pads of my feet, I swung to my left at the sound of Constantine's rumbled greeting. I touched my nose to his, then stretched out on my front paws, ducking my head in an instinctual gesture of obedience. Hunger knotted my belly, and together we paced the perimeter of the walls in search of a weakness. The fresh air filtering through the broken roof teased us with its promise of the outside world; the walls were too high and too smooth to scale, and the ground too packed for digging.

The sound of approaching footsteps froze us both, and we crouched low to the ground, tails lashing. Brenner kept his camp free of human influence. How was someone out there, walking around on two legs?

The door to our prison rattled and a key turned in the lock. It swung open to reveal Delacourte, visibly trembling, sweat streaming down his face. He had taken wolfsbane—a near-toxic dose, by the looks of it—to resist the change. A low whine escaped my throat as the scent of him piqued my hunger, but Constantine, fully in control, loped forward to rub his flank against Delacourte's legs. I stood out of my crouch, ears pricking forward as he spoke.

"Most of them went north, I think." He forced out the words between chattering teeth before collapsing to the ground and curling into fetal position. I vaulted over his body, and together, Constantine and I looked on as Delacourte writhed in the dirt while the wolfsbane and the moon competed for dominance in his blood. Thankfully, his beast won out within moments, and where the man had trembled in agony stood a large gray bear. When he shook his massive head and bared his teeth in a snarl, I took a few steps backward. But Constantine stood his ground and growled back. For a moment, the panther and the bear faced off, until Delacourte's snarls subsided and he sank to his haunches in acquiescence of Constantine's authority.

Constantine loped into the night and turned south. We fell in behind him. The bear lumbered beside me, foliage crackling under his huge paws, and I knew if any of the enemy were nearby they would hear our passage. Fortunately, Delacourte was also a formidable combatant.

Just as I was feeling a glimmer of hope that we would not, in fact, be detected, Constantine slowed to a stop and raised his nose to the air. When I followed his lead, the faint scent burned my nostrils: Katya and two other lions, downwind and approaching. Hoping to divide their force, we split, Constantine and I taking off toward the west and Delacourte heading east.

We ran more swiftly than before, but with ears flickering back and forth in an effort to catch wind of our pursuers. I had expected that they would leave Delacourte behind in favor of us, but within minutes, we heard his roar as they caught him up. Constantine stopped so quickly I was forced to leap over him before skidding through grass and weeds to a halt.

As one, we took off in the direction from which we'd come, racing to Delacourte and the fight. He had risked his life to save us, and we would do no less for him. The sound of snapping and snarling grew ever louder, and when we broke into a clearing in the trees, I took stock of the situation without slowing my pace. Katya menaced Delacourte from the front, while her male companions tormented his flanks. One had already scored a hit—a deep, three-point gouge just in front of Delacourte's left leg. Blood matted the hair around the wound and trickled onto the forest floor, and he was favoring that entire side of his body.

Several yards ahead of me, Constantine leapt for the closest lion and I set my sights on the one who had already injured Delacourte. As I approached, the lion turned from his prey and struck without prelude, aiming straight for my jugular. I leapt over him nimbly, digging my claws into his back as my momentum carried me dangerously close to one of the trees that encircled the clearing. He roared in pain and lashed out with one of his hind legs, very nearly catching me in the head. Panting, I circled back to face him.

This time, when he leapt forward I met him in midair, butting him in the chest as he once again went for my neck. I closed my jaw around the top of one of his forelegs, but he curled his hind legs forward and ripped open a shallow furrow in my belly. I twisted away, barely feeling the sting. He was bigger and stronger than me, but I was faster, and I used that to my advantage now.

I dashed beneath him and tore open a gash in his chest, then darted away before he could react. I returned over and over, never letting up on my attacks, forcing him to spin in a defensive circle. When he finally lunged at me, maddened by the pain, I avoided his attack and raked my claws deep into the muscle of his hindquarters. He stumbled, and I took full advantage, spinning to sink my teeth into the soft flesh below his jaw. He collapsed, twitching, and I fought back the demands of my overwhelming hunger with difficulty. Constantine and Delacourte were still fighting. I had to help them.

But I was too late. Even as I raised my muzzle from the lion's body,

Delacourte went down like a tree felled by an avalanche, Katya clinging to his throat. Blood gushed from the fatal wound, spraying her face and coat with crimson gore. With a roar of my own, I raced to confront her, determined to avenge my friend and rescuer, but Constantine was several steps ahead of me.

She had swung toward me at my bellow of rage, and he took advantage of the opportunity, leaping astride her back and sealing his formidable jaws in the thick folds of skin that protected her spinal cord. Once, twice, three times he shook her, until, with an audible snap, she collapsed.

A hush fell over the forest. I loped gingerly to Delacourte and pushed my nose against his, hoping for some sign of life. But that vital spark within him was gone. Only the shell, ravaged and bloody, remained.

At the sight of Constantine feeding from Katya's corpse, I returned to my own kill and gorged myself. As my hunger began to subside, I grew increasingly conscious of the pain in my belly. The wound would hamper my ability to run and would lay down an easy scent trail for Brenner's forces. I had to shift back to human form so that it could heal.

The cool, dry breeze raised gooseflesh on my naked skin, but I didn't shiver. Curling a stray lock of hair behind one ear, I ran one hand over the slight curve of my stomach. Not a mark marred its smooth surface. The healing power of the change never stopped being miraculous.

I looked over at Constantine and saw his form, too, beginning to blur. As the transformation took him, I walked toward Delacourte's motionless body and crouched to lay a hand on his huge head.

"You saved our lives twice tonight," I said. "Thank you. I'm sorry I couldn't do the same." Hearing Constantine's footfalls behind me, I rose to face him, unperturbed by my nakedness. "What now?"

He stared at Delacourte for a long moment before answering. "There is a Consortium safe house in Marrakech, a day's run to the southwest. If we press hard."

I stalked past Katya's mangled corpse, barely resisting the urge to spit. Beyond, the ascending moon still pulled at my blood, her call all the more enticing for not being an imperative.

"Then let us press hard," I said. And breaking into a run, I called my panther forth.

❖

Under cover of night, we slunk from shadow to shadow before settling down to lie in wait in an alley near a busy discotheque. When two drunken tourists stumbled out of the establishment and past the mouth of our hiding place, we brought them down silently and dragged them out of sight. They were both men, and even the smaller one's clothing was several sizes too large for me, but I made do. The clothing would grant us safe passage farther into the city, where the streets were brightly lit and more heavily trafficked.

"What are you looking for?" I asked Constantine as he paused to peer down two consecutive side streets off one of the main thoroughfares. Hiking up my stolen pants for what felt like the thousandth time in the past half hour, I hoped he would find the safe house soon. My toes were banging painfully against the fronts of my too-large sneakers, and I could already feel the blisters forming. Then again, blisters were far better than being the captive of Balthasar Brenner.

"I have only been here once," Constantine said testily, as though he had heard my unvoiced complaint. "Be patient."

Thankfully, he paused five minutes later at the mouth of a narrow winding street, and I followed him for several blocks until we stood in front of a shabby hotel. Its shingle bore the faded emblem of a growling lion, and I thought of Malcolm. Was it folly to believe that we might be safe now? That I might see Val soon—perhaps only in a matter of days?

Constantine knocked five times on the door, and a few moments later, I sensed someone peering out at us through the keyhole. When the door was flung open, my panther flinched in alarm.

The curly-haired boy who greeted us was barely an adolescent—certainly not someone to whom I would have entrusted the keeping of an important outpost. "The rumor is true!" he exclaimed, rocking back and forth on his heels. "You've escaped!"

Constantine stepped inside, and I followed him quickly. The short foyer spilled into a comfortable sitting room, and I had the insane desire to kick off my borrowed shoes and bury my toes in the plush carpeting.

"I'm fine," Constantine was saying. "Where is your father, Jasper? And the others?"

"Everyone was deployed to Sybaris four days ago," Jasper said, staring wide-eyed between the two of us.

Constantine frowned. "Why? What happened?"

"It burned."

Jasper's simple statement wrung a curse from Constantine's throat in his native French. He threw himself into one of the armchairs and propped his head in one hand. "So that's what Brenner meant by 'vampire casualties.'"

"What on earth is Sybaris?" I said, my thoughts turning to Val.

"It is one of the great vampire strongholds—a secret city, like Telassar in some ways. And now Brenner has somehow destroyed it."

When his voice quavered in disbelief, I had a sense of the magnitude of this catastrophe. It seemed as though Brenner planned to pursue his vendetta against all vampires everywhere with deadly force. My heart stuttered at the thought of Valentine in danger from him.

"We have to get to New York," I said. "As soon as possible."

"Agreed." Constantine turned to Jasper. "Your father did well to leave a man of your talents in charge."

At the praise, the teen's chest puffed with pride, and I found myself wondering whether Constantine had any children of his own. His rapport with Jasper was effortless.

"What can I do?" the boy asked.

"Alexa and I are going to need passports. And a secure line to New York Headquarters."

For the first time since opening the door, Jasper looked confident. His smile was broad. "I can set up the call right now," he said eagerly. "And you'll have the passports by morning."

"Excellent. Thank you."

When Jasper disappeared into an adjoining room, Constantine went to stand in front of the mahogany cabinet next to the fireplace. It was stocked full of fine liqueurs, and that simple fact made me miss Val even more intensely. She would have loved the chance to examine a collection of this caliber.

After extracting a very expensive-looking brandy, Constantine raised the bottle in my direction. At my nod, he reached for two snifters and poured a few fingers of smoky liquid into each.

I raised the glass that he handed me, and we stared at each other silently as the subtle aroma filled the air between us.

"Well," I said, feeling that the moment was utterly beyond words. "Cheers."

The hint of a tired smile curved his lips. And then we drank.

CHAPTER FIFTEEN

When the plane's landing gear touched down, I eased my grip on my hand rests. The slate gray of the runway blurring beneath the wheels, the directional markers decipherable only to pilots, the hint of Newark's skyline between squat airport buildings...my vision blurred and I swallowed hard to hold unexpected tears in check. *Home.*

"We're not out of the woods yet," Constantine said.

I forced myself not to react, refusing to allow his pragmatism to dampen my relief. Against long odds, we had made it back to New York. Within a few hours, I would be reunited with Val, where I belonged. Brenner could do his worst after that, and silently I dared him to try. Together, Val and I were unstoppable.

When I realized that my foot was tapping a muted staccato against the floor, I stilled my leg and focused on the Fasten Seat Belt sign. As soon as it turned off, I jumped to my feet. All around me, people were wrestling with the bags they had crammed under their seats or stowed into the overhead compartments. Suddenly self-conscious, I dipped my fingers into the right pocket of my jeans, just far enough to touch the passport Jasper had handed me as we'd left the outpost, bound first for Casablanca and then for home. It was all I had, aside from the clothes on my back. Thankfully, I had found some that were my size in one of the hotel's closets.

"Let's go." Constantine's soft command jolted me out of my introspection, and I followed him into the emptying aisle. As we left the jet bridge and entered the maze of corridors leading to Customs, he leaned in close. "Stay in the middle of the hall, away from any doors."

I inclined my head, wondering if he was just being cautious or whether he actually expected some kind of attack in one of the busiest airports in the world during broad daylight. Then again, I had already paid the price once for underestimating Balthasar Brenner.

After several twists and turns, we emerged into the Customs hall. As Constantine and I moved to the front of the snaking line, I ran through every relaxation technique I'd been taught as a new Were: light meditation, breathing exercises, visualization. I was about to enter the United States of America with forged documentation. The lawyer in me was screaming about crime and punishment. The rest of me longed for Val's embrace with a ferocity that overrode every moral qualm.

When we were ten feet away from the guards directing people toward the customs officers, Constantine slipped an arm around my shoulders. "You look a little stiff, sweetheart. Muscles sore from the flight?"

I pressed close, playing the part. "My shoulders," I said, lacing the words with a whine. "Those seats are so uncomfortable."

Constantine rubbed my shoulders obligingly. "Maybe we can take a hot bath once we get home, hmm?"

I let my arm curl around his waist and my mouth hover near his ear. Val loved when I closed my lips around her earlobe, when I gently sucked and flicked at it with my tongue. Once, I had been so ardent that I had bruised her there.

Constantine's fingers tightened on my waist, and I shuddered out of the memory. "Mmm, that sounds wonderful."

At a gesture from the guard, we walked together to one of the several glass booths separating us from free access to the city. Constantine gestured for my passport, and I turned it over to him after only the briefest of hesitations.

"Hello," he said as he handed over both documents to the officer behind the glass.

After flipping open each passport, the man, just shy of balding, looked up at us each in turn. "Where do you live?"

Before I could open my mouth, Constantine once again took the initiative. "We have a walk-up in the Meatpacking District. It's a gorgeous little place, right on Chelsea Park."

"And what were you doing in Morocco?"

"We were on vacation," I said, trailing my fingers up and down Constantine's arm. "Marrakech was so lovely, and the discotheques were great fun. That is," I tapped his chest lightly, "until this one drank too much at the Palace."

He rolled his eyes. "Are you going to tell everyone we meet, hon? Really?"

The officer flashed him a sympathetic grin and stamped our booklets before handing them back. "Welcome home."

We passed into baggage claim, where another burst of anxiety followed close on the heels of a relief I had not betrayed. "We don't have any luggage." I linked my arm through his. "That's going to seem suspicious."

But Constantine only shook his head and strode toward the guards at the exit. Once again, he turned over our passports for inspection. When one of the guards met my eyes, I smiled despite the knot of tension tightening in my throat.

"No bags?"

Constantine waved his free hand lazily. "You wouldn't believe how much shopping she did. It was far more convenient to just have everything shipped."

A curt nod was the only response. "Have a nice day."

When we made our way through the exit, I moved to disengage my arm, but Constantine's grip was firm. "Not yet," he whispered, almost too softly even for me to hear. "We may still be under observation."

Forcing my muscles to relax, I swept my gaze over the people waiting beyond the security barrier and struggled to hold back an exultant smile when I caught sight of Darren's hulking form, leaning against a nearby pillar.

"There he is," was all I said as I steered Constantine in his direction, wondering at Helen's decision to send her personal bodyguard to greet us.

"Good afternoon," said Darren as we approached, and I bit my lip as I realized he was playing the role of our driver. "How was your flight?"

Constantine clapped him on the shoulder. "Fine, just fine. But long."

"I am so ready to be home," I added. It had never felt so good to tell a simple truth.

"I'll get you there just as soon as possible," said Darren. "This way, please."

He guided us outside to where a heavy black car was idling at the curb. I slid into the back behind the pale, slender man who sat at the wheel. I'd never seen him before, but he was unmistakably a vampire, and I frowned. It was dangerous to send full vampires out in the daylight. If forced outside the protection of the car's treated windows, he would die in a matter of minutes. Why hadn't Helen sent another Were to drive?

Once Darren had folded himself into the passenger seat, the driver pulled away from the curb. When identical black cars fell into line both in front and behind us, I realized we had a security escort.

"Expecting trouble?" I asked, shrugging my shoulders in an effort to ease some of the tension that had gathered there. I needed Val's hands to relax me, soothe me, and then make me tense in an entirely different way. *Soon.*

"Yes," was all Darren said.

I knew he wouldn't elaborate, so I finally asked the question that had been burning in my brain since Brenner's forces had arrived under cover of the morning mist at Telassar, nearly two weeks ago. "Darren, is Val—"

"She's at the Consortium."

"I was going to ask how she was, not where."

"Even here, we're not secure. Ms. Lambros will answer all your questions as soon as you arrive."

Bristling, I opened my mouth to insist before reason overrode my impatience. If Darren was being obfuscatory, it was only because he was following orders. Slumping back into my seat, I stared out the windshield at the New York skyline. It grew before my eyes, the metallic spires of Downtown and Midtown bracketing the part I loved best—Alphabet City and the Village, sprawling with glorious laissez faire between the pinnacles of civilization.

"It is striking," Constantine said, his tone one of grudging admiration. I was suddenly struck by the knowledge that while this was my homecoming, it was his exile. He had no way of knowing whether he would ever see Telassar again.

Half an hour later, the car pulled up to the back entrance of the Consortium. My pulse had been rising since our exit from the Lincoln

Tunnel, and as I climbed out of the vehicle, I looked around eagerly for Val. But she was nowhere to be found. No one had come to greet us.

"I've been instructed to direct you to the War Room," Darren said, ushering us through the heavy door and down a corridor toward a stairwell. *The War Room?* I had never heard of such a place in Headquarters. Had it even existed before Balthasar Brenner's attacks on Sybaris and Telassar?

After ascending several flights of stairs, we emerged into another corridor, this one a dead end. But when Darren held his hand up to a scanner on the wall, a panel opened to display a keypad. His large fingers moved with a surprising lightness over the keys, and then the very wall itself swung inward to reveal a room, perfectly square, that blazed in the artificial light of at least a dozen plasma screens. Ignoring the allure of the flickering pixels, I looked around in anxious anticipation for Valentine. But still, she was nowhere to be found.

"Constantine." Helen materialized out of the shadows to lightly embrace him and kiss him on both cheeks. "You are very welcome."

"Generous words," he said with a tired but genuine smile. I wondered again about the nature of his allegiance to Helen Lambros. "Generous deeds. Thank you for your hospitality."

Helen turned then to acknowledge me, and her gaze was measuring. "Ms. Newland. I hear our mutual enemy has taken a special interest in you."

I ignored her invitation to discuss Brenner. "Your help has been invaluable, Helen." I was even more deeply in debt to her now, but I wasn't going to give her the satisfaction of hearing those words come out of my mouth. "Where is Valentine?"

When her eyes narrowed, I felt a twinge of anxiety that I tried to keep from my face. I didn't want Helen to know she could intimidate me. "She is here. In the building. You may see her once you have both been debriefed."

"Thank you," I said, finally willing to betray the depth of my gratitude. Val was here. She was all right. I would see her soon, talk with her soon, touch her soon.

"Come with me." Helen led us across the bustling chamber and into a small, windowless conference room. Its walls were visibly padded. She gestured for us to sit at the circular table as Darren closed the door from the outside.

"I will tell you what I know," she said, bracing her palms against the edge of the table. Ebony hair cascaded over her shoulders to curl around the lapel of her charcoal blazer. "And then you will be so kind as to fill in the gaps."

I glanced at Constantine to see if he had taken umbrage at Helen's presumptiveness, but instead of looking offended, his lips were curled in the ghost of an amused smirk. He wasn't just tolerating her brusqueness. He liked it.

"Almost two weeks ago, Balthasar Brenner—or more accurately, a force loyal to him—laid siege to Telassar. Several days later, after burning the city of Sybaris to the ground, he and his elite guard joined the bulk of the army. He promised peace if the two of you would surrender yourselves to him.

"You escaped the city, but were later apprehended by Brenner. He detained you for several days until you escaped again and made your way to the outpost at Marrakech." Helen pushed back from the table, then, and gracefully sank into a chair. "Now. Tell me what you learned as Brenner's captives."

"First, a question," Constantine said, pressing one fingertip against the tabletop. "What are your intentions regarding Telassar?"

Helen raised one perfect eyebrow. "To see that you are reinstated, of course. Brenner has declared war on vampires, yes, but his attentions appear to be focused specifically on the Consortium. He is seeking a dissolution of our alliance."

Constantine laughed darkly. "He was bold enough to call me your 'pet.' His animosity toward any Were who is in league with either vampires or humans is significant." He glanced at me, then away. "Hence his utter disgust with Alexa."

"I still don't understand why he wanted me alive." I managed to hold my voice steady, but the memory of Brenner's barely contained ferocity in my presence made my panther uncoil once again into alertness.

"Presumably," Helen said, "he was hoping to use you to get to Valentine."

I struggled not to betray my panic at her words. "Why her? What could she have that he would want?"

Helen sat back and crossed one leg over the other. "Valentine is now the last descendant of the clan of the Missionary—the vampire clan that has lived in and ruled Sybaris for centuries. Her very existence represents Brenner's failure to annihilate an entire branch of our species."

Stunned, I could say nothing. The news that Brenner was after Valentine specifically—that he wanted to assassinate her in order to complete a mass extermination of her kind—was beyond my comprehension. I had to stop him. But how did we put a halt to the juggernaut of a man who commanded legions and razed entire cities? Clutching at the table edge to steady myself, I struggled to pay attention to Constantine and Helen's heated discussion. Brenner was a powerful alpha, true, but as long as the Consortium remained intact, I would have powerful allies.

"Just because he eliminated one grade of the Order," Constantine said, "does not mean that he intends to do the same to the rest."

Helen's glance was scornful. "Do you honestly expect me to believe he will not come after each clan in turn? Especially given his success at Sybaris?"

"Perhaps. Or perhaps he will now use the threat of genocide as a bargaining chip."

She bared her sharpened teeth. "Unacceptable, either way."

In the ensuing pause, Constantine crossed his arms over his chest. "Give me a place on your tactical operations team."

"Of course." Helen stood. "In fact, I am going to have to insist that both of you remain in this building, under Consortium protection, for the foreseeable future."

My stomach dropped. All summer, I had been looking forward to the moment when I would step across the threshold of our apartment, small and ramshackle though it was. *Home.* And now I wouldn't see it for who knew how long.

Suddenly, I panicked. Had Helen been lying? She wasn't going to keep me from Val, was she? I couldn't, wouldn't stand for that. Even if forbidden, I would find her. "I need to see Valentine now," I said as evenly as I could around the lump forming in my throat.

Helen's gaze bored into me, equal parts disdain and anger. I had seen the disdain many times before, but the anger was new. What had I done to incur it?

"You are only Brenner's bargaining chip. Valentine is his target. She has also been secured." She walked around the table and pulled open the door. "Do not forget the terms of our original agreement, Ms. Newland. You have not done an exemplary job of upholding them these past few months."

As she swept out into the main chamber, she instructed Darren to take me to Val's room, and I sighed in relief. Constantine lingered behind, regarding me curiously. "What was that about?"

I flashed back to the day on which I had persuaded Helen to help me to become a Were. Val and I had gone to her office. At first, she had refused her assistance. When she'd finally changed her mind, she had issued an ultimatum. *If you promise to do everything in your power to keep her satisfied, I will do this.*

Everything in my power. The words were a semantic minefield. Val had seen my desire to learn more about the other half of my psyche, to reach a deeper understanding with my panther-self. She had wanted that for me, had encouraged me to go to Telassar. But had I made the wrong decision? This summer had been difficult for her. Painful. Because of me.

The fierce longing for Val's touch rose in me and I turned away from Constantine's searching gaze. Whether I had erred or not, I was back now. I could be what she needed.

"A promise," I said over my shoulder. "One that I've been remiss in keeping."

I had never visited the fifth floor, so I didn't know whether it had always been a maximum-security facility, or whether it had just recently been transformed into one. Darren shepherded me through the warren of hallways, locked doors featuring palm and retina scanners greeting us at every corridor junction. Each security measure added to the dread and anger that churned in my stomach. To finish what he had started, Balthasar Brenner needed to kill Valentine. I was never going to let him. High-tech gadgets were all well and good, but I wasn't going to feel better until I could add my claws and teeth to the arsenal protecting Val.

The memory of Brenner looming over me in that café, his sneering fury targeted at me, triggered my panther's rage. Mentally snarling and spitting, she made a furious bid for control, and I stumbled into Darren as I channeled my focus into subduing her.

"Whoa, whoa," Darren said, catching me and holding me at arm's length. "Jesus, even I can feel her pushing."

I barely registered the pressure of his hands around my biceps, but my panther felt our constraint and thrashed even harder. *Easy, easy. Not now. Soon, I promise, but he is strong and we have to be patient. To wait.* The words were meaningless to her, but the emotions accompanying them slowly began to have an effect. When I was able to spare enough attention for my own body, I shrugged off Darren's grip.

"You're making it worse," I said. "I've got this. Sorry."

"She really wants out." Darren was looking at me with grudging admiration, and I remembered just how easy it had been to force him to shift all those months ago when Helen had convinced Valentine to break up with me.

"It's been a rough few weeks." I felt my heart rate slow as the panther subsided into the dark reaches of my psyche. Once Val and I had reunited—once we had talked and made love, once she had taken her fill from me—I would go to the hunting grounds and allow my cat free rein.

Darren pointed to a door just a few feet away on the left. "Well, you made it. Room five-thirty-three."

I didn't thank him. I didn't say good-bye. I took three quick steps to the door and knocked, holding my breath.

When it opened a few moments later, shock pushed the breath from my lungs. At long last, after so many days when I had thought I might never see her again, Valentine stood within arm's length. She wore her standard summer fare—a tank top and cargo shorts—but the tank hung loosely over her torso and the shorts hung low on her hips. Her eyes carried a hint of bloodshot and her face was paler than it should have been. *Oh, my God. What have I done?*

As if on cue, she grew even whiter.

"Val," I breathed, stepping forward into the room. She had let go of the door, and I closed it behind me. "Sweetheart..."

I didn't know what to say, and I didn't know why she wasn't

moving. Why wasn't she pushing me against the wall, kissing me, allowing her hands to roam all over my body, loving me the way we both needed? Why was she standing stock-still, trembling?

She looked like she was in shock. Was this a surprise? Had Helen told her nothing—not even that I was safe and on my way home?

Finally, her hands closed around my waist. But she didn't pull me close. She kept me at bay.

"Alexa." Her eyes were dark and wild not in desire but in terror. "Please, you can't be here. You have to go. Now."

CHAPTER SIXTEEN

Go?" I pushed against Val's grip and her arms trembled even more violently. She was weak. I could break her hold if I had to. "What are you talking about, Val? I've been trying to get back for weeks. I need to be here. With you. God, I've missed you so much."

But Val shook her head. "You're in terrible danger. Baby, you have to—"

My temper snapped. "What could possibly be more dangerous than being the hostage of Balthasar Brenner?" I pulled her hands away from my waist, then stepped forward and crushed my body to hers. Every muscle in my shoulders relaxed as I surrendered to the perfect fit of *us*. "You're not making any sense," I said, tucking my head beneath her chin. "I love you."

Her arms came around me then, pulling me even closer than I already was. "I love you," she whispered raggedly against my ear. "I love you, Alexa. I was so damn worried."

"I know. Me, too." For a moment, I allowed myself to simply exist—to let all my fears and anxieties melt away in the shelter of Valentine's arms. I had known from our very first date we were something special, though I had kept that conviction to myself until much later. Val was my soul mate. My one and only. I would fight through hell as many times as it took to return to her. But I hoped that now, after so much time apart, we could fight side by side, together. The way we were meant to.

With a sigh, I pushed back just enough to meet her wounded gaze. "Did Helen not tell you I was coming home?"

"Helen doesn't trust me." Her laugh was hollow. "She wants me to be the Missionary now. To be the thing that made me this way! And she knows I'll have no part of it."

Against my will, the memories cascaded through my brain: the Missionary draining his willing victims at the Circuit; the Missionary crouched over Devon Foster, her blood staining his lips; the Missionary savagely looming over Val as she lay broken on the floor of his apartment. My grip on her tightened.

"You're not him," I said, making my voice as soothing as I could. "You'll never be him. Helen can't force you to do anything."

Val nodded. "Yeah," she said, but I could tell she didn't mean it. Despite wanting to. "I know." She swallowed hard. "Anyway. The only news I've been getting is what Karma learns from Malcolm. She heard about the siege, but then we didn't know anything more until yesterday, when you got to Marrakech. I thought you were still there. Safe."

"Safe?" I looked at her incredulously. "He was hunting us, Val. This is the first time I've felt safe in weeks."

"Helen didn't tell you." Her voice was flat but her eyes were anger-bright.

"Tell me what?" I took a deep breath to combat my rising frustration. "I've just come from her War Room. We talked about Brenner's plans." I raised my hands to cup Val's face. "You're the one in terrible danger, Val. He's after you."

"What I'm worried about has nothing to do with Brenner. Or hell, maybe it does. I don't know." She turned her head just enough to kiss one of my palms. "Let's sit down, and I'll explain."

I didn't want to sit down; I wanted her to take me to bed. But right now, whatever she was afraid of had overruled both her desire and her thirst. That fact alone frightened me enough to let her lead me to the far corner, where two chairs flanked a small table. I sat, but kept my hand on her knee. Her muscles quivered beneath my touch.

"New York isn't safe for you. Or for any Were." She threaded her fingers through mine and I could feel the clamminess of her palm against my knuckles. "There's a pathogen. As far as I know, it only affects Weres. But it can be fatal." Her hand tightened. "At least two people are dead. One of them is Gwendolyn."

My pulse leapt and I worked to keep my breaths slow and steady. "Gwendolyn. The tiger, from the Circuit?"

"Yes. She died trying to break the Record." Val shuddered, and I leaned in closer to her. "She couldn't shift. I think—I think that's what killed her."

"But I thought you said it was some kind of pathogen?"

Val scrubbed her free hand through her hair, a familiar gesture of frustration. "My current theory—which is just a goddamn educated guess because everyone else is covering this whole thing up—is that the pathogen stops a Were from shifting. And not being able to shift is what eventually…kills."

My panther growled as my anxiety rose, and I felt fortunate that she couldn't understand Valentine's words. "Helen is covering this up? Why?"

Val shrugged. "To stop a panic, probably. But I'm not sure that's the only reason." She tucked a strand of hair behind my ear. That simple, loving touch made my heart stutter in a surge of emotion.

"Do you see now? You can't stay here, baby. It's too dangerous. This is going to turn into an epidemic, and as far as I know, there isn't a cure."

I captured her hand and brought it to my lips. If I focused on her, I could ignore my own fear. "How many sick have you seen?"

"Personally? Four. But I'm sure there are more out there."

"Still," I said, "four hardly seems like an epidemic."

Val's jaw clenched. "When Gwendolyn died last week, there were at least two hundred people in that room with her. Who knows how this thing even spreads? I don't know anything about it. If it's respiratory, it's already everywhere. Even if it isn't, given the way our people share blood and sex and needles…" She pulled her hand away from mine and rubbed at her temples. "This is a fucking nightmare. You may already have been exposed!"

I blew out my breath on a long sigh. "I know you're scared, Val. Frankly, so am I. But I'm not leaving you again. I never should have in the first place."

"But—"

I put two fingers to her lips "Don't push me away. Haven't we already learned this lesson? That we're so much stronger together than apart?"

"This is qualitatively different, and you know it."

"It isn't," I said, determined to be even more obstinate than she was. "If I run, either Brenner will catch up with me, or this mystery disease will. Probably both. If I stay, we can limit my exposure to other Weres, and I can help you figure out what the hell is going on."

I moved my fingers away from her mouth and readied myself for her tirade. But she sat silently staring—not at me, but through. Or maybe beyond.

"Before you make a final decision, there's something else I have to tell you." I watched her hands clench where they rested on her thighs. "A few days ago, I—I lost control. I attacked Karma."

"Oh my God." I leapt out of the chair and knelt before her, scanning her body for marks of injury even as my rational brain told me that if Karma had shifted, Val would be dead. "Did she hurt you?"

Val shook her head. "She knocked me out. She didn't change. When I woke up, I was here." She wouldn't meet my eyes. "Clavier... he had me transfused."

"Transfused?" I frowned in confusion. "But I thought you said she didn't hurt you."

"She didn't."

And then the words struck home. Clavier had given her blood. Someone else's blood. Fury rose in me, sharp and blazing. The panther flexed, and if Clavier had been in the room, I would have let her come. *Mine.*

"He did this while you were unconscious?" When Val nodded, misery etched in every line of her face, I gripped her legs tightly. "That's like rape, damn it!"

"That's what I said when I woke up. That's what it felt like. Feels like." She looked away again, her jaw working. "He insisted that he had only done it for my own good—that without the blood, I would have been too dangerous. And maybe he's right. I was...it felt like I was going crazy."

"What does this mean?" What was happening in Val's body? Would my blood still be able to keep the parasite in check? Or had Clavier jeopardized all of that? "For you? For us?"

"I don't know." Val's whisper was agonized. "I don't think anyone knows."

In the ensuing silence, I battled back my rage by focusing on the possibilities. If my blood stopped being effective, the parasite would eventually complete its conquest of Val's circulatory system. She would lapse into a brief coma and emerge from it a full vampire: stronger, faster, more ruthless. Unable to walk in the sunlight. Some believed that in the transition, a full vampire lost her soul.

I wanted to promise her that I'd never let that happen. I wanted to reassure her that receiving someone else's blood hadn't changed the potency of mine. It broke my heart to know I could do neither. But Val was acting as if this news would change the way I felt about her, and I couldn't stand that. My love for her wasn't attached to any conditions. When would she believe that?

"I love you," I said. "And I am not leaving you, Valentine." They were the only truths I had.

She stared at me for a few moments before burying her head in her hands. When her shoulders hitched, I rose to my feet and gently pulled at her wrists. She made a sound deep in her throat, and the sheer animal nature of it stirred my panther's protective impulses alongside my own.

"Come lie down," I said, tugging insistently until she stood. I maneuvered her until the backs of her legs were pressing against the bed, and then pushed on her tight shoulders. Obliging me, she stretched out on top of the comforter, one arm thrown over her eyes. Her chest rose and fell rapidly, and the first thing I did when I slid into place next to her was to rest my palm against the fluttering skin over her heart. Her next breath sounded more like a sob.

I curled into her then, my face against her neck and my arms wrapped tightly around her. Val rarely cried, but she needed to right now, and I wished she would just let go of all the emotions that were strangling her like a vine choking a tree. Instead, she fought them, her body taut against me as she struggled to rein in her tears. I stayed still and quiet, doing nothing more than holding her and occasionally letting my lips skate across her pale skin, until she began to relax.

As her muscles loosened, I raised myself up on one elbow and pulled her arm away from her face. Her eyes were still shadowed by fear, but when I traced one cheekbone with my thumb, she smiled wanly.

"I'm—"

Not wanting her apology, I sealed my mouth to hers. The kiss was our first in weeks, and it seared my soul. Val felt it too, her fingers clutching at my shoulders as though she were drowning and I was her lifeline. In a way, that was true. But her need echoed mine, and

I was determined to prove it in every way that I could. I lost myself in her mouth, remembering her fully in the dance of our tongues and the wet slide of our lips, and I didn't pull away until I felt her tugging at the hem of my T-shirt. I trapped her body between my knees, then sat up and ripped off everything separating my breasts from hers. She followed me, the muscles in her stomach contracting as she kissed the skin I revealed.

Not to be outdone, I undressed her, my knuckles skimming over her torso as I divested her of first the shirt and then the sports bra beneath it. I sucked in my breath as Val's full, beautiful breasts were freed. She gasped as I cupped them in my hands and lightly rubbed my thumbs over her nipples. They were the loveliest shade of dusky coral, and they hardened at my touch.

"Oh, Val," I murmured between the kisses I placed along her jawline. "Val, you feel so good."

When I pinched her between my fingertips, her strength gave out and she called my name, collapsing back onto the mattress. I followed her down, marveling at the power I held over her in this sensual moment, and brushed my breasts across her glistening mouth. The loving swirl of her tongue inspired a groan from deep in my throat. She always made me feel so desirable. So cherished. But in that moment, I didn't want tender romance. I wanted to feel the potent depth of her need for me—a need beyond pleasure, beyond even love. I needed her teeth in my skin.

Giving in to gravity, I slid down until my mouth was next to her ear. "I want you slow, Valentine. I want you to take your time with me. But not right now." Her body went taut and I punctuated my words with a sucking kiss to her sensitive earlobe. "Right now, I need you not to hold back. Right now, I need to feel you come with your teeth in my neck." She shivered, and I hid a triumphant smile against her skin. "Take me. Please."

The weakness, the hesitancy, the doubt—all of it disappeared in one powerful surge of her muscles. And as I stared into her handsome face, her cheeks flushed with desire and her eyes dark in passion, the world righted itself. This was where I belonged.

"Off," Val growled, making quick work of the buttons on my jeans. She kicked away her shorts and then there were no barriers between us.

She cupped my cheek as she slid one thigh against me, and I knew the moment she felt how very wet I was by the thirst that twisted her lips.

Her hand against my face began to move, sliding down over my shoulder and along the outer curve of my breast—Valentine mapping me, anchoring me with her possessive touch. As her fingers slid between my legs, I closed my eyes in pleasure.

"No," she said harshly, stilling her hand. "Keep them open."

"Val…" her name left my lips on a groan as I obeyed. When my eyes locked with hers, she stroked me, a whisper-light touch. I cried out, my entire body clenching, the pleasure made all the more powerful by the intensity of her hungry gaze.

"You're mine," she said, lowering her head as she continued to tease me. Overwhelmed with sensation, my back arched. And then she was kissing me—a fierce, bruising, possessive kiss. She stole my breath before trailing her lips down, down from the corner of my mouth, over my jaw, down along my neck where the staccato of my racing pulse was strongest.

"So beautiful," she said, tracing the lines of my veins with her lips. "Alexa. I need you."

The sharp flash of pain as her teeth broke my skin merged with the inexpressible pleasure of her fingers pushing deep into my body. She claimed me fully, and I screamed. I pulled her closer as every muscle contracted, tangling my fingers in her hair and twining my legs with hers. Her hips surged, and through the blazing tide of my release, I rejoiced that she had found hers.

Val drank and drank, coaxing every last shudder from me until I lay quiescent. When she stilled her hand and withdrew from my neck, I shivered at the loss. She stayed where she was, pressing me into the mattress, tenderly licking the tiny wounds closed as she eased her fingers from my body.

Peace suffused me and I drifted, dimly aware of Val turning down the covers and sliding me between the sheets. She wrapped herself around me and I turned into her embrace.

"So good," I slurred, burrowing my face into her neck and breathing in the fragrance of her familiar, beloved scent. "Don't you see? No more pushing me away. Promise."

She stroked my hair. "I can't live without you," she said, and though she meant the words to be reassuring, the note of sorrow in her voice made my heart ache.

"Val—"

She shook her head and deepened her touch, massaging my scalp. "Sleep now, baby."

"But what about everything that's happening?" I said, struggling to muster my thoughts. Helen might have told both Val and me to lie low, but I knew Val wouldn't be content to cool her heels while the maelstrom raged around us. And neither was I. "First Brenner, and now this disease. What are we going to do?"

I expected her to stop then, to turn her focus from me to what our plan of action should be. But the soothing rhythm of her fingers never faltered. "We'll figure it out later," she said. "Rest. You need it. We both do."

Sighing, I let myself relax into her touch. We were together again. Everything would be all right. I knew it. I'd prove it to her, day after day, until every one of her doubts disappeared. Surrendering to my own exhaustion, I let the cadence of her words pull me under.

"I love you, Alexa. Sleep."

CHAPTER SEVENTEEN

The conference room adjacent to Karma's office was barely large enough to fit us all, but it had been the only viable option. Trying to be circumspect, I moved my chair to the right to put just a few more inches between myself and Sebastian. My panther, sensing his connection to the powerful alpha who had terrorized us across the ocean, was on high alert. She radiated distrust and suspicion, and had it been up to her, we would have been on the other side of the building by now. Her unease was compounded by my own; Sebastian still regarded Val with the kind of propriety look that wasn't appropriate on anyone but me. Had he not been our ally, I would have been tempted to teach him a lesson.

Karma patted my knee in reassurance as I edged closer. We had just spent an hour in her office, catching up over coffee. For a good day and a half, I hadn't had the urge to leave Val's bed. Wrapped around each other, we had slept long and hard, waking only to eat and make love. But the stronger I began to feel, the more stir-crazy I became. It had been a relief to leave the narrow confines of our room, though Val had vehemently protested.

Only when I forced her to admit that Karma had yet to show any sign at all of being ill had she relented. I didn't like making her upset, and I never wanted to hurt her. But if I'd remained sequestered for much longer, the panther's claustrophobia might have won out over my own ego.

I had several reasons for wanting to talk to Karma in private. I'd missed her over the summer and wanted to share stories of my time at Telassar. But more importantly, I wanted her take on what had happened that night, almost a week ago now, when Valentine had lost control. Once I'd satisfied her curiosity about what it had been like to confront Balthasar Brenner, I asked her to tell me about Val.

"I went to your apartment," Karma had said. "Malcolm had just received news about Telassar from Nadia—you must have met her? She called in once she reached safe haven in Djerba." When I nodded, she went on. "I knocked on your door, and then again when Val didn't answer. She finally opened it. I think she had been sleeping."

I smiled at the thought of sleepy Valentine: her features soft and vulnerable, the slow blink of her blue eyes as she tried to make sense of the waking world. But that was my Valentine, the one who woke in my arms after a restful night of sleep. I could only imagine how frantic Val had looked when she'd opened the door for Karma.

"I went inside. I told her about the siege, and Brenner. That you and Constantine were missing." Karma had reached out for my hand. "I think I made a mistake then. She was upset, so I put my arm around her. As we kept talking, she grew more and more tense. I attributed that to her being worried about you."

The panther's hackles had risen as jealousy flared beneath my skin, hot and sharp. I didn't blame Karma—she had only been trying to comfort Val—but it had been a struggle not to react. "What happened after that?"

"She was telling me about a dream she'd had. About Brenner. I was asking questions. And then…" She had trailed off, and I'd wondered if she was reliving the memory. "Sometimes I think that we—that vampires and Weres—have more in common than we realize."

"How so?"

"Valentine fought against the impulse to drink from me. She lost." Karma had shrugged. "How many times have I fought my jackal and lost?"

"You won that night," I'd said, allowing the gratitude that I felt to saturate my voice.

Karma had shuddered. "It was a close thing."

"You knocked her out and brought her here?"

"Directly to Clavier, yes."

Another lance of anger had shot up my spine and set my panther snarling. "He gave her blood."

"What?" She'd sounded shocked. Most shifters believed that my relationship with Valentine was perverted—a kind of slavery. But Karma knew the idea had been mine from the beginning. She saw how much we loved each other, and she respected it. "I went in to see her as soon as Clavier would let me. She wasn't hooked up to anything then."

I still wanted to rip him limb from limb for violating Valentine— for believing he had the right to ignore her wishes when it came to the nature of her very existence.

"Val made him take it out when she woke up."

"Alexa, I am so sor—"

"No," I had said gently, squeezing her hand. "You are not allowed to apologize. You did everything you could to help her, and in a way, you even saved her life." I had shaken her fingers lightly to get her to meet my gaze. "Thank you."

"Is everything going to be all right?" she'd asked after a moment of hesitation.

I had wanted to say yes—a confident, unequivocal yes. But I couldn't. "I hope so."

"We have a problem," said Val, startling me out of my memory. As she paced the length of the small room, my gaze lingered with appreciation on the defined muscles of her upper arms, the gentle swell of her breasts beneath her tight gray T-shirt, the pale band of skin between its hem and her low-slung jeans. Even in the midst of so much chaos, she stirred my body and my heart.

"Just one?" Sebastian's words were heavy with irony.

Val shot him an irritated glance. They had grown close in my absence, and I didn't like it. While I wasn't about to begrudge Val a friendship, I would never be convinced that Sebastian didn't have some kind of design on her.

"We know there's a pathogen out there. We know that it's killed. We know that the Consortium is covering up its existence." She stopped behind my chair and her fingers brushed my neck—to reassure either herself or me, I couldn't tell. At her gentle touch, I closed my eyes. The panther purred.

"Let's take a step back," Karma said into the silence. "Helen and Malcolm have been distracted by the ADA's inquiries into Consortium business practices for most of the past month. Without any warning, Brenner razes Sybaris and seizes Telassar in the space of a week. And now, Weres are dying mysteriously."

I frowned at the logical conclusion. "A three-pronged attack, and not a coincidence?"

"Where my father is concerned," said Sebastian, "it's always best to assume the worst."

"Both Helen and Malcolm are completely preoccupied by his movements," said Karma. "Malcolm has encouraged me to investigate the disease, but his primary concern seems to be that Brenner will attempt a takeover here."

"Here?" I was incredulous. "He can't risk that kind of exposure."

"What if this disease is a forerunner?" Sebastian said. "If it creates a large enough vacuum, he can waltz right in to power, virtually unopposed. By Malcolm, anyway."

"Why only target Weres, then?" I asked. "It doesn't make any sense. I got the distinct impression, after listening to him rant and rave, that he wants vampires out of the picture. Categorically."

"At this point, I don't care what he wants." Val looked grim. "What I care about is that there's some kind of pathogen out there and we still know virtually nothing about it." She scrubbed a hand through her hair. "I don't think it's airborne, but I can't be sure, and I've been worse than useless since Helen put me under house arrest. If I could get to my lab, I'd have at least a little more information. I put in a call to my friend who is running tests on Shade's blood, but he hasn't gotten back to me yet."

"It's definitely spreading," Sebastian said. "Especially among the hardcore user crowd."

"Two of Malcolm's lieutenants fell ill last week," Karma added. "But they don't fit that profile."

"The rumors are spreading even faster than whatever this thing is," Sebastian said. "Luna has been emptier by the night."

"Rumors?" I asked.

"My people have heard it compared to HIV on several occasions." He bared his teeth in a mirthless smile. "So much for stopping a panic."

My pulse spiked and the panther instinctively shoved at the

boundaries of my psyche. I turned in my chair and met Val's troubled gaze. "Is there any truth to that analogy?"

"Yes and no." She began to pace again. "It's probably transmitted in the same ways as HIV. And I suspect that, like HIV, the pathogen itself isn't fatal. But unlike HIV, this doesn't seem to be an immune disorder. My best guess at this point is that what killed Gwendolyn, for example, was…well, the tiger."

Karma leaned forward, clearly alarmed. "Her other half killed her?"

"She couldn't make the change," said Sebastian. "But she couldn't stop it, either."

Karma reacted by speaking several words in a language I didn't recognize. They didn't sound good. I reached for Val's hand and squeezed tightly.

"That must have been a terrible way to die."

"The next full moon is a few weeks away." Karma's voice wavered. "What will happen to the ones who are infected? Will they also die?"

Silence greeted her question. I imagined what it would be like— feeling the full glory of the moon as it rose above the horizon and pulled at my blood, wanting nothing more than to surrender to the wild beauty of the hunt…only to be blocked, over and over, from obeying its insistent call.

Torture. It would be torture.

"I don't know," Val said angrily. "God damn it, I don't know."

We were interrupted by a knock at the door, and as Karma got up to answer it, I drew Val's hand to my lips. Pressing a gentle kiss in each space between her knuckles, I willed her to focus on me, alive and well. On us, back together again. As frightening as this illness was, especially on top of everything else, I felt confident that I would be safe. I didn't inject drugs, and I certainly wasn't sleeping with anyone except Valentine.

"Sebastian Brenner." A familiar voice reverberated off the close walls, and I looked up to the sight of Darren and another member of Helen's guard, the vampire who had accompanied them both to the Missionary's loft, so many months ago. The one who, I suspected, had set fire to the place afterward. He was looking at Sebastian, who lounged in his chair, feet propped insouciantly on the table.

"This can't be good," Val muttered, moving even closer to me.

"We are under orders to detain you." The vampire wore a gun clipped to the waist of his dark jeans, and I wondered whether its chambers were filled with bullets or tranquilizer darts.

"To detain me?" More quickly than my eyes could follow, Sebastian was on his feet, his knees bent as though poised to flee. Or fight. Across the room, Karma tensed. "On whose orders, exactly?"

"Mine." Helen stepped into view behind her crony and rested a hand on his shoulder. He moved aside just enough for her to enter the room, but his gaze never left Sebastian.

"Unsurprising." Sebastian cocked his head, and I could almost hear the debate that raged between him and his wolf. To strike out? To escape? To yield?

"On what grounds?" Karma asked, outrage seeping into her voice.

Helen didn't so much as spare her a glance. "Suspected sedition."

Sebastian's devil-may-care smile hid a snarl. "You're an idiot. And this is an act of desperation. In my case, the apple landed quite far from the tree."

I didn't particularly like him, but in that moment, my respect for him increased tenfold. It was refreshing to hear someone stand up to Helen. And I had no doubt that evidence of any involvement in his father's activities didn't exist. Helen was running scared. So was Malcolm, if he had signed off on what essentially qualified as internment.

"Are you going to come quietly?" said the vampire, palm poised above his gun. "Or not?"

Sebastian widened his eyes dramatically. "My, my, you do seem eager to put that weapon to use. I'd better not give you an excuse." When he reached the doors, Darren cuffed his hands behind his back. I wondered whether he felt torn in his loyalties.

Sebastian glanced over one shoulder, the fake smile still plastered to his lips. "Feel free to come visit me at camp," he said sarcastically before turning back to his captors. "All right, gentlemen. *Arbeit macht frei*, eh?"

They marched him down the hall, but as the echoes of their passage faded, Helen remained behind. Her gaze traveled over my body like a forced caress, and I struggled not to shudder. Finally, she turned the spotlight of her attention away from me and onto Val.

"You're looking better, Valentine," she said, her tone mocking.

Val ignored the bait. "Where will you hold him?"

"You are blowing this out of proportion, as usual." Helen smoothed the front of her gray blazer. "We just want to ask him a few questions."

Her patronizing tone made my panther lash her tail. Karma was struggling, too—I could tell from the white-knuckled grip that she had on the back of the nearest chair. But if she was able to sense our unrest, Helen was totally unfazed by it. She glanced at her watch, then back at Val.

"Be safe."

And then she was gone.

As soon as the door closed, Karma collapsed into her chair. "I need to talk to Malcolm," she said. "Now." But her shoulders trembled, and she made no move to get up.

"Do you think Helen's acting alone?" I asked. "Or would he sign off on detaining Sebastian?"

Karma looked up, poised to answer…and froze.

"What?" I said, frowning. "What is it?" When she didn't move, I turned to Val, only to watch the blood drain from her face. She even wavered on her feet, as though she might faint.

"Oh God," she choked out. "No."

And that's when I felt it—the tickle against my nose, familiar from the aftermath of a jog on a cold winter's day. When I reached up to brush the moisture away, the side of my index finger came away red.

Red. I stared at it, first in confusion and then in disbelief. My nose was bleeding. How could my nose be bleeding? I had only returned to New York three days ago. I hadn't engaged in risky behaviors. I was sick, but it didn't make any sense.

I had been confident in my invulnerability. I had promised Val that everything would be fine. And now, when the next full moon rose into the sky, the power of its tidal forces would rip me apart. I would die. I knew it.

Deep inside my mind, the panther howled in fury.

valentine

CHAPTER EIGHTEEN

If Alexa hadn't been sleeping in our bed after taking a mild sedative, I would have torn the room apart in fury. Instead, I sequestered myself in the Consortium's gym and hammered at a heavy bag until sweat sluiced down my face like tears and every muscle burned. My brain was a storm of anguish and fear. I couldn't think, but I had to. I had to figure out a way to find a cure.

How had she gotten sick? If the pathogen were airborne, Karma and Sebastian would have come down with it weeks ago. Had Brenner somehow infected her with it in Africa? But she hadn't been drugged or even unconscious—only imprisoned.

I stopped my frenzied dance around the bag and held it in place as my breathing began to slow. On the edge of tears, I rested my forehead against my gloved hands. Why had I let her convince me that she was safe? My instincts had known better. I should have found a way for her to escape. Or better yet, we could have escaped together...

Together. I pushed off the bag as the horrifying epiphany lanced through me. Over the past few days, we had been together in every way possible. We had made love more times than I could count, and Alexa, determined to satisfy my desperate thirst, had urged me to drink from her repeatedly.

There was only one logical conclusion. She had gotten it from me. I had been the one to make her sick.

All of the fight went out of me, and I sank to the floor. Beyond thought, I stared into the abyss of despair that had opened in my brain. Ever since I'd been turned, I had been nothing but a danger to her. No matter what she did to try to change that fact, or how often she tried to deny it, the truth continued to slap us both in the face. And now, that truth was going to kill her.

"Val!" I raised my head at the sound of Karma's voice bouncing off the cement walls. She hurried across the room. "I've been looking everywhere for you. Are you—"

Cutting herself off, she stopped a few feet away and watched as I got to my feet. She didn't make a move to touch me. I was in no mood for comfort. Beneath the despair, anger churned sluggishly, awaiting its chance to burst into the open.

"I made her sick," I said without preamble. "I did. Me."

Karma took a step backward, every muscle taut as the fear washed through her. I didn't think it was possible to feel worse, but that simple gesture of rejection made my gut churn.

"What are you talking about?"

"It's the only explanation that makes sense." I kept my eyes on the wall past her shoulder, so I wouldn't have to see the incrimination on her face. "This thing isn't airborne, or you'd be sick. And Alexa doesn't shoot up. The only person she's been sleeping with is me."

"But vampires haven't been falling ill. You haven't demonstrated any of the symptoms, have you?"

I shook my head. "Vampires must be able to carry it."

The doubt didn't leave Karma's face. "Even so. How did *you* get infected?"

There was only one logical answer, and its implications made me want to scream. "The transfusion. Has to be." My thoughts were spiraling into binary. Either Clavier had infected me on purpose, or he had not. The answer didn't really matter. The only thing that mattered now was Alexa. And she was sick because of me.

"Oh, Val."

She crossed the gap between us and grasped my shoulders. "We are not giving up. Do you hear me?"

Her eyes were beautiful—chocolate flecked with gold. I let the conviction in them anchor me against the nihilistic winds of my own despair.

"In our meeting, you said something about lab results. Can I help you get them?"

Her resolve set my panic temporarily at bay. She was right. There was something I could do. Right now. I could be proactive, instead of continuing to wait for Sean to send along the results. "I'll make a call."

"Good," she said, her hands falling away from me. I leaned against the wall and dialed Sean's extension at the lab, praying that he had chosen to work late tonight.

"Hi, Sean," I said, certain that my voice betrayed my gratitude at hearing his. "It's Val."

"Val, hey. We've missed you. Are you hanging in there?" Like the rest of my lab, Sean thought that I'd had to leave suddenly because of a family emergency. Which wasn't all that far from the truth, now.

"Yeah. Hanging in. Actually…remember those tests I asked you to run last week? The results would be handy right about now."

"You have good timing," Sean said. "I just got them back a few hours ago. Was about to e-mail them to you. I'm sorry they took so long to come in—I had to run them on the DL, and it's been a busy week."

"I understand." I tried to keep my tone light. "And thanks again."

"Sure thing. Hurry back, Val."

I glanced at Karma as I ended the call on my phone and tapped over to my mailbox. "He's going to e-mail what he's got."

She nodded, bent over her own PDA. "And they're holding Sebastian in the cells on level two. Along with several of his siblings?" Karma was staring at the screen as though she couldn't believe what she was reading.

I frowned at the implications. "Jesus. Do you think they've rounded up every one of Brenner's whelps who lives in the city?"

"As collateral." Karma's eyes were troubled. "Every piece of correspondence I'm reading has Malcolm's digital signature on it alongside Helen's, but I don't like it."

"Do you think they'll stop us if we try to visit him?"

When Karma only shook her head, I realized just how upset she was. I was willing to bet that locking up Sebastian and his siblings had been entirely Helen's idea. I wondered if it had been easy for Helen to convince Malcolm of her desperate wartime logic. Or had he been reluctant to enforce martial law on his own people?

Deeply unsettled, I continued to refresh my inbox every second until Sean's message came through. The wait while my phone downloaded his spreadsheet was interminable, but when I was able to inspect the data, I found more questions than answers. As expected, Shade had significant levels of both bipolar and antipsychotic medications in her bloodstream.

She was also pregnant.

"This can't be right," I said, even as I scanned the supporting data. Shade had been grieving for Gwendolyn. She hadn't mentioned anything about a baby. Hell, she had practically resigned herself to dying from the same affliction to which her lover had succumbed. Besides, the drugs she was taking presented significant risks to a fetus. I couldn't believe she had been pregnant. But the hormones in her blood couldn't lie.

Or could they?

I flashed back to nearly a month ago, when I had first seen the devastating effects of the Were pathogen while at Luna. After watching the agonizing spectacle of Vincent's aborted transformation, I had tapped into the Consortium's research on Weres, hoping to find a logical explanation for why he had been unable to shift. All I had discovered was that, by an unknown mechanism, pregnant Weres did not transform. But what if that was how the pathogen operated—by tricking the host body into believing it was pregnant?

"What?" Karma's voice was laced with the urgency we both felt. "What did you find? Val?"

I looked up as I realized there was a very simple way to test my hypothesis. All it required was a trip to the nearest pharmacy. Helen wouldn't let me go anywhere, but Karma was free to move about as she wished.

"You asked how you can help," I said, reaching into my back pocket for my wallet and then pulling out a twenty. "I need you to buy a home pregnancy test."

I sat on the edge of the bed, listening to the rustles of movement in the bathroom as Alexa followed the instructions of the pregnancy kit. The whole scenario was a daydream turned nightmare. There had been many sleepless nights over the past few months when I had tried to calm my body and my soul by imagining Alexa pregnant with our child—the gentle bulge of her belly, the peace that would radiate from her face, the quirky cravings I'd trek across the city to satisfy. Now the pathogen lurking in Alexa's blood had put every dream in jeopardy.

The bathroom door opened and she stepped out, holding the test strip. "Hey." She sat next to me, and together we stared at the indicator, waiting for either a plus or minus sign to appear.

"I love you," I said, brushing a tentative hand across her knee. She trapped it and held it to her body.

"Stop blaming yourself. I'm the one who wouldn't listen." When I nodded without meeting her gaze, she gripped my chin. "I mean it, Val. I don't regret making love with you. I don't regret begging you to drink from me. I need you, and I need to be here, *with* you. We'll figure out how to beat this."

"I know," I said hoarsely, not because I did, but because I knew she was trying to convince herself. I wrapped an arm around her shoulders and leaned in to kiss her temple. "I know we will, baby."

I kept my eyes closed and savored the smoothness, the fragrance of her skin—until she tensed. "Well." The single syllable trembled. "That's surreal."

I looked down to the sight of a blue plus sign but felt no exultation at being right. Despite knowing what to expect, it was a shock. I rubbed Alexa's back until I found my voice. "I'm going to take this to Clavier and Helen, okay?"

She nodded, and when I stood, she pulled up her feet so that she was curled on the bed facing the window. I pressed a kiss to the nape of her neck. "Is there anything I can get you?"

"I was planning to hunt tonight," she said after a moment's hesitation. "The panther has been restless for days. I kept promising that I would give her a chance to run. And now…"

Swallowing hard, I glanced at the bottle of pills on the nightstand. "Do the meds help?"

She rolled over and reached for my hand, and I sank back onto the bed. "I'm not sure. I'm afraid if I take them too often, the panther will feel trapped. Which would only make this whole situation worse." She brushed my knuckles against her cheek. "But they do seem to stop me from getting too anxious."

I wanted to cry. I wanted to punch something. Instead, I reached over her for the television remote. "It sounds like a distraction is in order. You know, crime shows can be pretty effective."

The ghost of a smile played along her lips. "Oh yeah?"

"Mmm-hmm." I spotted her phone behind the pills, and scrolled through the contacts list until I found Karma's name. "And I'm going to put you on the line with Karma, okay? I know she would love to bring you a few books. Or some tabloids to poke fun at."

Alexa tugged at my hand until I was close enough to kiss. "You are very good to me," she said before brushing her lips across mine.

"I love you," I said, keeping my voice soft so she wouldn't hear the snarl of tears in the back of my throat. "See you soon, okay?"

Pushing the call button, I handed her the phone and walked out of the room, determined to make Clavier see reason. But when I arrived at his office, he wasn't there. Perhaps he was in the restricted basement facility. I wondered if they had put up increased security precautions around the makeshift hospital after I'd stumbled into it. As I was turning toward the doors at the end of the corridor, though, I saw Tonya leave one room and walk down the hall. Quickly, I moved to intercept her.

"You're back," she said, a smile of recognition spreading across her face. "You know, when you didn't tell me your name the other day, I had to ask my friends. Kyle told me all about you, Valentine."

I ignored her flirtation. "I'm hoping you can tell me where to find Dr. Clavier."

She rested one palm on my sternum and plucked at the collar of my shirt. "Harold is in a meeting with Ms. Lambros. Since he can't be disturbed, maybe I can help you?"

"Actually," I said, removing her hand, "I'll take my chances with disturbing him." I sidestepped, and was several paces closer to the exit before her human reflexes registered my movements. "Thanks for the help," I called over my shoulder as the fire doors closed behind me.

❖

Darren stood outside Helen's office, his massive arms folded across his chest. "You can ask," he said, "but I can tell you right now you're not going to be able to see her. At least a dozen people have been turned away already today."

Those dozen people must have stood on decorum and the conventions of polite society. I had no intention of doing so. I barged into the antechamber and blatantly ignored Helen's secretary. But when I closed my hand around the doorknob to her office, I found it locked.

In that moment, the door epitomized everything that was blocking me from discovering a cure for Alexa. The rage I'd been holding back since the morning finally boiled over, drowning out the secretary's indignant words, the scrape of her chair against the floor as she stood, Darren's heavy footfalls behind me. For the first time, I embraced the strength that was my right as blood prime of the line of the Missionary.

I twisted. The knob snapped off, splintering the wood around it, and the door swung open to the sight of Helen rising to her feet, face dark in anger. Clavier sat in the chair in front of her desk, and when he saw me, he grimaced. I didn't let any of them speak, but held up the plastic indicator.

"Alexa is 'pregnant.'"

Darren's hand landed on my shoulder, but I stood still, eyes locked with Helen's. Silence reigned for several seconds, broken only by the ring of Helen's private line. She didn't answer.

"Shut the door," she said, gesturing sharply for me to come inside. Her voice was ice, but I didn't care. I shrugged off Darren's grip and stepped over the threshold, easing the battered door closed behind me. As soon as we were alone, she pointed an accusing finger.

"That little stunt was absolutely ridiculous. You need to learn—"

Refusing to be cowed, I cut her off and focused on Clavier. "The pathogen tricks its Were host into a chemical pregnancy. I don't know how. But maybe that's the key to stopping it."

Clavier folded his hands on top of his crossed legs. "I've known this for weeks, Valentine. But congratulations on figuring it out all on your own."

Red tinged my vision at his sneering words. He had known? And he hadn't done anything to stop it? My frayed temper snapped again and I lunged forward to twine my fingers in the expensive material of his oxford shirt. I lifted him into the air and shook him, hard.

"You fucking bastard!" When he struggled, choking, I shook him again. "Tell me how to fix this, God damn it!"

"Enough." Helen's voice carried a venom that sliced through the roar of my heartbeat. "Release him. Now."

When I let go, Clavier fell back into his chair, clutching at his throat. I could have killed him. I still wanted to. Trembling as the rage and adrenaline swept my blood, I balled my hands into fists.

"We have known how the pathogen operates for some time, Valentine," Helen said. "And we have tested several treatments. But none of them have been successful."

"You *gave* it to me!" My arms ached with the effort it took to keep my fists at my sides. I wanted to make Clavier bleed. Dimly, I registered Helen's phone ringing again, but again, she didn't pay it any mind. "If you hadn't, Alexa would still be well!"

I'd only seen surprise cross Helen's patrician features one other time—also in this office, several months ago, when Alexa had asked to become a shifter so that she could sustain me for eternity. Maybe her expression was false, and maybe it wasn't. Either way, I rounded on Clavier.

"It was the transfusion that you administered."

"Accident," he said, coughing.

I braced myself on the armrests of his chair. "Why should I believe you? Why, when you keep blocking me?" I looked back over my shoulder to Helen. "Is this some kind of punishment for refusing to be your goddamn Missionary?"

At that moment, the door banged open again. Malcolm Blakeslee stood at the threshold and he was trembling—not in fear, but with the effort it took to restrain his beast. Instinctively, I pushed off the chair, out of his way.

"You haven't been picking up your phone," he said to Helen.

"As you can see, I've been engaged. What is it you—"

"I have *him* on the line." Malcolm held aloft the device in his right hand. "He is demanding to speak to the both of us. And he is growing impatient."

Helen bared her teeth. "Fine. Put him through." As Malcolm laid the phone on the desk and keyed it to speaker, I watched her take a deep breath. "We are both present, Balthasar."

"Helen." His voice was a rich baritone, and he sounded almost jovial. No doubt having the upper hand put him in excellent mood. "It has been so long."

"Not long enough." Despite the animosity I'd felt toward Helen recently, I admired the way she stood up to Brenner. "Say your piece, and be gone."

He laughed sonorously. "Oh, that's not quite how it's going to work. I have terms to propose, you see. For your surrender."

Helen and Malcolm exchanged an inscrutable glance, and Malcolm's grip on the desk tightened enough for the wood to protest. "I'm afraid you won't find us amenable, Balthasar," was all he said.

"Perhaps not you specifically, Malcolm," Brenner mused. "But certainly, most of your followers will accept my offer. You see, even as we speak, my agents are spreading my message throughout the Were community in every corner of New York, by all available media.

"A few months ago, my people raided a Consortium research facility and recovered an experimental virus that, if contracted by one of us, would cause that Were to be unable to shift. The Consortium had engineered this pathogen without a cure."

Brenner's words pierced my heart. The Consortium was *responsible* for creating the plague now threatening Alexa's life? Malcolm seemed just as surprised as I was, but the grim look shared by Helen and Clavier convinced me of the proof of Brenner's claim. How had the virus gotten loose? Had Clavier purposefully introduced it into the Were community? Or had it been another "accident"?

"Thankfully, my people were able to develop an effective treatment," Brenner said. "And we are willing to share that treatment with any Were, in exchange for the head of a vampire."

Shock reverberated up my spine, and I took another step away from Malcolm before I realized what I was doing. I couldn't believe what I'd just heard. In a matter of minutes, Brenner had dissolved an alliance that had taken the Consortium decades to engineer.

"This is madness, Balthasar." I had no idea how Helen maintained her preternatural calm in the face of Brenner's catastrophic threat, but her voice did not so much as falter. Then again, in the face of annihilation, what more did she have to salvage than her pride?

"In three days, I will release a modified version of the virus that is airborne. Within hours, every Were in the city who has not yet joined me and received the vaccine will be infected. When the next full moon rises, those not under my protection will be dead."

Helen's knuckles were white against the dark mahogany of her desk. "You wouldn't dare to launch an offensive of this magnitude when I've detained all of your offspring. Call off your attack, or they will die. By your hand."

When Brenner didn't reply immediately, I thought that her counterthreat might prove to be effective.

"This is a cleansing of the species," he said, and there was no hint of hesitation or conflict in his voice. He had paused for dramatic effect, not because he was conflicted. "Only the fittest will survive. There will be no negotiation. You have my ultimatum."

He severed the connection, but none of us moved. Was nothing sacred to that madman? Not even family?

"Our bet was misplaced." Malcolm turned to Helen, anger deepening the lines on his brow. "His claim about the origins of the virus. Is that the truth?"

"Half true. Like everything he says." She sighed, exchanging another glance with Clavier. "For years, we have been trying to create a medication that will block the change for those shifters who either wish to do so for personal reasons or need to remain human during a full moon. That virus represents a failed attempt, not a biological weapon."

"It was destroyed," said Clavier. He sounded genuinely confused, but I wondered if it was an act. "According to my records, we destroyed it last year, when its side effects proved fatal."

"Clearly, those records were falsified." Malcolm's jaw clenched. "And we have a traitor in our midst."

"Am I to presume, then," Helen said, sounding for all the world like ruling royalty and not a beleaguered combatant, "that you will not be offering my head to Balthasar on a pike?"

Malcolm raised one hand in a gesture of placation. "Our priority must be a fortification of this facility, and a plan of escape in case that fails. There are plenty of Weres who will remain loyal to our alliance."

"But more who will not." Only when Helen relaxed her stance had I realized that she had been tensing for conflict. "Thank you, Malcolm." She looked past him to me. "You have your wish, Valentine: my permission to do whatever you deem necessary in order to find a way to block the effects of Brenner's virus. I know that Harold will help you however he can. Perhaps your fresh insight will precipitate a breakthrough."

I nodded, biting the inside of my cheek to keep myself from making a caustic retort. She should have enlisted my help from the beginning. Then maybe we could have stopped Brenner from giving every Were in the city a reason to turn against the vampires. Now we were going to need a miracle to keep every loyal shifter alive past the next full moon. To keep *Alexa* alive.

"And arm yourselves," Helen added. "There will be blood in these halls before long."

CHAPTER NINETEEN

Helen's secretary's phone was ringing off the hook as Clavier and I passed through the antechamber and into the hallway. Once we were outside, I rounded on him.

"I'm not going to apologize. What you did to me was unconscionable, and now that Alexa is sick—" The urge to strike out at him welled up in me like a flash fire, and I braced my hand against the wall so as not to give in to the impulse. "I want access to everything. And your full cooperation. I am going to make this right, damn it, whatever it takes."

He stared at me coldly. "Save your self-righteous invectives for someone who will be moved by them."

I took a menacing step forward, despite my determination to remain poised. "Hoping for a repeat performance? You must get off on asphyxiation." At the spark of anger in his eyes, I laughed. "The first thing that's going to happen is that I am going to talk to Sebastian. And *you* are going to call whoever you need to call to make that happen. Right now."

Without waiting for a response, I turned sharply and headed for the stairwell. The elevators would no doubt be a mess as panicked Weres and vampires either fled the building or tried to get answers. It wouldn't take long for someone to get hurt. Even the shifters who remained loyal to the Consortium would be on edge and likely to lose control. And I'd left my gun in our room. Great.

Our room. I paused on the edge of the stairs, wondering whether I should go there first. Since Alexa was with Karma, I had no doubt she'd already heard Brenner's announcement. She had to be even more anxious than before. And I could only imagine how stir-crazy she was getting. But if I went up there, my tension would add to her own. I had to focus—to concentrate on the one way in which I could truly help her. If Brenner had a cure, we could steal it. We just had to figure out how to get to him. And where.

As I exited onto level two, I found myself face-to-face with the vampire who had arrested Sebastian. He held a pistol in his right hand and barred my way with his left. Halfway down the corridor, two other guards flanked a door.

"Valentine Darrow." He looked me up and down. "We've never been formally introduced. Leon Summers."

Tall and muscular, his dark hair cut close to the scalp, Summers looked the part of a military officer. "Pleasure," I said drily. "Now let me pass."

He cocked his head but otherwise didn't move a muscle. "Come to rescue your wolf boy?"

"I've come to speak with him. To ask about his father."

"Futile." He spat on the ground near my feet. "Believe me, I've already tried."

I frowned. "What's your role in all of this?"

"I collect intelligence."

I rolled my eyes at his obtuseness. "Well, I'm Sebastian's friend. And Helen has authorized my involvement, so you're going to let me speak with him."

I expected an argument, but instead, he lowered his weapon and stepped aside. "Suit yourself. But heads up: there are quite a few of them in there. We may not be able to get to you in time if things go... south."

The bastard was threatening me. Everywhere I went, people were trying to push me around, to shut me out or give me orders. I'd been low man on the totem pole since being turned, and my monogamous blood relationship with Alexa made me look weak in the eyes of some. But now, I was blood prime and the Missionary, and I was going to start demanding the respect to which I was entitled.

Refusing to dignify Summers's threat with a response, I brushed past him and stopped in front of the door. "Open it."

One of the guards produced a key from his pocket. The door was heavy and creaked as he pushed it open. I stepped into a low-lit room that was devoid of furniture except for benches along three of the walls and a toilet in the corner. Sebastian was sprawled out on his back along a bench, one arm dangling, the other covering his eyes. Over a dozen other occupants ranged throughout the room—some alone, some clustered in small groups. A few were clearly high-powered executives, their expensive suits contrasting with their bleak surroundings. Others were dressed casually in jeans or shorts. One man, particularly muscle bound, had almost as many tattoos as the Circuit's gatekeeper.

They stared at me in silence. I had spent enough time around Weres to know that announcing myself to Sebastian was redundant; his keen senses had already picked up my scent.

"Valentine," he said with a sarcastic joviality as he unfolded himself from the bench and stood stiffly. His hand swept the air in a grandiose gesture. "Meet my biological family. Some of them, anyway. Really, there are more of us here than I had thought were living in New York. Helen's intelligence is very good."

Someone snarled at the mention of Helen's name. I didn't blame him. Or her. "The situation has just gotten more precarious," I said, deciding that at this point, honesty was the best tactic. If any of Sebastian's siblings were even half as ambivalent about their father as he was, they wouldn't want to see Balthasar's plan succeed. "I need your help."

"More precarious?" A golden-haired woman near the back of the room took a few steps toward me. Clad in a tank top and tight shorts, she had obviously been interrupted during her morning workout. Annoyance and frustration rolled off her body in waves. "What is that supposed to mean?"

"Your father just took responsibility for the deadly illness that's been spreading through the Were community," I said. "And he delivered an ultimatum. Any Were who brings him the head of a vampire will receive an inoculation against the virus."

A gasp. Low murmurs. I waited until they had subsided to continue. "In three days' time, he'll release an airborne version. Anyone who has not received treatment will die in the next full moon."

Some stared at me in silent shock. Others cursed.

"But why?" one asked. Young—perhaps even younger than I—he sported a wrinkled sweater and worn jeans that screamed graduate student.

"Why?" The blond woman rounded on her half-brother. "Because he's a megalomaniacal tyrant, that's why."

I blinked. Indeed, Sebastian wasn't the only one harboring ill will toward his father. Just how many of his own whelps had Brenner alienated? And why hadn't he sought to make amends, or at least contact, before infiltrating the Consortium's ranks?

"I need your help," I said again over the muted squabbling that had begun.

Sebastian moved until he was close enough to force me to look up at him. "My siblings and I are not feeling very charitable toward your kind at the moment." The current of anger beneath his words made me want to take a step backward. I resisted the impulse.

"I don't agree with this strategy," I said, indicating their prison. "But you know as well as I that the decision to put you here was made cooperatively, between vampires and Weres. Your father wants to dissolve the Consortium and force our species into another war. Malcolm wants to preserve the current power structure. Helen wants to save her own head."

Sebastian looked skeptical. "And you don't, Val?"

"I want to find a treatment for the plague," I said, unable to keep the emotion from my voice. "Alexa is sick. I want…I need to save her life. And if I can find a cure fast enough, before too much blood has been shed, it will undermine your father's entire plan."

"What do you want from us?" asked one of the men in suits. "We've already been subjected to interrogation from Helen's lieutenant."

"Your father has a cure. I want to steal it. I need his location."

"We don't *know*." The blond woman's voice was tight with frustration. "None of us know. When will you bloodsuckers believe us?"

I knew that my skepticism registered on my face, but her claim seemed impossible. How could Balthasar Brenner not be in touch with any of his kin? Didn't he want to include them in his plans? Or at the very least, protect them from coming to harm?

"Our father uses us, like he uses everyone else," Sebastian said. "Apparently, in this case we were a liability. I have no doubt there are those in this room who would have joined with him, but he knew the Consortium would suspect us. Letting us in on his plan was too risky."

My skin crawled. According to Sebastian, his own father didn't have a modicum of paternal instinct. "Not only did he not let you in on it," I said grimly. "He didn't protect you from it. Are any of you displaying symptoms?"

Heads shook around the room. No one spoke up. I frowned. There were almost twenty Weres in this room. Some of them looked like they routinely engaged in risky behaviors, and most of them probably did the same even if they didn't look the part. How improbable was it that none of them were sick?

Adrenaline shot through my blood as the last puzzle piece clicked into place. I pressed my fingers to my temples, trying to focus through the storm of revelation.

"You're all purebloods."

"Of course," Sebastian said, looking at me as though I'd gone crazy. "Our father seems to think it's his responsibility to populate the world with born Weres."

"And none of you are sick. No nosebleeds." I sat down hard on one of the benches, watching as each shifter in turn felt the puzzle pieces click into place. "My God. You're immune. He didn't have to protect you because you're immune."

"What does this mean?" Sebastian asked. His voice sounded like it was coming from far away. I cradled my head in my hands and stared down at my knees, trying to think it through. Purebloods were immune. There were two options: something about their genetic makeup either made them resistant to the virus, or it killed the virus off before it could take hold. If I could discover the mechanism, maybe, with Clavier's help, I could synthesize it into a cure.

I started at the sensation of a light touch on my leg, and raised my head to the sight of Sebastian crouched before me, regarding me with concern. "Val. Are you okay? What are you thinking?"

It was difficult to organize my thoughts. "I think...I think this means that a cure is possible. There's something going on inside all of you that either kills the virus or prevents it from affecting you." A new thought occurred to me and I jumped up, beginning to pace. "Maybe it has to do with you all being purebloods—or maybe it has to do with you sharing genetic material with Balthasar. I won't know for sure until I test your blood."

The blond woman sneered. "A vampire asking for blood. How predictable." She planted her hands on her hips. "Why should we help you?"

I almost lost my temper at her selfishness. Even if we did discover some aspect of the purebloods' biology that would be useful, it would still take time to mass-produce a treatment. Alexa might not have time. The moment she lost control to her panther, she would die—full moon or no.

Taking a deep breath, I tried to slow my racing pulse. Everyone in the room was having a monumentally bad day; apprehended out of nowhere, detained, and interrogated, they were stressed and angry. Probably even afraid. Just like me.

"I'm willing to bet that every one of you have friends or loved ones in the city who were turned, not born Were. Those people are in grave danger now. If they're not sick already, they will be in a matter of days. And in two weeks…" I trailed off, certain that their imaginations could do a better job of picturing the repercussions of the next full moon than any words I could find.

"You can take a sample of my blood," Sebastian said into the silence. "As long as I'm free to go afterward."

I didn't have any authority to make that call, so I decided on a compromise. "We'll need to test everything first. But I'm confident that you'll be allowed to leave tomorrow, once we've done the testing. And the same deal goes for anyone else who volunteers."

When Sebastian nodded, I pulled out my cell, determined to argue my case to Clavier, Helen, or whomever it took. But I wasn't about to have that conversation in front of Brenner's kin.

"Thank you," I said, taking the time to survey the room. To telegraph the magnitude of my appreciation. Maybe it wouldn't make a difference. Then again, maybe they would remember that my lover's life was also on the line. "I'll be back soon, with supplies."

❖

As swiftly as I could, I pushed the tube onto the needle and inserted it into Sebastian's arm. He watched my every movement attentively, and my hands sweated under his scrutiny.

"I've wondered what it would be like," he said, too softly for any but me to hear.

"What?" I watched the tube fill with red. When it was time, I replaced it with another, feeling the irony of my role as phlebotomist.

"You. Taking my blood." Startled, I met his gaze. His eyes were dark and intense. "But not this way."

I refocused my attention on the tube. Alexa had once claimed that Sebastian wanted me. I had laughed her off, dismissing his flirtation as a game that amused him. I played along sometimes, as I had at that fund-raiser a few weeks ago. But what if Alexa was right, after all? How was that possible? Men like Sebastian, who had their pick across genders, were not traditionally attracted to me. What did he see? And why wouldn't he give up the ghost, having witnessed the magnitude of what Alexa and I shared?

Once the second tube was full, I pulled the needle from his skin and reached for a Band-Aid, hoping he would take the hint and let the subject drop. But he grasped my wrist. "No need."

I watched in awe as the tiny hole squeezed out one last drop of blood and closed before my eyes, Were physiology asserting itself against the unwelcome intrusion. Sebastian smeared the crimson drop onto his index finger and held it up to my lips.

"Taste."

The scent of his blood was wholly unlike Alexa's—redolent of musk, reminiscent of a pungent forest floor at the first spring thaw. My mouth watered. I couldn't help it. But I could still control myself. I turned my head away.

"I appreciate your generosity." The words sounded taut, constricted, even to me. Breathing shallowly, I loosened the tourniquet and rose to my feet. "Thanks to your precedent, we'll have a lot of samples to compare."

All around the room, Clavier's staff were drawing blood from the other shifters. Once they were finished, we could run a battery of tests on every tube and try to isolate whatever factor was making Brenner's kin immune. I labeled both vials and placed them in the insulated case at my feet, intent on moving on to my next patient. But Sebastian blocked me.

"What can I do now?"

I blinked in surprise. "You're asking *me*?"

"As far as I can tell, you're the only one who has been able to make any sort of breakthrough in this whole mess."

I considered the options. "Malcolm and Helen seem intent on making sure that Brenner can't stage a coup here. But whatever fortifications they come up with will be ineffectual if they don't find the traitor."

"So you're certain there is one?"

"The virus came from a Consortium lab that was trying to create a way to temporarily block the change." When Sebastian's eyes narrowed in suspicion, I hurried to continue. "Only for shifters who wanted to. Or needed to, so as not to endanger their covers. But the virus proved fatal, and Clavier thought he destroyed it."

"And you believe him?" Sebastian sounded incredulous.

"I think so. I've seen him lie plenty, and this time, he honestly looked confused. He and Helen are convinced that someone stole the virus for your father and falsified the records."

"In which case, that person is probably still hanging around. And you want me to try to find him?" He looked around the room. "While I'm locked up in here?"

I shrugged. "It's the only thing I can think of. Maybe when you're talking to your siblings you can ask around? See if they've heard or noticed anything unusual?"

He seemed skeptical. "Not much to work with, but I'll try my best. What's your plan?"

I hefted the cooler. "Once we finish collecting here, I need to take one set of samples to NYU. My lab at Tisch has more sophisticated equipment than the facility here."

"You're going out? Doesn't my father have a price on your head?"

A fresh surge of anxiety buzzed beneath my skin at the reminder and I patted the gun concealed at the small of my back for reassurance. "I'm armed."

He stared at me for several silent seconds before resting a hand on my shoulder. "I'll see what I can do. Be careful, Val."

I watched him walk toward a group of his kin at the back of the room, his strides long and confident, as though he were the jailor rather than the prisoner. It bothered me that he'd been acting as though he had some kind of claim on me, when nothing could be further from the truth. I didn't like it. Shrugging off the sensation, I turned to my next patient. The sooner I ran these tests, the sooner I could make Alexa well again. The sooner everything would go back to normal.

Normal. Right.

CHAPTER TWENTY

I waited until after ten o'clock to arrive at Tisch, hoping my lab would be vacated for the night. There was no way I could justify to my boss the kinds of tests I needed to run on the shifter blood samples. They involved commandeering technologies and techniques that I had helped use but had never operated by myself, and the uncertainty was making me anxious. Distracted. Which is why I didn't notice Olivia until she put her hand on my arm, a few feet from the front door.

"Val? Is that you?"

"Olivia?" She was dressed in a loose T-shirt and frayed jeans, as though she'd thrown on clothes as an afterthought. But Olivia never did anything as an afterthought, and she never jeopardized the carefully coiffed image she'd been sporting ever since landing her job in the DA's office. Besides, why was she pacing the sidewalks outside the hospital late at night?

"Are you here to see Abby, too?" she asked.

"Abby?" The more she spoke, the more confused I became.

"Oh—you're not?" Flustered, Olivia began to babble. "I'm sorry, I just thought that, well, when I mentioned her at that gala it seemed like you knew who she was so I thought that maybe..."

Abigail Lonnquist. I remembered now. She was the daughter of the ambassador to China. At the charity gala back in January, Olivia had told Alexa and me about the savage attack that had landed Abby in the hospital. Caught up in our hunt for the Missionary, I'd never followed up on whether he had successfully turned Abby.

"I know her," I said, cutting Olivia off. "What happened?"

"She's come down with something and the doctors have no idea what it is."

A sick vampire? Had Brenner found a way to modify the virus to affect us, too? Or was this unrelated? "What are the symptoms?"

"At first, it seemed like a fairly harmless upper respiratory thing," Olivia said. "But then…" Swallowing hard, she wrapped her arms around her stomach as though to literally hold herself together. Clearly, she cared a great deal for Abby. "Early this morning she went into these convulsions, like a seizure. She fell and hit her head, and now she's unconscious."

I frowned in confusion. Olivia was listing almost every known symptom of the Were virus. If Abby was a shifter, then it was likely that she was only alive because she'd knocked herself out. But then the Missionary hadn't been the one to turn her, all those months ago. What the hell was going on?

"I want to see her," I said. "Will they let us in outside normal hours?"

Olivia nodded. "My job does have a few perks."

I let her lead the way into the hospital and across the lobby to a bank of elevators. "How is Alexa?" she asked as we waited. And then she turned to me in alarm. "You're not here to see her, are you?"

"No," I said, my insides twisting at the memory of Alexa lying in our bed, pale and frightened and trying not to show it. "I'm here to work. I've been interning at a microbiology lab."

"Oh," Olivia said as we got into an elevator.

I expected her to follow up on my inadequate answer—to press me on why I was working in the middle of the night—but she just stared at the panel of lights as we ascended. Where was the seasoned investigator and hard-ass attorney that had plagued the Consortium for the past month? She had gone from borderline panicked to withdrawn and distracted in a matter of seconds. Just how long had she known Abby, anyway? Were they in love? I didn't know whether to hope so or not, because it sounded like Abby didn't have a very strong control of her animal half. She would probably lapse right back into the seizures if she regained consciousness.

"Here we are." Olivia opened Abby's door and we slipped inside. The room was dim but my eyes adjusted almost instantly. Abby lay motionless in the bed, her long blond hair draped across the pillowcase like some kind of halo. Her eyes were closed, but they flickered rapidly in REM. I wondered what she was seeing, feeling—whether her inner beast was pushing her consciousness, shoving her toward wakefulness.

Suddenly, instead of Abby I saw Alexa as she would appear on the cusp of the full moon, less than two weeks away. Alexa lying pale and wan, locked in a deadly internal struggle with her feline half. Alexa, losing the fight.

Swallowing down a surge of bile, I forced back my panic. "Has she been getting nosebleeds?"

Olivia, who had taken a few steps into the room, spun to face me. "How did you know?"

I shook my head. "It doesn't matter."

"Bullshit, Val!" She was on me in seconds, fingers wound tightly in the material of my T-shirt. I could have broken her grip easily, but I let her shake me. "You know something. What do you know?"

"Get a hold of yourself," I said, more harshly than I'd intended. "I'm not the one responsible. I'm trying to piece it all together myself."

"Responsible?" Olivia's voice was shrill. I'd never seen her lose control like this. "Someone did this to her?"

I considered my options. Maybe, just maybe, I could make this situation work to the entire Consortium's advantage. "The investigation you've launched into Helen Lambros and Malcolm Blakeslee—I don't know why you're doing it, but I need you to call off your watchdogs. And I need to know who's feeding you information."

Olivia's mouth worked silently. "Are you telling me, are you honestly saying, that my investigation has something to do with Abby getting sick?"

"They're related, yes. I can't tell you more than that." When she withdrew her hands from my shirt and took a deep breath, I realized she was going into full-on state's prosecutor mode. I held up one hand. "I mean it. There are things I cannot and will not tell you. You're going to have to trust me."

Her face darkened. "If you don't start talking, Val, so help me God I will call a detective and—"

I made a snap decision and cut her off. "Alexa is sick too. Like Abby. I'm here trying to find a cure."

The self-righteousness left her like air from a balloon. "Alexa is sick?"

"Yes. And they will both die if I don't get to my lab soon." I ran my free hand through my hair. "I'm close to figuring this out. But I'm not there yet. Let me do my work. And please, I need that name. You've been tricked, Liv. You've been used as a diversion."

Olivia took a few steps back and collapsed into one of the chairs next to the bed. For several seconds, she stared at Abby's expressionless face. And then she squared her shoulders.

"I don't have a name."

I set down the cooler that I'd packed full of pureblood Were samples and took the chair next to hers. "What do you have?"

"A routine." She hesitated but I didn't push, not wanting to give her an excuse to clam up. "Every morning on my way to the office, I pass an Irish pub. If there's a flag hanging in the third window, then I step into the coffee shop two doors down."

"And then?"

Again, Olivia glanced at Abby, as though hoping she would wake up and render this entire conversation moot. But the only motion came from her restless, dreaming eyes.

"Just outside the coffee shop is a bus stop. He waits there, reading a paper. When he sees me, he ducks inside the store and I follow. While we're in line, he hands me a memory card. We never talk."

"What's on the card?"

Olivia shrugged. "It varies. Names and dates, sometimes. Copies of tax returns. Very occasionally, account numbers." She leaned into my space. "How are you mixed up with Lambros and Blakeslee, Val? They have some really shady business practices going on. You should get out."

I almost laughed. My fate had been sealed when the Missionary had sunk his teeth between my ribs, almost a year ago now. There was no such thing as "getting out" for me. Ever. And as for the Consortium's business practices, I was betting they had illegal deals dating back five centuries.

"It's not what you think," was all I said. "What does he look like?"

"I've never even fully seen his face. Only in profile." Olivia closed her eyes. "Tall. Very muscular—like a body-builder. Brown hair. Wearing a black suit. Black T-shirt most of the time."

For a moment, it seemed as though my heart might stop. It stuttered painfully before breaking into a gallop against my rib cage, forcing me to gasp for breath. *Darren.* God damn it. How could Darren be the traitor? It was incomprehensible and perfectly intelligible, all at once.

"You know him?"

I had to stop him, to shut him down, to alert Helen. Except if I did that, then the game would be up, and Balthasar Brenner would know that we held his traitor. He would accelerate his plan. But what then? Should I let Darren continue to walk unthreatened among those whom he was betraying?

I scrambled to my feet and lurched toward the door. I couldn't think this through by myself, but I didn't want to call Alexa and risk making her upset. The result could be deadly.

I had to talk to Sebastian.

"I have to go."

"But, Val—"

"No." I consciously channeled the Missionary, for once cowing Olivia into silence. "We're running out of time." I gestured toward Abby. "Call me if something changes. Until then, leave me alone. I'm trying to save her, and Alexa. You have to trust me."

"I don't have to do anything," she whispered as I crossed the threshold into the hallway. She probably didn't think I could hear her. But I could.

❖

As soon as I exited onto the twelfth floor, I pulled out my cell phone and dialed Sebastian's number. He picked up on the first ring.

"It's Darren," I said without preamble, walking as quickly as I could toward my lab. "It's fucking Darren."

"Are you sure?" Even Sebastian sounded surprised. The low buzz of voices in the background reminded me that he couldn't speak freely right now, surrounded as he was by his own kin and the Consortium guards.

"Oh, I'm sure." When I twisted my key in the lock, metal protested, and I eased my grip before I broke something. "Bulky, black suit, black T-shirt. Sound familiar to you?"

"Mm."

"He's been feeding information to Olivia."

"Son of a bitch!" His interjection was quiet but vehement. For one strange, disconnected moment, I wondered whether he meant the epithet in canine or human terms.

"I don't know what to do," I said. "But my gut says to keep a lid on this for a while yet."

"Agreed. Though it may be wise to tell Karma."

My racing thoughts ground to a halt on the mental image of Helen and Malcolm lying dead in their offices, killed by the traitor they never suspected. How had Darren managed to fool them for years?

"Get Karma to stick to Malcolm. And Helen, if she can. I don't think Darren would make a move against either of them until it's time for whatever invasion Brenner's planning, but…"

"But the clock is ticking," Sebastian finished.

I almost dropped the cooler as an even more horrifying thought crossed my mind. Alexa wasn't just in danger from the virus. She trusted Darren implicitly. A soft groan left my throat before I could contain it.

"Are you all right?" Sebastian sounded even more alarmed than he had at my news of the traitor. "Val? What—"

"Alexa," I said, through teeth that wouldn't unclench. "What if he—"

Sebastian cut me off. "I'll make sure she knows. I promise you." He lowered his voice even further. "Focus, Val. You have to focus. There's only one way to put an end to all of this."

Leaning against the door, my hand still on the knob, I took one deep breath and then another. Sebastian was right. I couldn't afford to panic. "Yeah," I said as soon as I had myself back under some semblance of control. "I know. With any luck, I'll be back in a matter of hours."

As the call disconnected, I shut the door behind me and set the cooler onto the closest lab bench. My hands were trembling, and I braced them against the edge of the counter, forcing my thoughts away from the panic. *Focus.* I needed to test the blood of several of Brenner's children against the virus in Alexa's blood, and in order to see exactly what was going on when they interacted, I was going to have to image them using the scanning electron microscope.

After powering up the machine and the monitors to which it was attached, I prepared my slides. I started with the blood from three different Weres, each exposed to the virus via Alexa's blood. Giving them time to interact, I prepped the microscope, checking and rechecking each step. It was one of the most sophisticated pieces of technology in the lab, and I'd never used it without Sean's supervision.

Once I had the parameters set, I returned to my samples. I needed to spread each of them onto an electron microscopy grid, and then rapidly freeze them by immersing them in liquid ethane. The technique, called cryo-electron microscopy, was the best way to image biological processes. While the samples would freeze, no crystals would form, and I would be able to observe a snapshot of the interacting blood specimens that was virtually indistinguishable from their natural, liquid states.

The first grid contained Sebastian's blood mingled with Alexa's, and I bent close to the monitor, both eager and fearful of what the scope would reveal. I had observed specimens this way before, but even so, I was unprepared for the complex and delicate beauty of the image that appeared onscreen. The virus seemed mathematically impossible, its spirals and sharp edges coalescing in a deadly geometry. But as I scanned across the field of view, hope began to fill the cold vacuum of fear in my chest. Sebastian's blood had already produced immunoglobulins, and they had begun their work in earnest before I had frozen the sample. They were IgM antibodies, large and five-pronged, and several had bonded to the menacing virus in order to render it impotent.

"Don't get too excited," I said, swapping out Sebastian's sample for another. It would be no good to leap to any conclusions before I had multiple data points. But after examining two more grids that looked virtually identical, I allowed myself to smile. The pattern was clear: Brenner's children all had innate immunity to the virus. Given that IgM antibodies were the first to be expressed in a fetus, it made sense that they were the ones who swarmed to the attack. In fact, those very antibodies were probably the mechanism whereby pregnant shifter women didn't go insane during the nine months when they couldn't transform into their animal halves.

The scientist in me was clamoring to run an extensive battery of tests to try to prove my hypothesis. But the rest of me was driven by the ticking clock. To develop an effective treatment, I was going to need a lot of the pureblood antibodies—many more than I could get from only one sample. The question was whether a combination of samples would remain effective against the virus, or whether the different immunoglobulins would attack each other instead.

I glanced over at the clock on the wall. Almost three thirty in the morning. Blinking back my fatigue, I worked up one more grid, this one a combination of four different samples. After adding Alexa's blood, I waited for as long as it took me to empty the coffeepot into my mug and then froze the specimen.

The results were disastrous. Cursing, I scanned the field of view for so much as a speck of good news, but chaos reigned throughout the mixture. IgM antibodies predominated, but most of them were locked in a struggle against each other instead of the virus. Clearly, the genetic marker of each separate shifter's antibodies made them appear as antigens to the others.

Sighing, I shut down the microscope and rubbed my eyes. There was only one solution. The cure was going to have to come from one and only one shifter. In order to produce enough antibodies for harvesting, I was going to have to expose that shifter to a significant amount of virus.

I perched on the nearest stool and stared into my cooling coffee in an effort to quiet my mind so that I could think this through. Over time, given the right equipment and some expert direction, I could synthesize both a cure and a vaccine from a single pureblood's sample. But Alexa and every other infected shifter didn't have time. They couldn't wait for scientific finesse. They needed a treatment now.

Frustrated, I got up to rinse out the pot only to find myself distracted by the waterfall I'd created in the sink: a clear stream falling from the faucet into the drain. I thought of the vast network of pipes that crisscrossed the hidden interior of the hospital—a circulatory system made of steel and PVC. Cocking my head, I stared transfixed at the steady stream of water and felt logic reassert itself despite my exhaustion. There was a quick and relatively easy way to create the necessary antibodies in vivo. Transfusion. If I transfused infected blood into one of Brenner's offspring, their immune system would react to the invasion of the virus by mounting a swift and sweeping immunoglobulin response. I could then harvest their antibodies in sufficient quantities to produce a cure.

It was a plan. Theoretically, it would be successful. But it would also pose a significant risk for the Were who offered their body as an antibody breeding ground. They would be exposed to massive quantities of the virus, perhaps enough to overwhelm even their natural immunity. That much of the virus could provoke their animal half into a deadly reaction.

Working quickly, I cleaned the lab benches that I'd used and returned my samples to the cooler. I had to get back to the Consortium.

I had to find a pureblood who would take that risk.

CHAPTER TWENTY-ONE

Alexa called as I barged into the sweltering night, scanning the street beyond for waiting taxis. Hope and fear warred in my chest as I put the phone to my ear. If she was calling, she was still okay. But what if something else had happened?

"Hi, love," I said, trying to keep my voice soothing. "How are you doing?"

"I'm all right. But Constantine got a nosebleed today." When her voice wavered a little on the syllables, my stomach clenched. I had met her sire only in passing, but I knew Alexa cared about him deeply. His illness would only contribute to her anxiety.

"Oh, baby. I'm so sorry."

"Where are you?"

"Just leaving the hospital." At the intersection half a block away, I saw a cab with its lights on and raised my hand.

"I know you're so busy right now," Alexa said, "and I feel selfish for asking this, but do you think I could see you soon? Just for a few minutes? I miss you."

"Of course. I feel terrible that I've had to be apart from you, especially right now." I scrubbed at my heavy eyes. "How about meeting me in the room where they're keeping Sebastian? I have a proposal for him and his siblings. And it's something you should hear."

"Good news?"

"I think so." I climbed into the cab and leaned my head against the window. "I hope so."

"We could all use some of that." She paused and I took comfort from the steady rhythm of her breathing. "Is it really true, about Darren?"

Alarm shot up my spine at the simple mention of his name, the rush of adrenaline forcing my free hand into a fist. "It looks that way. There's no hard evidence yet, but in this case—"

"Better to presume guilt before proving innocence," Alexa said.

"Exactly."

"This whole thing feels like some kind of elaborate nightmare. The kind I used to get after we'd been out all night drinking pitchers of cheap sangria."

I laughed. It felt so incongruous to laugh in the middle of all of this fear and uncertainty, but that was part of Alexa's magic. My laughter prompted hers, and in that moment, I fell even more in love with her.

"You're amazing," I said when I could speak again.

"No, you."

I smiled. "Go downstairs, babe. I'm almost there. I'll see you soon, okay?"

"Okay. I love you, Val."

Within minutes, I was stepping out of the elevator on the second floor. Once again, Leon Summers stood in my path. This time, I had a message for him. "We have a serious problem," I said before he could mouth off at me again. I dropped my voice. "And his name is Darren."

I watched Summers's face as he processed my words. I tensed to subdue him if he showed even the slightest indication of being in league with the traitor. It would be utter folly for a vampire to throw in with Balthasar Brenner, but I had to be sure. Shock rippled across his face only to be replaced by an icy determination.

"You're certain?"

"No. But my intelligence is very good. I informed Karma Rao several hours ago, and since then, she's been trying to keep an eye on both Malcolm and Helen. But that can't be easy."

"Why don't I go and give her a hand," Summers suggested.

"Don't alert him. If he doesn't think he's under suspicion, we can use him."

Summers sneered as he brushed past me more quickly than any human could have moved. "I'm not an idiot, Valentine." And then he was gone.

As soon as I stepped into the room, Alexa was at my side. Blocking out the nearly twenty pairs of watching eyes—many judgmental—I threaded my arms around her waist. "Hi, baby."

Her answering kiss was brief but firm, and I drew strength from it. "I love you," I whispered against her temple as she stepped back to let me speak with Brenner's whelps.

Squaring my shoulders, I turned to face the expectant crowd. "Thank you all for letting me test your blood. Your generosity will lead to a cure."

"Are we immune?" someone in the back asked.

"You are. Every pureblood Were is, in point of fact. Each of you has antibodies against this virus by virtue of being conceived and not turned. I'm happy to explain the details to anyone who is curious, but first I have another request to make."

I took a deep breath. "Each one of you has developed a slightly different version of the antibody against the virus. This means that we can't just combine the samples you've provided in order to create a cure. Your antibodies are different enough that in such a case, they destroy each other instead of the antigen. With time and help, I'm fairly confident I could synthesize a treatment for the virus out of one sample. But we're running out of time before your father makes his move—and more importantly, before the next full moon."

"So what do you want from us now?" one of the women asked, sounding put out. My temper surged, but Alexa squeezed my hand, grounding me.

"There's only one way to do this quickly. I need one of you to volunteer to undergo a transfusion that contains a large amount of the virus. That Were's immune system will mount a corresponding immune response, allowing us to harvest enough of the antibodies to treat the infected population here in the city.

"But this is a risky procedure. A large dose of the virus may overwhelm your body's natural immunity. It's possible the volunteer's animal half will rebel, which could lead to the seizures many of you have witnessed in the infected. Often, those seizures are deadly."

The room was still. No shifter but Sebastian would meet my eyes. Finally, one of the men in suits spoke up. "So you're asking us to risk death for a procedure that *might* produce a cure. For something that doesn't even affect us."

"I'm asking one of you to take a risk in order to save lives." This time, I reached for Alexa's hand. "Her life. And the lives of hundreds of others who either have been infected or will be infected when your father releases the airborne mutation."

I knew that every single one of them could hear the staccato of my heart in my chest, pounding rapidly as I waited in anxious anticipation. I knew they could read the sincerity of my body language—my honest desire to halt the monstrosity that Brenner had unleashed upon their close cousins. But none of them spoke. Perhaps they were more like him than they had thought.

And then Sebastian stepped forward. "I'll do it."

"Since when are you a martyr?" the woman sneered.

He ignored her and focused on me. "Just so we're clear: I'm doing this more out of the desire to stonewall my father than for any other reason." He faced his kin. "And any of you who are planning to run straight to him once they let us out of here can go ahead and quote me."

I pulled Alexa in close, relief threatening to overwhelm me. I didn't want to cry in front of this pack of power-hungry dogs. "Thank you," I said.

Sebastian nodded. "What happens now?"

I forced my chaotic thoughts into order. "Now...now we need to find somebody with the virus who can transfuse you. Do you know your blood type?"

"O negative."

"Seriously?" When he nodded, I had to hold myself back from punching the wall. O negative was the hardest type to transfuse, since people with that type could only accept blood from other O negatives, who were rare to begin with. Finding someone who was O neg, infected, and willing to donate several pints of blood was not going to be easy.

"Well, this is going to be easy," Alexa said.

I frowned at her, confused by the dissonant echo of my own thoughts. "What—"

"I'm O negative, too."

❖

I didn't argue with her until we were out of earshot of Brenner's kin. After asking Sebastian to meet us in half an hour in the medical wing, I had called Karma to see whether she could get the other shifters released. Given the level of animosity toward the Consortium in that room, some of them might, as Sebastian expected, try to find their father. If Helen and Malcolm put tails on all of them, maybe they could discover his location.

Besides, they had fulfilled their end of the bargain. I owed them their release, and I wanted them to have the memory of a vampire who had kept her word.

But once Alexa and I were back in our room, I let all pretense at calmness drop. Pressing my back to the closed door, I opened my mouth to beg her to change her mind. We could find another match. It would take some additional time, but someone would—

"Don't, Val. Don't say it." She drew me just far enough from the door so that she could wind the fingers of one hand in the short hairs at the back of my neck. She cupped my face with her other hand, and I leaned into her touch.

"I know what you're thinking. I know that my giving as much blood as you'll need for Sebastian's transfusion might incite the panther. But *you* know that I have a much stronger control of her than most other shifters do over their beasts. I can do this. I should be the one to do this."

I wanted to be strong. I wanted to be supportive. If I opened my mouth, I would be neither. So I buried my head in the gentle dip between her shoulder and neck and inhaled deeply, imprinting her scent in my cells, my soul.

"I can't lose you," I whispered against her skin.

"You're not going to." She pulled far enough away to meet my eyes. "This is going to work."

She couldn't know that. Alexa was asking me to have faith—not in the science, but in her. And the fact of the matter was that if our roles had been reversed, I would have asked for the same thing. She was my partner, my equal, and as much as I wanted to protect her, I had to honor this decision.

Her lips pressed gently to my chin, then skated along my jawline. When she kissed me fully, I met her with everything in me. Cradling her face in my palms, I drank her in without breaking flesh. *Mine.*

If my cell phone hadn't rung, we might never have stopped. But at its persistent buzz, we reluctantly parted, Alexa smoothing her thumb across my wet mouth as I fumbled in my pocket. The phone quivered in my hand like a captured hummingbird. As I connected the call, I put it on speaker.

"Sebastian."

"I'm ready," was all he said.

When Alexa reached for my hand and squeezed, I squared my shoulders. It was time to finish this. Time for the Consortium to assert itself against the specter of Balthasar Brenner—to prove to him that we would not be cowed by his threats. That we were stronger and smarter even than the juggernaut of his tyranny.

"We're on our way."

Sebastian and Alexa lay parallel to each nother, their beds separated by only a few feet. Soon, they would be intimately connected, Alexa's poisoned blood flowing into Sebastian's veins. Focusing in on Alexa's monitor, I noted the slight dip in her heart rate. It was a good sign. For the past hour, they had both been under a gradual sedation—slow enough, I hoped, to keep their inner beasts from raising an alarm. By this point, they were both nearly unconscious.

The door opened to admit Kyle, and I did my best to smile in welcome. "Thanks for coming."

"Of course," he said, and I watched his gaze shift between the two prone bodies on the beds before us. "What can I do?"

"We're going to be transfusing Sebastian with Alexa's blood," I said. "I want an extra pair of hands, just in case." I would have preferred to have Karma keeping me company. If anything did happen, she would be better equipped to react with a show of strength. But she had to work at keeping Helen and Malcolm safe, especially with Darren still free and able to do his master's bidding.

"Wouldn't Dr. Clavier be a better choice than me?" Kyle sounded uncertain, and he looked hesitant. I held his gaze.

"I don't trust him. I do trust you."

His eyebrows arched in surprise, but all he said was, "Okay."

"I need you to monitor their vital signs during the procedure, while I focus on harvesting the antibodies that Sebastian should produce. If this goes according to plan."

"So I'm watching the monitors. What do I look for, specifically?" The steadiness of his voice and the specificity of his question were reassuring. "Just keep me appraised of any fluctuations that you see. I've set the alarms for anything below sixty or above one hundred and twenty." They were fairly conservative parameters, especially since I didn't know Sebastian or Alexa's normal resting heart rates, but I wanted to err on the side of caution.

"All right." Metal grated against tile as Kyle pulled one of the free chairs in between the feet of the beds. From there, he would have a clear view of both machines. I felt him scrutinizing me as I prepped Alexa's right arm and Sebastian's left hand. "You're going to pump her blood directly into him? I've never seen anything like that before."

"It's actually a more rudimentary technique." I bent over Sebastian and inserted a peripheral IV line into the large vein that bisected the back of his hand, then closed off the port. The monitor didn't register any sharp change in heart rate, and I nodded in satisfaction. So far, so good. "Back in the old days, before doctors knew how to preserve blood, all transfusions had to be done directly."

When I turned to Alexa, I had to fight back the instinctual surge of anxiety that attended the sight of her motionless body. *Focus.* I raised her bed as high as it could go by pressing a button near her head. Gravity would carry her blood into his vein.

I ripped open the package of a sterile cannula and connected one end to Sebastian's port. And then, as gently as I could, I inserted the other end into Alexa's arm. In the instant before her blood began to flow down the insulated line, its rich tang pierced the air and set my throat afire. A tremor ripped through my body, jostling the needle in her vein, and her heart rate jumped. I froze, watching as frown lines appeared across the bridge of her nose and her head shifted restlessly against the pillow. Was the panther starting to push already?

"What's happening, Val? Are you all right?"

I breathed through my mouth and forced back my thirst. "I'm okay. Just had a moment there. How is she doing? Going back to normal?"

He nodded, his eyes riveted on the monitor. "Slowly, yes."

"Okay." I took a few more breaths before turning back to Sebastian. "Here we go." Ignoring the panicked voice in my head that was screaming at me to stop this madness, I opened the port and watched the crimson thread slide those final few inches home. They were connected.

In an effort to make the procedure as un-traumatic as possible, I had chosen a high-caliber line, which would deliver Alexa's blood more gradually than the normal cannula that was most often used for transfusions. For the next several minutes, as Kyle kept his attention on the monitors, I prepped the materials that I needed to draw and store Sebastian's blood. Someone donating blood would usually give one unit—perhaps two at maximum. I was hoping to get three or even four from Sebastian before his body, or his wolf, rebelled.

When one of the monitors began to beep more insistently, I forced myself not to look up from the bags that I was hanging on the rack below Sebastian's arm. I had told Kyle that I trusted him, and now I had to.

"It's Sebastian," he said. "His heart rate just jumped and now it's accelerating steadily."

"Good," I said, opening more packages of line.

"Good?"

"His body is reacting. Producing antibodies." It felt strange to be pleased that the deadly virus was already starting to affect Sebastian, but I couldn't afford to look at that bed and see him as my friend. It was hard enough watching Alexa's eyes move beneath her fragile lids, unable to tell anything about her mental state but fearing the worst. At that moment, her head thrashed once again on the pillow, as though she were fighting off some kind of nightmare.

"Her pulse just spiked," Kyle said. "And now it's increasing. Faster than Sebastian's."

"Keep an eye on it. Let me know when either of them hits one hundred." I chose the number as a benchmark more than anything else, hoping I was right to believe that they weren't likely to shift unless their heart rates surged close to two hundred. In the meantime, I knelt on the floor next to Sebastian's bed, arranging the bags and the cooler in which they'd be stored as efficiently as possible. I might have to get his blood out of the room in a hurry, if one of them did end up shifting.

"Alexa's at one hundred," Kyle said into the terse silence. "And Sebastian's getting close."

"Damn it." I had wanted to hold off for a few more minutes, but if Alexa's condition was already deteriorating then I couldn't wait.

Working quickly, I secured a tourniquet around Sebastian's right arm and ripped open another package of line. He flinched under my touch, and I did my best to keep my hands gentle, even as I slid the needle into his bulging vein. Within moments, his blood—hopefully swarming with antibodies—was running steadily into the first bag.

Now I was faced with a dilemma. Sebastian's body was being attacked from two sides—by the virus flowing into his system and the precious fluids draining from it. Would it be wise to keep transfusing him so his blood supply didn't drop precipitously? Or would it be best to halt the influx of the antigen? I had no idea, and making the wrong decision might jeopardize this entire operation.

As I watched, his lips grew taut, the grinding of his teeth audible beneath the accelerating beeps of the monitors. Swallowing down a surge of dread, I looked over him to Alexa. Her head twitched against the pillow and her hands seemed to be trying to clench into fists. I didn't want to restrain her, but if I held off, she might hurt herself.

The first bag was almost full and I forced myself to stay put until I could change the line. But once Sebastian's blood was streaming into the second bag, I hurried to Alexa's side and wrapped the bed's cuffs around her arms with as much tenderness as I could manage.

"You're doing great, baby," I said, smoothing the hair back from her forehead. When my hand came away moist with sweat, I knew we didn't have much time.

A muted groan, low and animal, worked its way out between her clenched lips. Tears rose up to blur my vision and I dashed them away with one swipe of my arm as I entwined the fingers of my free hand with hers. But they felt more like claws, scrabbling against my palm in search of freedom. The alarm on her monitor pierced the air as her pulse surged over one-twenty, and her whole body flinched at the noise. I scrambled to turn it off, then bent to press a kiss to her cheek. Her skin was fevered.

"I am so sorry, love. So sorry." The words came out a harsh whisper.

"The second bag, Val," Kyle said. "It's almost full."

Reluctantly, I returned Alexa's hand to the bed and went back to tending Sebastian. He had grown restless too, and subtle shudders ran beneath his skin every few seconds. This couldn't go on much longer. I would have to stop at three bags. I switched the line and double-checked the integrity of the two full units before placing them into the cooler.

"Just hang on for a few more minutes," I said. And then, suddenly, the door opened. I stood and turned.

And froze.

"Hey, Darren," Kyle said.

CHAPTER TWENTY-TWO

"What the hell do you think you're doing?" Darren glared at me, the veins in his neck standing out like blue cords against his flushed skin.

"Whoa, take it easy," Kyle said, stepping forward as he raised a placating hand. He probably thought that Darren had taken umbrage at what I was doing to Alexa and Sebastian. "Val is just trying to hel—"

Abandoning all pretense, Darren swept Kyle aside with one powerful shove that lifted him off his feet and sent him crashing into the wall, where he stayed, wheezing at the force of the impact. In another moment, I knew, Darren would set his sights on me. Or worse—Alexa, Sebastian, and the precious blood I had collected. I had to get him out of the room.

I vaulted over Sebastian's bed, marshalling every ounce of strength and speed at my disposal, and barreled into Darren. When I made contact, I wrapped my arms around his thick waist and forced him out into the hallway. Sebastian's monitor erupted into shrill alarm, and I had a split second in which to wonder whether he and Alexa could sense Darren's presence, before I was preoccupied with defending myself.

"Get that needle out of Alexa's arm!" I shouted to Kyle, then slammed the door shut in the process of dodging Darren's heavy fist. But his next punch was already incoming and caught me squarely in the stomach. My breath left me all at once, and I barely evaded being put into a headlock.

I backpedaled, but not fast enough. Darren's knuckles caught me just under my left eye, and as I staggered backward, tasting blood in the back of my throat, he kicked me in the sternum. I went flying down the hallway, landing hard on my tailbone and gasping for air. My stomach and chest cramped and my lungs refused to fill. I would faint soon if I didn't manage a clear breath.

He advanced deliberately, and even through my blurred vision I could tell he was gloating. Fortunately, that bought me some time, and I focused on taking shallow breaths until my muscles relaxed.

"I have no idea what Helen sees in you," he said as he loomed over me. "You're pathetic. A shadow of what you could be. Blood prime, and a member of the Order, but I don't even have to shift to tear you to shreds."

"Why?" I choked out, needing to keep him talking. Gradually, my strength was returning. The pain in my face was sharp, but my chest felt worse, and I suspected a bone might be fractured.

"Why?" He crouched down to snarl into my face. "Your kind should have died out centuries ago. Why the Consortium was ever created is a mystery to me. And to *him*. It's survival of the fittest, Valentine. And we are the fittest."

When a cruel grin spread across his face, I realized just how good an actor Darren had been. In all the time I'd known him, he had seemed reticent. Taciturn, even. His loyalty to Helen had been automatic and unquestioning. And a total farce.

"When I'm finished with you," he said, "I'm going to do our entire community a favor and put your bloodsack of a girlfriend out of her misery. She's a disgrace to all of us."

Darren's words were like his fists, hitting me precisely where it hurt the most. Streaks of red shot through my vision at his threat, and at the adrenaline surge, I could breathe freely again. How dared he appoint himself the arbiter of who lived and who died?

Tensing every muscle in my battered body, I pushed off the floor as hard as I could when I saw him reach down to grab me. I darted beneath his grasp and spun behind him, then leapt onto his back, wrapping my arms around his thick neck to close off his windpipe. Pain spiked through my chest as my injured breastbone clashed against his shoulders, but I didn't let go. Roaring in outrage, he reached over his shoulder and yanked at my hair, trying to pull me off. Beneath my hand, his pulse beat a furious staccato.

The last time I had fought a man hand-to-hand, that man had been the Missionary. Like Darren, he had threatened to kill Alexa. Like Darren, he'd had superior strength—delighting in pummeling me and breaking my bones before moving in for the kill. Then Alexa and I had worked together, alternately engaging and distracting him until I'd been able to fire a kill shot. Now I was alone. Now I was weaponless.

But now *I* was the Missionary.

Darren crashed backward into the wall, smashing me into the plaster. My grip loosened at the dizzying spike of pain that pierced my chest. Scrabbling for purchase, my nails raked furrows into his neck, and he bellowed again, taking a step forward in preparation for another pass against the wall. Beyond thought and reason—beyond anything but the instinct to preserve myself and defend Alexa—I bent and sank my sharp teeth into his jugular. He howled in pain and rage, slapping and scratching and pulling at every inch of me that he could reach. But I didn't let go.

I drank.

His blood was hot and thick, liquid strength sluicing down my throat. I was always careful with Alexa, but I didn't have to be cautious now, when my thirst was also my greatest weapon. I delighted in gorging myself—in the coppery tang that liberally coated my throat; in the temporary cessation of the thirst that was my constant goad; in the power, the raw potential, that seeped into my starving muscles.

I felt the moment when his wolf began to enrage; Darren's movements became clumsy, and tremors crawled up his spine like the shocks of an earthquake. He fell to his knees, his entire body shuddering as his wolf surged to the surface. Reluctantly, I withdrew my teeth from his skin. Helen had said that the blood prime's appetite was enhanced, and I wondered if I could have drained him entirely. I would never know. There was only one imperative now: to put him down before he could change.

Shifting the position of my hands on his neck, I called upon my new reserves of strength, and then I twisted. The audible snap was satisfying. Darren's lifeless body crumpled beneath me, but I didn't so much as stumble, leaning forward into the pitch of his corpse to land on the balls of my feet. Blood still trickled from his neck, and I watched the flow grow sluggish, then stop. His heart was motionless, his spinal cord severed. He was dead.

Alexa.

I threw open the door, barging in on a scene of chaos. Both Sebastian and Alexa were convulsing in their beds, writhing like creatures possessed. Alexa's heart rate was pushing two hundred already. Kyle had taken the line from her arm, but clumsily. The crook of her elbow was covered in crimson. He knelt next to Sebastian, frightened but trying to concentrate on disengaging the line from the third bag, which was almost full.

When he saw me, he jumped up. "Oh my God, Val! Are you—"

I ignored him. I had no doubt that I looked terrible, but I felt strong. Already, the pain in my face and chest had eased, muted by the high I had found from Darren's blood. My vision was clear. Even the metallic grays and blues of the room's décor seemed vivid.

As quickly as my sharpened eyes took in the facts, my brain was processing them. Alexa would die soon if she couldn't shift. Sebastian was on the verge of the change himself. Only his blood could free her panther. In an instant, I was next to Kyle, bending to detach the line from the final unit of his blood. I pointed to a package in the box of supplies next to the bed.

"The syringe. I need it."

Kyle fumbled with the plastic but finally ripped it open, handing me the barrel. I connected it to the line, and when it had filled, jammed a needle onto the threads. "Now. Help me hold her."

I was at Alexa's side in two seconds. Her convulsions were increasing in magnitude now, and her eyes had rolled back in her head. My heart contracted painfully, but my head remained clear. Kyle's human movements were ponderous, but finally he was next to me, pressing down on Alexa's shoulders as I found a vein in her unbloodied arm. "Stay with me, baby," I said, pushing down steadily on the plunger.

The seizure that shook her as the syringe emptied was the strongest yet, and would have broken the needle off in her arm if I hadn't been able to react so quickly. She threw off Kyle's grip, but when he tried to restrain her again, I waved him away. Her body was starting to blur around the edges.

"Get out of here!" I shouted, tossing the used syringe to the floor. "Before they both change!"

He ran for the door as I gathered her into my arms, praying I hadn't been too late and that a vial full of Sebastian's blood would be enough. Alexa thrashed against my chest and her fingernails scratched my face, but I clung to her and darted for the hall. I had to get her away from the wolf that Sebastian was on the verge of becoming.

Once outside, I dropped to my knees and released her. Her face was a mask of agony as the seizures grew stronger. "Come on," I said, clenching my fists hard enough to break skin. And then, a memory intruded—dusk falling on the Serengeti, the scent of blood on the air, and Alexa summoning her panther to fight the threat. Calling her forth, with a single Swahili imperative.

"Uje!"

Her body stilled. No breath, no heartbeat, not even a muscle twitch. *Gone.*

As the seconds ticked by, despair sliced me open like a blade. I had killed her. Again. As I stared at her twisted, motionless form, I returned to the night, nearly a year ago now, when I had taken too much of her blood. When I had believed her dead. And now she truly was.

The air suddenly shifted as her body arched into a perfect, impossible bow, like a marionette wrenched up by its strings. Her mouth opened in a scream of primal pain and rage, only to be choked off as her limbs collapsed in on themselves, giving way to the panther. Dark fur bristling, she rolled fluidly onto her paws and loomed over me, snarling.

Gleaming, white teeth curved over her crimson gums, but I felt no fear. She could tear me to shreds in the next moment, and it would be no more than I deserved. She was alive. That was all that mattered.

But then I heard the growl. Low and canine, it rumbled from behind me, and I knew Sebastian had also transformed. Tearing my gaze from Alexa, I took in the sight of the huge black wolf crouched just beyond the threshold of the doorway. Hackles raised and trembling, his red-gold eyes gleamed under the harsh artificial lights. He was truly formidable. And he was fixated on Alexa.

As she focused on this new threat, her belly brushed the floor and her tail lashed dramatically. When the muscles beneath her sleek fur quivered in anticipation of the pounce, the rumble in Sebastian's throat grew louder. His hind legs flexed, and I knew what would happen next. They would meet in midair, snapping and snarling in a fight to the death. A battle that Sebastian, a born Were and powerful alpha, would undoubtedly win.

I lunged for the door, slamming it home just as Sebastian leapt forward. The force of his impact made the hinges groan, but they held. As I watched through the small window, he lay on the floor panting heavily, ears flat against his head. He would recover soon enough, and I had to get him tranquilized before he tore the whole room apart—including the units of his own blood.

Turning so that my back was against the door, I faced Alexa once again. Her tail still quivered, but now her attention was divided between me and Darren's corpse, several yards away. I smiled grimly. The thought of her tearing into his body to gain the energy necessary to make the change was satisfying. Poetic justice.

"That's right," I said, hoping that my voice would penetrate to wherever Alexa's human consciousness resided. "Take him. And come back to me."

She padded on silent paws to where Darren lay prone. The sounds of her feasting didn't turn my stomach, and I watched dispassionately as she rent the meat from his bones. I had taken my own sustenance from him, after all.

But at that thought, the first trickle of guilt seeped into the front of my mind. Twice now, I had taken blood from someone other than Alexa. The first time had been Clavier's doing, but drinking from Darren had been wholly intentional. Entirely my decision. And I hadn't so much as hesitated.

What did that mean?

"Valentine."

I blinked. Where moments ago the panther had crouched gorging herself, now Alexa stood naked. My mouth went dry as I took her in—jet-black hair brushing her shoulders; the delicate arches of her collarbone that gave way to perfect, rose-tipped breasts; the pale expanse of her stomach enticing my gaze lower to the dark triangle of hair between her shapely runner's legs. A wash of heat engulfed me, rising from my gut to set my throat aflame.

Exquisite. Alive. *Mine.*

"You're hurt," she said and quickly moved forward, her hands closing around my forearms as she inspected the damage Darren had inflicted on me. My whole body trembled at her touch.

"It's not as bad as it looks." I freed one of my hands to stroke the curve of her cheek. "You're alive."

She smiled. It felt like forever since I'd seen her smile. "I feel wonderful, actually."

The memory of her motionless body intruded, making me flinch. "You almost died again."

"But I didn't." She rose to kiss me and my arms automatically threaded around her waist. I could feel the flutter of her heartbeat against my own chest. So warm. So vital. *Alive.* A groan escaped me at the softness of her mouth over mine, and I pulled her against me, ignoring the flare of pain in my chest. I returned her kiss with everything in me, needing her to claim my very soul.

Behind me, a throat cleared. I spun to face the sound, shielding Alexa's body with my own.

"I thought you said they were in danger, Kyle." Karma's expression was serious, but her voice was rich with amusement.

"I...but..." Kyle's jaw worked soundlessly.

Trailing them, Helen and Malcolm looked wary. Leon Summers stood close to Helen's side, his palm resting on the butt of his gun. In the ensuing moment of silence, our collective attention was drawn to the sound of scrabbling at the base of the closed door.

"Darren is dead," I said, maneuvering myself and Alexa to the side so that our visitors could have a clear glimpse of the mangled corpse. I heard Kyle swallow hard. The others didn't so much as flinch.

"Sebastian?" Malcolm's normally smooth voice was tight with anxiety.

"He seems fine," I said, "but he needs to be tranked so I can get to my supplies."

"What supplies?" Even in the midst of utter chaos, Helen managed to look and sound like a queen.

"Sebastian's blood will form the basis of a cure. I was able to take three units before he turned. The bags are inside, with him."

Malcolm waved Karma toward the door. "Take care of it."

Drawing a small gun, Karma headed for the door. "You may want to move away," she said, and I tugged at Alexa's hand to pull her flush against my back as we took several steps toward the group. I didn't want them to see her nakedness.

Karma trained her gun on the door, then flung it open and fired in one smooth movement. Sebastian collapsed at her feet, his massive paws twitching as the sedative took effect. Karma stepped over him and returned a moment later with the blankets from Alexa's bed.

"You're all right?"

"I am." Alexa's gaze shifted to the unconscious wolf as she covered herself. "Thanks to Sebastian."

"Thanks to you both." I pressed a kiss to her temple, then made my own foray into the room. It was a mess. Streams of blood adorned the floor and most of the furniture had been upended. The cooler had been knocked onto its side, but when I opened it, all of the units were intact.

"The blood is fine," I called over my shoulder before sealing the cooler and returning to Alexa's side.

"What do you need to make a cure from that?" Malcolm asked.

"Nothing the Consortium lab doesn't have already," I assured him, shifting my weight from one foot to the other. I still felt amped up from Darren's blood, and I wanted to put that energy to good use.

Helen moved close to me, her fingertips trailing over my bruised face and then down across my breastbone. "Let Harold do this, Valentine," she said. "You're injured. It won't be long before you crash."

When our gazes locked, one of her brows quirked knowingly before she looked away. Had she realized how I had subdued Darren? Would she hold that knowledge against me?

"But—"

"She's right, love." Alexa spun me to face her. "You've done so much. You've saved us all. Let someone else take over now. Come and rest with me."

Her gaze pleaded with mine, and I capitulated without a fight. After so many weeks of fear and anguish, after the insurmountable distance that had gaped between us, after nearly losing her a second time…she was right. We just needed to be together.

Heedless of our audience, I dipped my head and brushed my

lips across hers. "All right," I whispered against her mouth. "I'm all yours."

But the taste of Darren's blood still lingered in my throat, and a small, niggling part of me couldn't help but doubt the truth of that claim.

CHAPTER TWENTY-THREE

As though by some unspoken agreement, we were silent as we made our way toward our room. My thoughts spun in the aftermath of the day's events, and Alexa's grip on my hand was a welcome anchor. When we reached the door, she raised her free palm to the scanner and tugged me inside. Only then did she let go, taking a few steps back to survey me from head to foot.

"Let's get you cleaned up."

"You'll come with me?" I asked, not wanting to be separated from her for even a moment.

"Of course."

While I undressed, Alexa perfected the water temperature. "Ready when you are," she called as I painfully peeled off my bra and stared at myself in the mirror, steam clouds billowing around my head. My eye was swollen half-shut, the skin beneath red and puffy, and a deep bruise was already forming above my breasts.

"Oh, baby," she said as I stepped into the shower. Her fingertips trailed tenderly along my chest. "That seems painful."

"It's not as bad as it looks."

She smoothed her hand across the back of my neck, urging me closer. "That, or you're still too keyed up to really feel it." Her kiss was lingering. "Good thing I have exactly what you need to heal."

I pulled back, frowning. She couldn't be suggesting that I drink from her now, when only an hour ago she had almost died. "Baby, no, I—"

"I'm fine," she cut in. "Better than fine. I feel great. So does the panther. It was such a relief to make the change."

"Your *heart* stopped," I said, regretting the harshness of my words even as they left my mouth. Looking down at the floor, I swallowed hard, back in those terrifying moments when I had believed her to be gone. "I'm sorry, I just—"

She gripped my chin and raised my head until I had to meet her eyes. "I know, Val. I know how scared you were. But I wish you could feel what it's like, to change back." She smiled. "The best way I can describe it is like...like a whole-body reset. Like waking up from a dream fully rested."

She poured a dollop of shampoo into her palm. When I braced myself against the tiled walls, she began to massage it into my hair. "You're not going to hurt me, love. You healed me. Now let me do the same for you."

My heart constricted, and I very nearly confessed to drinking from Darren. I had hurt her yet again. She just didn't know it. But what else could I have done? Weaponless and weakening, I had resorted to the only defense I'd had left. If I hadn't bitten him, he would have killed me, Alexa, and Sebastian, and he would have destroyed our best hope of creating a cure.

Oblivious to my inner turmoil, Alexa drew a bar of soap over my body. As she worked the lather over my skin, I began to feel the slow ebb of the blood high that had swept me along for much of the past hour. The pressure in my chest increased, and I focused on taking shallow breaths so as not to irritate the damaged tissue.

Alexa noticed right away. "The pain has gotten worse, hasn't it?" When I nodded, she shut off the faucet and reached for a towel. "Step out, love." She dried herself briskly and then focused on me, patting me down with gentle hands. I stood still, feeling the exhaustion creep over me, and surrendered to her loving touch.

Once we lay together under the bedcovers, I turned onto my side to face her, struggling not to wince as the movement aggravated my injuries. She lightly kissed the inflamed skin beneath my eye before trailing her lips down to brush over mine.

"Drink me," she said against my mouth, her lips curling as my body tensed. "Don't be afraid, Val. I want you to. I need to do this, to be this for you."

I pulled back just enough to see the truth in her eyes. Alexa was my soul mate, and the events of the past few weeks hadn't changed that. I loved her like no other, thirsted for her like no other. No one—not Clavier, not Darren, *no one*, could touch that.

I moved over her and braced myself on sore arms, then bent my head to her ear. "Thank you," I whispered, before following the graceful line of her cheek down, down to where the large vein in her neck pulsed tantalizingly beneath my mouth. Never more than in that moment—the instant before my teeth pierced her willing flesh—did I *know* that she was mine and I was hers.

I slid into her with none of the violence that had attended my attack on Darren, and as the ambrosia of her blood touched my lips, she arched beneath me—not in pain, but in passion. Bright on my tongue, she flowed through me and the world regained its sharpness. The intoxicating scent of her, the sweetness of her skin beneath my lips, the rich tang of her life's blood—all were magnified as my senses opened.

To taste her was to find myself.

My pain forgotten, I surged against her, groaning as I felt her wetness coat my thigh. Desire flamed down my spine, compelling me to draw more deeply from her vein.

"Oh God, Val." Alexa's hips rose and fell as she met my fervor with her own. "Please, touch me. Please, I need you, please…"

Her begging drove me wild. I skimmed my hand down along the curves of her torso, lingering in the dip between her abdomen and leg before entering her fully. I wanted her passion and took what I craved, feathering my tongue over her broken skin even as I curled my fingers deep inside her body. She cried out her assent, and I kept my movements strong and steady, driving her inexorably to the edge.

"With me," she gasped, and I knew she was close. "With me, Val, please—"

I gloried in the sensation of her closing hard around me as the ecstasy took her, the white-hot rush of sensation sweeping over me just a few moments later. I raised my head as the pleasure coalesced and allowed the beauty of her release to push me to mine.

❖

I woke from a dead sleep, blinking in the muted daylight that filtered through the window curtains. Tucked into the curve of my body, Alexa breathed deeply, her slumber undisturbed by whatever had awakened me. I smiled against the nape of her neck and tightened my arm around her, already sliding back into unconsciousness. I didn't know what time it was and didn't care; we both needed all the rest we could get.

And then I heard the buzzing. My phone. As smoothly as I could, I slid off the bed and grabbed it, checking the display. Karma. I darted into the bathroom in hopes of not waking Alexa.

"Hey," I whispered.

"Val? Are you all right?"

"Yes, fine. Just trying to be quiet. Alexa's sleeping."

"I'm sorry to wake you," she said. "But I thought you might want to know that Dr. Clavier has developed a successful treatment. He's already administered it to the infected Weres in-house, including Constantine."

Only when I exhaled in relief did I realize that the pain in my chest was a mild twinge. When I inspected my reflection, I was gratified to see no swelling at all; instead of turning into a prodigious shiner, the skin around my eye was tinted a muted yellow and green, as though the bruise was already a week old. Alexa's blood truly was miraculous.

"That's great news," I said. "Is there some kind of plan in place for getting the word out to Weres across the city?"

"A press conference, I think. I'm not sure of the details, but I imagine Helen will want you to be there."

"Maybe," I said, still uncertain about the nature of my new relationship with Helen. Now that I was both blood prime and the Missionary, I had a feeling she was going to try to manipulate me much more rigorously than she had been.

"How are you doing?" I asked, hearing the fatigue that weighed down her voice.

"I'm tired," she said. "But now that we have a cure, I can see the light at the end of the tunnel."

"That's good. That's really good."

"We all have you to thank," she said.

"And I have you to thank," I countered. "For helping me. For helping Alexa. Especially while she was sick."

"I'm so glad she's okay." When the sound of knocking intruded on Karma's end, I heard her get to her feet. "I have to go, Val. Talk to you soon."

When I opened the bathroom door, I stood still for a moment, enjoying the sight of Alexa, now curled around one of the pillows, blinking adorably at me from across the room and looking for all the world like a sleepy cat.

"How do you do that?" I asked, sitting next to her so I could comb my fingers through her dark hair.

"Do what?" She abandoned the pillow and curled herself around me instead. When she rubbed her forehead against my thigh, I laughed.

"You really have contracted some feline mannerisms."

"You like it," she said, and kissed my knee.

"Mm." I continued to stroke her, loving the feel of her breasts against my lower back, the comforting sound of her deep, even breaths. And then, it hit me: the nightmare was really over. Now we could be together again—not once every few weeks, but every single day. Healthy. Whole. The way we were supposed to be.

"What did Karma say?"

"She had good news." I twisted to reach her shoulders, and she let out a deep sigh as I began to massage. "Clavier was successful in developing a treatment. They administered it to Constantine, and he seems to be fine."

"Thank God," she said, and even though her voice sounded more alert, she made no move to get up. I was glad. We needed this time—just the two of us, relaxing, free for the moment of any pressing demands.

After a while, she uncurled herself and pulled me down beside her. "What do you think will happen now?" she said. "Now that we have a cure, I mean. I can't imagine things just going back to what passes for normal. Not with Brenner still out there."

"Still gunning for the Consortium," I added.

"Still gunning for *you*." Alexa slid half on top of me. "We're going to have to be careful."

I looked up into her eyes, now dark in anger, and wished for the thousandth time that the Missionary hadn't chosen me all those months ago. I had wanted us to have a good life together, a busy life made joyous by the fulfillment we found in each other and our work. Not

NELL STARK AND TRINITY TAM

a life in which we were continually beset on all sides by forces that wanted us separated or dead.

"Much as I hate to suggest it, maybe we should stay here for the time being." Our apartment was vulnerable. Though apparently, so was the Consortium.

Alexa looked uncertain. "Maybe." She rolled onto her side and I wrapped my arm around her shoulders. "God, I wish I knew who we could trust. I mean...I have total faith in Karma, but not in the information she receives from Malcolm. You know?"

"I know. I still can't believe how long Helen managed to cover up that virus."

We were silent for a while each lost in our own thoughts...until Alexa's hands began to wander over my skin, tracing delicate patterns on my upper arm before shifting toward my breasts.

"How is your chest feeling today?" She brushed a kiss across the light bruise. "It looks much better. Your eye, too."

"The pain is almost gone." I shifted restlessly against the sheets as her lips skated lower.

"Almost gone. Hmm." She raised her head, and my throat flared at the sensuous curve of her lips. "That's not quite good enough for me, you know. I'm a perfectionist."

"No," I said, surrendering once again to her seduction. "You're perfect."

❖

Later, while Alexa paid a visit to Constantine, I arranged to meet Olivia at a café two blocks from the hospital. She was already there when I arrived, cradling a cup of coffee as though it was the Hope Diamond. The smudges beneath her eyes were darker and I'd never seen her so pale. It was clear that she hadn't slept in the day and a half since we'd last met. When she saw me, she threw her shoulders back and frowned, gathering the shreds of her energy around her like a ragged cloak.

"Val, what the hell is—"

I slid into the booth and grasped her hands. Her eyes went wide and her words petered out as she felt the vial I had concealed in my palm and was now pressing into hers.

"What's this?"

"The only thing that will save Abby. She needs it as quickly as possible." I shook my head when Olivia would have spoken again. "Listen to me. What you're holding right now is an auto-injector, like the ones used for severe allergic reactions. All you have to do is remove the safety at the top and then press the tip firmly against Abby's thigh. Hold it there for ten seconds."

Olivia's jaw clenched, and I could sense her inner struggle, the war between her personal and professional selves. "You're sure this will work?"

"It worked for Alexa."

Sudden tears blurred Olivia's eyes. She stood quickly, taking the vial with her, and turned her back to me. "I don't know what to say."

I knew how difficult it was for her to take me at my word, to trust me blindly. I also knew that once Abby had recovered, Olivia wouldn't rest until she had discovered the whole truth. The truth that would shatter her world.

"Go, Liv. We can talk later."

She turned just enough for me to see the grim resolve that had overtaken her relief. "I'll hold you to that, Val."

I watched her push through the crowd in front of the door, then pick up her pace once she was outside. It was strange to feel older than Olivia—strange to sense the envy and admiration I'd always felt toward her give way to pity. She wasn't going to let sleeping dogs lie, and one of them—perhaps even Abby—would bite her.

I stood slowly, my muscles still a little sore from the events of the past few days. My throat was sore too, the thirst a constant ache that never fully abated. I needed Alexa again. Already. Was that normal for a blood prime? Or was the parasite responding in some way to my having drunk from Darren?

The knot of anxiety tightened between my shoulder blades, and I tried to shrug off my foreboding. Alexa was probably finished speaking with Constantine by now. She would let me have her again. Her blood, her body, her heart—I would reclaim them all until the memory of being parted was distant and dim.

Eager for the sanctuary of her embrace, I stepped out into the sunlight.

EPILOGUE

A lexa and I filed onto the stage behind Constantine and Clavier, and as we turned to face a room crowded with people and cameras, I felt an odd kind of empathy with my father. He often stood with the president during press conferences and occasionally even held his own. Now we were standing with Helen and Malcolm to demonstrate our support for them as the Consortium rallied in the face of Brenner's unsuccessful coup. The conference would be encrypted and sent via satellite to key vampire and Were leaders throughout the world. They, in turn, would get the word out to their constituents.

Suddenly feeling very exposed, I scanned the room for any suspicious activity. The audience had purportedly been vetted, but without having been part of the process myself, I wasn't about to trust it. When I cast a sidelong look at Alexa, I could tell she was doing the same thing.

In the next instant, the buzz of noise subsided as Helen stepped out from the wings and walked to the podium. She was joined there by Malcolm. Cameras flashed and my anxiety ratcheted up a notch.

"Good evening," Helen said, her melodious voice bouncing off the close walls and ceiling. "As you are all aware, two days ago, Balthasar Brenner sought to dissolve this Consortium between wereshifters and vampires by threatening the release of a virus deadly to turned Weres. In so doing, Brenner hoped to create chaos in our organization, and a power vacuum into which he could step.

"I am here today to inform you that he has accomplished neither of his goals. Our medical team has produced a treatment for the virus that will be made available, first to Weres throughout the New York

City metropolitan area and, soon, to shifters around the world. Anyone who wishes to receive this treatment must simply report to the medical wing at the Consortium headquarters in their respective nations."

She paused, then, and I watched her grip on the podium tighten. "Anyone seeking to join the enemy and abandon the longstanding alliance that Malcolm and I have cultivated, however, will be prosecuted according to the fullest extent of our law. Already, we have ferreted out and executed a traitor in our midst. Balthasar Brenner has declared war on this institution, and we will answer in kind.

"To that end, I am announcing a task force dedicated to improving Consortium security and meeting this new threat to our livelihood." Helen gestured toward each person in turn. "Constantine Bellande, Master of Telassar, will serve as chief of tactical operations. Leon Summers will continue in his role as chief intelligence officer."

She paused again, and I felt Alexa turn beside me. I was still focused on the press of people in front of the stage, and I jumped when she squeezed my hand, hard.

"Oh my God, Val. Look!"

I spun in the direction she was facing and stifled an exclamation. The woman who was emerging from stage left to join the two members of the team was smartly dressed in a white blazer and slacks that accentuated, rather than hid, the impressive gun belt at her waist. She was thinner than I remembered. She was also alive. When last I'd seen her, she had been lying prone on the floor of the Missionary's apartment. Dead, I had thought. How, then, was she walking across the stage toward Helen and Malcolm, shaking each of their hands before stepping into line next to Summers?

"What the hell is going on?" Alexa spoke so softly that only I could hear.

"I don't know," I said. "But Helen has a lot of explaining to do."

"And finally," Helen announced, "I would like to introduce our new chief of security—former NYPD detective Devon Foster."

About the Authors

NELL STARK is an assistant professor of English and the director of the Writing Center at a small college in the SUNY system. TRINITY TAM is a marketing executive in the music industry and an award-winning writer/producer of film and television. They live, write, and parent a rambunctious toddler just a stone's throw from the historic Stonewall Inn in New York City.

Books Available From Bold Strokes Books

Whatever Gods May Be by Sophia Kell Hagin. Army sniper Jamie Gwynmorgan expects to fight hard for her country and her future. What she never expects is to find love. (978-1-60282-183-5)

nevermore by Nell Stark and Trinity Tam. In this sequel to everafter, Vampire Valentine Darrow and Were Alexa Newland confront a mysterious disease that ravages the shifter population of New York City. (978-1-60282-184-2)

Playing the Player by Lea Santos. Grace Obregon is beautiful, vulnerable, and exactly the kind of woman Madeira Pacias usually avoids, but when Madeira rescues Grace from a traffic accident, escape is impossible. (978-1-60282-185-9)

Midnight Whispers: The Blake Danzig Chronicles by Curtis Christopher Comer. Paranormal investigator Blake Danzig, star of the syndicated show Haunted California and owner of Danzig Paranormal Investigations, has been able to see and talk to the dead since he was a small boy, but when he gets too close to a psychotic spirit, all hell breaks loose. (978-1-60282-186-6)

The Long Way Home by Rachel Spangler. They say you can't go home again, but Raine St. James doesn't know why anyone would want to. When she is forced to accept a job in the town she's been publicly bashing for the last decade, she has to face down old hurts and the woman she left behind. (978-1-60282-178-1)

Water Mark by J.M. Redmann. PI Micky Knight's professional and personal lives are torn asunder by Katrina and its aftermath. She needs to solve a murder and recapture the woman she lost—while struggling to simply survive in a world gone mad. (978-1-60282-179-8)

Picture Imperfect by Lea Santos. Young love doesn't always stand the test of time, but Deanne is determined to get her marriage to childhood sweetheart Paloma back on the road to happily ever after, by way of Memory Lane-and Lover's Lane. (978-1-60282-180-4)

The Perfect Family by Kathryn Shay. A mother and her gay son stand hand in hand as the storms of change engulf their perfect family and the life they knew. (978-1-60282-181-1)

Raven Mask by Winter Pennington. Preternatural Private Investigator (and closeted werewolf) Kassandra Lyall needs to solve a murder and protect her Vampire lover Lenorre, Countess Vampire of Oklahoma— all while fending off the advances of the local werewolf alpha female. (978-1-60282-182-8)

The Devil be Damned by Ali Vali. The fourth book in the best-selling Cain Casey Devil series. (978-1-60282-159-0)

Descent by Julie Cannon. Shannon Roberts and Caroline Davis compete in the world of world-class bike racing and pretend that the fire between them is just professional rivalry, not desire. (978-1-60282-160-6)

Kiss of Noir by Clara Nipper. Nora Delany is a hard-living, sweet-talking woman who can't say no to a beautiful babe or a friend in danger—a darkly humorous homage to a bygone era of tough broads and murder in steamy New Orleans. (978-1-60282-161-3)

Under Her Skin by Lea Santos. Supermodel Lilly Lujan hasn't a care in the world, except life is lonely in the spotlight—until Mexican gardener Torien Pacias sees through Lilly's facade and offers gentle understanding and friendship when Lilly most needs it. (978-1-60282-162-0)

Fierce Overture by Gun Brooke. Helena Forsythe is a hard-hitting CEO who gets what she wants by taking no prisoners when negotiating— until she meets a woman who convinces her that charm may be the way to win a battle, and a heart. (978-1-60282-156-9)

Trauma Alert by Radclyffe. Dr. Ali Torveau has no trouble saying no to romance until the day firefighter Beau Cross shows up in her ER and sets her carefully ordered world aflame. (978-1-60282-157-6)

Wolfsbane Winter by Jane Fletcher. Iron Wolf mercenary Deryn faces down demon magic and otherworldly foes with a smile, but she's defenseless when healer Alana wages war on her heart. (978-1-60282-158-3)

Little White Lie by Lea Santos. Emie Jaramillo knows relationships are for other people, and beautiful women like Gia Mendez don't belong anywhere near her boring world of academia—until Gia sets out to convince Emie she has not only brains, but beauty…and that she's the only woman Gia wants in her life. (978-1-60282-163-7)

Witch Wolf by Winter Pennington. In a world where vampires have charmed their way into modern society, where werewolves walk the streets with their beasts disguised by human skin, Investigator Kassandra Lyall has a secret of her own to protect. She's one of them. (978-1-60282-177-4)

Do Not Disturb by Carsen Taite. Ainsley Faraday, a high-powered executive, and rock music celebrity Greer Davis couldn't be less well suited for one another, and yet they soon discover passion has a way of designing its own future. (978-1-60282-153-8)

From This Moment On by PJ Trebelhorn. Devon Conway and Katherine Hunter both lost love and neither believes they will ever find it again—until the moment they meet and everything changes. (978-1-60282-154-5)

Vapor by Larkin Rose. When erotic romance writer Ashley Vaughn decides to take her research into the bedroom for a night of passion with Victoria Hadley, she discovers that fact is hotter than fiction. (978-1-60282-155-2)

Wind and Bones by Kristin Marra. Jill O'Hara, award-winning journalist, just wants to settle her deceased father's affairs and leave Prairie View, Montana, far, far behind—but an old girlfriend, a sexy sheriff, and a dangerous secret keep her down on the ranch. (978-1-60282-150-7)

Nightshade by Shea Godfrey. The story of a princess, betrothed as a political pawn, who falls for her intended husband's soldier sister, is a modern-day fairy tale to capture the heart. (978-1-60282-151-4)

Vieux Carré Voodoo by Greg Herren. Popular New Orleans detective Scotty Bradley just can't stay out of trouble—especially when an old flame turns up asking for help. (978-1-60282-152-1)

The Pleasure Set by Lisa Girolami. Laney DeGraff, a successful president of a family-owned bank on Rodeo Drive, finds her comfortable life taking a turn toward danger when Theresa Aguilar, a sleek, sexy lawyer, invites her to join an exclusive, secret group of powerful, alluring women. (978-1-60282-144-6)

A Perfect Match by Erin Dutton. The exciting world of pro golf forms the backdrop for a fast-paced, sexy romance. (978-1-60282-145-3)

Father Knows Best by Lynda Sandoval. High school juniors and best friends Lila Moreno, Meryl Morganstern, and Caressa Thibodoux plan to make the most of the summer before senior year. What they discover that amazing summer about girl power, growing up, and trusting friends and family more than prepares them to tackle that all-important senior year! (978-1-60282-147-7)

The Midnight Hunt by L.L. Raand. Medic Drake McKennan takes a chance and loses, and her life will never be the same—because when she wakes up after surviving a life-threatening illness, she is no longer human. (978-1-60282-140-8)

Long Shot by D. Jackson Leigh. Love isn't safe, which is exactly why equine veterinarian Tory Greyson wants no part of it—until Leah Montgomery and a horse that won't give up convince her otherwise. (978-1-60282-141-5)

In Medias Res by Yolanda Wallace. Sydney has forgotten her entire life, and the one woman who holds the key to her memory, and her heart, doesn't want to be found. (978-1-60282-142-2)

Awakening to Sunlight by Lindsey Stone. Neither Judith or Lizzy is looking for companionship, and certainly not love—but when their lives become entangled, they discover both. (978-1-60282-143-9)

Fever by VK Powell. Hired gun Zakaria Chambers is hired to provide a simple escort service to philanthropist Sara Ambrosini, but nothing is as simple as it seems, especially love. (978-1-60282-135-4)

Truths by Rebecca S. Buck. Two women separated by two hundred years are connected by fate and love. (978-1-60282-146-0)

High Risk by JLee Meyer. Can actress Kate Hoffman really risk all she's worked for to take a chance on love? Or is it already too late? (978-1-60282-136-1)

Missing Lynx by Kim Baldwin and Xenia Alexiou. On the trail of a notorious serial killer, Elite Operative Lynx's growing attraction to a mysterious mercenary could be her path to love—or to death. (978-1-60282-137-8)

Spanking New by Clifford Henderson. A poignant, hilarious, unforgettable look at life, love, gender, and the essence of what makes us who we are. (978-1-60282-138-5)

Magic of the Heart by C.J. Harte. CEO Susan Hettinger and wild, impulsive rock star M.J. Carson couldn't be more different if they tried—but opposites attract in ways neither woman can resist. (978-1-60282-131-6)

Ambereye by Gill McKnight. Jolie Garoul is falling in love with her assistant. The big problem is, Jolie is a werewolf. (978-1-60282-132-3)

Collision Course by C.P. Rowlands. Tragedy leaves Brie O'Malley and Jordan Carter fearful and alone. Can they find the courage to take a second chance on love? (978-1-60282-133-0)

Mephisto Aria by Justine Saracen. Opera singer Katherina Marov's destiny may be to repeat the mistakes of her father when she becomes involved in a dangerous love affair. (978-1-60282-134-7)

Battle Scars by Meghan O'Brien. Returning Iraq war veteran Ray McKenna struggles with the battle scars that can only be healed by love. (978-1-60282-129-3)

Chaps by Jove Belle. Eden Metcalf wants nothing more than to flee from her troubled past and travel the open road—until she runs into rancher Brandi Cornwell. (978-1-60282-127-9)

Lightbearer by John Caruso. Lucifer dares to question the premise of creation itself and reveals that sin may be all that stands between us and living hell. (978-1-60282-130-9)

The Seeker by Ronica Black. FBI profiler Kennedy Scott battles ghosts from her past, deadly obsession, and the evil that haunts her. (978-1-60282-128-6)

Power Play by Julie Cannon. Businesswomen Tate Monroe and Victoria Sosa are at odds in the boardroom, but not in the bedroom. (978-1-60282-125-5)

The Remarkable Journey of Miss Tranby Quirke by Elizabeth Ridley. When love enters Tranby's life in the form of a beautiful nineteen-year-old student, Lysette McDonald, she embarks on the most remarkable journey of all. (978-1-60282-126-2)

Returning Tides by Radclyffe. Insurance investigator Ashley Walker faces more than a dangerous opponent when she returns to the town, and the woman, she left behind. (978-1-60282-123-1)

Veritas by Anne Laughlin. When the hallowed halls of academia become the stage for murder, newly appointed Dean Beth Ellis's search for the truth leads her to unexpected discoveries about her own heart. (978-1-60282-124-8)

The Pleasure Planner by Larkin Rose. Pleasure purveyor Bree Hendricks treats love like a commodity until Logan Delaney makes Bree the client in her own game. (978-1-60282-121-7)

everafter by Nell Stark and Trinity Tam. Valentine Darrow is bitten by a vampire on her way to propose to her lover Alexa Newland, and their lives and love are placed in mortal jeopardy. (978-1-60282-119-4)

Beggar of Love by Lee Lynch. Jefferson is the lover every woman wants to be—or to have. A revealing saga of lesbian sexuality. (978-1-60282-122-4)